THE PORT FAIRY MURDERS

1943: The newly formed Homicide division of the Victoria Police has been struggling to counter little-known fascist groups, particularly an organisation called Australia First that has been festering since before the war. And now there's an extra problem: the bitter divide between Catholics and Protestants. Detective Joe Sable and Constable Helen Lord are working to track down the ruthless George Starling, who in turn is planning to wreak vengeance on them for the downfall of his nationalist group and mentor. At the same time, the duo is called to investigate a double murder in the fishing village of Port Fairy. The solution seems straightforward, but it soon becomes apparent that nothing about the incident is as it seems — and that investigations which appeared unrelated are tied by a disturbing thread.

ROBERT GOTT

THE PORT FAIRY MURDERS

Complete and Unabridged

AURORA
Leicester

First published in 2015 by
Scribe Publications

First Aurora Edition
published 2019
by arrangement with
Scribe Publications

A catalogue record for this book is available
from the British Library.

ISBN 978–1–78782–138–5

Published by
F. A. Thorpe (Publishing)
Anstey, Leicestershire

Set by Words & Graphics Ltd.
Anstey, Leicestershire
Printed and bound in Great Britain by
T. J. International Ltd., Padstow, Cornwall

This book is printed on acid-free paper

For my parents, Maurene and Kevin.
Always.

1

Wednesday 12 January 1944

George Starling hated Jews, women, queers, coppers, rich people, and his father. He loved Adolf Hitler and Ptolemy Jones. Hitler was in Berlin, a long way from Victoria, and Jones was dead. He knew Jones was dead because he'd stood in the shadows and watched the coppers bring his body out of a house in Belgrave. One of those coppers had been a Jew named Joe Sable, and that meant one thing, and one thing only — Joe Sable's days were numbered.

★   ★   ★

Detective Joe Sable knew he'd returned to work too soon. He sat, bruised and miserable, at his desk in the Homicide division of the Victoria Police in Russell Street, Melbourne. Detective Inspector Titus Lambert and Constable Helen Lord were out, but he wasn't alone in the office. Sergeant David Reilly sat on the opposite side of the room. Reilly was a recent acquisition, and Joe had yet to make up his mind about him. He knew Helen Lord resented Reilly, but her resentment was based less on his abilities and more on the fact that he threatened her position in the squad. She was there by the grace and favour of Inspector Lambert, who'd snaffled her by arguing chronic manpower shortages to his superiors. Under normal circumstances, a female constable could expect to languish unacknowledged for the duration of her career. Helen Lord was only too aware that Katherine Mackay, a woman she admired, had waited 13 years to be elevated to the dizzy heights of senior constable, and that was as far she would be suffered to rise.

The war had created unexpected opportunities, so that in mid-January 1944 Helen Lord remained seconded to Homicide — a fact that got up the noses of many in the force. Reilly, and any further additions to the squad, might end that secondment. Consequently, her relations with most of the male members of Homicide — who were destined to always outrank her, no matter how incompetent they might be — were fraught. She felt every sidelong glance, every raised eyebrow, every small sneer, with the force of an explicit verbal correction to her being there. She admired Inspector Lambert, and was grateful for his belief that her sex was irrelevant. Nevertheless, an ember of resentment that she was beholden to him could still be fanned by circumstances into something hot and restive. And then there was Sergeant Joe Sable. She needed to discipline wariness into her dealings with him. She was a much better detective than Joe — more instinctive, smarter, more observant — and yet she was acutely aware that her attraction to him might lead her into a deference she would otherwise abhor. She was, however, so easily lacerated by a careless remark, even by him, that she hadn't so far fallen victim to

2

obsequious agreement. Her return to the office, alone — Inspector Lambert was lunching with the assistant commissioner of police — interrupted Joe Sable's morose self-absorption. It was David Reilly who spoke first.

'Anything interesting?'

His tone was carefully, studiedly neutral. He was aware that he'd earned Constable Lord's displeasure without even trying. This would normally not have bothered him, but his position in Homicide mattered to him, and Constable Lord mattered to Inspector Lambert. Ipso facto, as he'd said to his wife, Constable Lord needed to be kept on side. Barbara Reilly thought that the idea of a woman willingly exposing herself to the kind of horrors that her husband spoke of was unnatural.

'She must be a bit mannish,' she'd said.

'She's plain,' David Reilly had said, and that had elicited a smug and knowing 'Ah' from Barbara.

Constable Lord sat down at a desk that had been pushed into a corner for her.

'Depends what you mean by interesting,' she said.

'Anything other than what I'm doing would qualify,' Joe said.

'We all have to do paperwork, Sergeant,' she said, 'and you know you look like you've gone 14 rounds with Jack Dempsey. You can't interview people. You'd frighten them.'

She smiled at him, but caught herself before it reached the arc of a grin. She was suddenly conscious of the jokey intimacy in her tone, and of David Reilly's eyes on her. She turned to him.

'Nothing interesting,' she said, and began ostentatiously transcribing notes. Reilly caught Joe's eye and raised his eyebrows. Joe gave the slightest of shrugs in return, but Helen Lord noticed it peripherally, and her mood darkened.

★　★　★

There were two men in the bar of the Caledonian Hotel in Port Fairy, a small town a good five hours' drive from Melbourne. One of the men was the bartender — a portly, wheezy, unshaven, easily rankled man named Stafford Giles. The other man, seated away from the bar near a window through which he watched a dust shower sweep down Bank Street, was George Starling. There was no one out and about, but an empty street was preferable to the view inside the hotel, which included the sight of Stafford Giles. Starling was repulsed by him, by his heft. Starling believed that fat people were lazy, complacent individuals who ate and drank more than their fair share. You couldn't rely on a fat person: he'd be driven by self-interest, and he'd be a stranger to self-discipline.

Starling was wearing a long-sleeved shirt, although its sleeves were rolled up. He was conscious of the smell of fish that clung to him, trapped in the shirt's cotton and in the thick hair of his arms. He liked the look of his arms; they were sinewy and masculine, and they intimidated people. They smelled of fish because he regularly scaled and gutted the catch brought in by a local

4

fisherman. This man, Peter Hurley, whose red hair and fair skin should have confined him to sunless indoors, had dropped nets and lines in the Southern Ocean for close to thirty years, and his face was the creased, blotched, and blasted testament to every hour he'd spent at sea. He was fifty, and could easily have passed for a ravaged seventy. Starling didn't like Hurley, although he didn't despise him, which amounted to a kind of approbation. Hurley paid in cash, and made no inquiries about Starling's private life. Starling offered Hurley the same incuriosity. This suited them both. Each had reason to preserve the lack of intimacy — Hurley because his catch was largely illegal, and illegally disposed of, and Starling because he was a person of interest to the police.

George Starling left the Caledonian Hotel and headed to the room he rented in Princes Street. The heat didn't bother him, and neither did the smell of wrack and fish-rot, mixed with an aromatic hint of eucalypt forests smouldering after fires, that drifted through the town. When he reached his room he stretched out on the sour-smelling bed and added up the number of people he wanted to, needed to, kill. He'd start with Joe Sable, but he wouldn't stop there.

★ ★ ★

When Inspector Titus Lambert returned to Russell Street, he asked Joe Sable to follow him into the privacy of his office.

'Close the door, Sergeant.'

Joe immediately felt uneasy. Lambert often made him feel uncomfortable, even incompetent. Now Joe faced his superior with the evidence of his incompetence writ large in the wounds he'd sustained in his first major investigation.

'How's the shoulder, Sergeant?'

'It's healing. The knife wasn't a long one.'

'I don't believe you should be back here yet. It won't make anything heal any faster.'

'Are you asking me to stay home, sir?'

As soon as the words were out of his mouth Joe realised they sounded sulky.

'No, Sergeant. There are things you can do here, and it frees Constable Lord to get valuable experience.'

Inspector Lambert's tone was uninflected, but in his words Joe heard a rebuff, a reminder that Lambert considered Helen Lord a better police officer — certainly a better Homicide officer — than he. A wave of nausea washed over him.

'Are you all right, Sergeant? You look ill.'

'I'm fine, sir. Tom? How's Tom?'

At the mention of his brother-in-law's name, Inspector Lambert leaned forward in his seat and stared hard at Sable.

'Tom Mackenzie is not now, and never has been, your responsibility. He joined you of his own volition. No one could have foreseen what was to happen to him. You can carry that weight if you want to, but it isn't rightly yours to carry, and it will crush you.'

'Mrs Lambert doesn't share that view, does she?'

'Maude, at the moment, is concentrating her energies on looking after Tom, not on blaming you.'

'So how is Tom?'

'He's comfortable, I think. He's walking, although he doesn't leave the house. He's in pain, and he doesn't say much. I won't lie to you; there's something vacant about him now. I catch Maude watching him — waiting, I think, to see a glimpse of the brother she remembers. We'll get him back eventually, Sergeant. Tom Mackenzie is as strong as his sister. He *will* recover.'

Joe felt his eyes well with tears and, unable to prevent it, he began to sob. He sat with his head bowed and his shoulders rising and falling. He made no sound, and Inspector Lambert made no move to intervene. As he regained control, Joe reached into his pocket and withdrew a handkerchief. He pushed it at his eyes and held it there.

'I'm sorry,' he said.

'Has that been happening much?'

Joe nodded. 'Well, a few times, and mostly it takes me by surprise. I'm sorry. You must think . . . '

'Don't presume what I think, Sergeant. If you'd walked away from that investigation without suffering any effects, I'd say you were as cold and insane as the man who stabbed you and tortured Tom.'

'Can I visit him, sir?'

'No. Not yet. He's not ready.'

'And Mrs Lambert?'

'No. She's not ready to see you yet, either.'

There it was — the confirmation that Maude

Lambert could not forgive Joe for the injuries to her brother's body and mind. Joe remembered with searing clarity the words she'd spoken to Inspector Lambert at the hospital.

'He's all broken, Titus,' she'd said. 'He's all broken.'

Joe looked up at Inspector Lambert, and although he recognised sympathy in his eyes, he also saw pity, or thought he saw pity. Another wave of nausea passed through him.

'Are you up to discussing a few matters relating to the case, Sergeant?'

This took Joe by surprise.

'Yes, yes, of course.'

'Good, because there are loose ends, and one of those ends in particular worries me.'

'George Starling.'

'George Starling. He's still at large. If Military Intelligence had picked him up, I assume they'd have told us, although professional courtesy isn't their strong point.'

'He'll have gone to ground, sir. Intelligence won't find him. I didn't spend much time with him, but he struck me as being as fanatical in his own way as Ptolemy Jones. And now that Jones is dead, Starling might want to pick up his leader's sword. Tom spent more time with him . . . '

'Yes, but it wasn't Starling who tortured Tom, was it? It was Jones.'

'I don't think for a minute that that points to any squeamishness or humanity in Starling. Whatever the reason for his not being there, I'd say he felt cheated, peeved, at being denied that pleasure.'

'He might also feel cheated because Germany

8

will lose the European war. That gets clearer every day. I think our home-grown Hitlerites will quietly reorganise themselves into something less dismal, or work to whitewash their inconvenient allegiance.'

'You don't think George Starling will call his mates to arms?'

'Ptolemy Jones was a deluded, fanatical psychopath. Those creatures are rare. George Starling is an acolyte. They're common. I'm guessing, despite your observation, that politics mattered to him only because it mattered to Jones. With Jones gone, Starling's hatreds are unfocussed and naked. He can't dress them up in a well-tailored ideology. I may be wrong, of course. I hope I am. If it's Nazism that fascinates him, I think we have a chance of catching him, because he'll make contact with others. If he's lost his taste for it, he'll be an unpredictable menace. He's out there, and I'm uneasy about that.'

'Maybe we'll never hear from him again. Maybe he'll lie low until the war is over and live an anonymous, miserable life.'

'Let's hope it's miserable, at any rate.'

★   ★   ★

Joe Sable sat in the late-afternoon light in his flat in Arnold Street, Princes Hill. He'd recently begun to scour newspapers and journals for news of the horrors being visited upon Jews in Europe, and his life-long indifference to his own Jewishness had begun to torment him. He spoke to no one about this. His sleep was troubled, and

9

his dreams, never remembered, left him waking each morning with a vague and lingering dread; and, to his mortification, he'd begun to cry in response to unpredictable, unrelated triggers.

He was twenty-five years old. Sometimes he thought of resigning, but what would he do? His arrhythmic heart wasn't acceptable to the military. Manpower would place him somewhere ghastly — a munitions factory, or some other war industry where his brains were of no interest to his employer.

This afternoon, his thoughts were interrupted in their dismal progress by the jangling of his telephone.

'I have a reverse-charge trunk call for a Joe Sable from a Fred — no other name. Will you accept the charge?'

Joe's body tensed.

'I'll accept,' he said.

'Putting you through. Go ahead, please.'

There was silence, although Joe could hear Fred's breathing.

'You should live every day like it's your last, Sable, because it might be.'

'We know who you are, Fred. We know your real name is George Starling. We know all about you. We'll find you.'

The line went dead, and Joe immediately regretted what he'd said. He'd thrown away what might have been an advantage — Starling's probable assumption that Homicide didn't know his real identity. Lambert would see this as unforgivable and, doubtless, typical thoughtlessness. Well, he saw no reason why Lambert had to be told the truth. He telephoned the inspector at home. Maude Lambert answered.

'Mrs Lambert, this is Sergeant Joe Sable.'

There was a devastating pause before Maude asked, 'How are you, Joe?'

He wanted to hang up. There was a mechanical quality in Maude's voice, as if she was going through polite motions.

'I'm doing all right. And Tom?'

'Yes?'

'May I speak to him?'

'No,' she said simply. 'I'll get Titus.'

Joe heard the handset hit the wood of the telephone table, and in the background he heard Tom Mackenzie's voice asking who was on the telephone.

'Nobody,' Maude said, and Titus's voice obscured any further exchange between them.

'Sergeant Sable? What's happened?'

Joe told him, and Titus instructed him to stay where he was until he could find out from the telephone exchange where the trunk call had originated. He hung up, and fifteen minutes later he called Joe back to tell him that the call had been made in Warrnambool.

'Starling's father lives there, or near there, doesn't he, sir?'

'An officer from Warrnambool is on his way to see Starling Senior. Did his son call himself Fred?'

'No,' Joe lied. 'He called himself George Starling.'

There was silence at Lambert's end, and Joe knew that his inspector suspected the lie. He didn't press Joe on the point and said quietly, 'I see.'

★   ★   ★

Mepunga might once have been substantial enough to warrant its designation on a map. By January 1944 it had been subsumed into the lush landscape until all that remained were a few dispersed structures — a schoolhouse, a church, a rarely used Mechanics Institute — and a handful of struggling dairy farms. No one would have dignified John Starling's property with the term 'farm'. There was a house that needed a new roof; a couple of out-buildings, one of which had lost a wall; and dry, sour paddocks, trampled from pasture into dusty aridity by two horses and a donkey. When Constable Manton began walking, in the gathering dusk, from his car to the house, the horses moved with ungainly haste from the far side of their paddock towards him. Constable Manton had grown up on a farm, and he knew that the horses must be hungry. He was immediately on edge. John Starling wasn't well liked in nearby Warrnambool, but nobody had ever suggested that he neglected his animals. On the contrary, Starling was thought to prefer them to humans. Manton knocked on the front door and waited. Nothing. He knocked again, more robustly, and a peel of paint fell away from the frame.

'Mr Starling?' The bark of Manton's voice caused two swallows to abandon the perch they'd taken for the night under the eaves. The small rush of their wings startled him. He peered through the grimy, curtained windows and saw nothing. No lights were showing. He tried the door, and it opened. He pushed it, and the house exhaled a warm, stale breath. Putting his head around the door, Manton sniffed the air and detected no telltale odour of putrefaction. He was relieved. At least Starling wasn't dead somewhere in the house. He called his name again, and when there was no reply he decided against entering, convincing himself that a quick search of the outside ought to be done first.

The yard at the back of Starling's house was a mess of small, broken machinery, tins, and rusting tools. A woodpile, stacked carelessly, threatened to topple over, and a splitter leaned against it. Manton couldn't understand people who treated expensive tools with cavalier indifference. The yard was sequestered from the paddock beyond it by a tatty fence. Manton passed through the single-hinged gate and stopped to locate a peculiar noise. '*The murmurous haunt of flies on summer eves*,' he thought, and was pleased to recall that verse from a poem he'd been forced to memorise at school. He couldn't remember who wrote it. Keats? Yes, Keats. The sound of buzzing insects wasn't insistent or remarkable — the fading light had calmed their frenzied work — but it was concentrated in one place, near a large, golden cypress. Manton crossed to it, and saw the legs first.

'Mr Starling?'

This was a pointless question; he knew that.

He'd caught a whiff of death on the wind. Not wishing to get too close to the body, Manton walked in a wide circle around the dark cypress. John Starling sat propped against the trunk, his head having lolled forward and his arms folded almost neatly in his lap. Manton put a handkerchief to his nose and approached. Earlier in the day, a dense, noisy aggregation of flies would have been busy feeding and breeding. A cursory glance at maggots dropping from the ears, eyes, and lips told Manton that Starling had been dead for several days at least. A closer examination could be left to the coroner. Manton checked the immediate surroundings for forensic evidence, and when he'd satisfied himself that there was nothing that needed collecting or securing, he returned to the vehicle and headed back to Warrnambool.

★　★　★

Helen Lord never spoke to her mother about her work in Homicide. Having been the wife of a policeman, Ros Lord had seen the toll the work had taken on her late husband. She'd never pressed him for information, but had always waited patiently for him to come to her when he'd needed to. So it was with her daughter. She didn't pry, or harry. She waited. For her part, Helen was determined to spare her mother both the disappointments and the satisfactions of her job. She thought, wrongly, that discussion of police work would serve only to poke at the wound left by her father's death. The resulting silence between them, except on trivial matters, although borne of mutual respect, was beginning to compromise the easy intimacy between them. There was something uncomfortable in the silence, something slightly poisonous, something that might overwhelm them. Helen was more conscious of this than her mother, who was used to waiting for an expression of trust, and was used to being rewarded.

Helen couldn't go to her uncle, Peter Lillee, in whose large house in Kew they lived. He'd taken them in after the death of Helen's father in Broome. There'd never been any sense of charity about this. He lived alone, was wealthy, and loved his sister, Ros. It had been no hardship for him to offer her a place as his housekeeper, and the fees he'd paid to educate his niece amounted to an insignificant impost on his income. He was kind, but distant, and when Helen had joined the police force she'd noticed a finely nuanced wariness in his dealings with her. She suspected he was homosexual — a preference she knew little about and which, prior to her relationship with her uncle, she would have been liable to address as a deviancy. The horror it excited in her male colleagues, and the cruelty it encouraged in many of them, created in her a prejudice in favour of homosexuals, in spite of her unworldliness. She would have liked to learn from her uncle, but such wasn't the nature of their relationship. He was a private man, without being secretive. Helen felt strongly that he had a rich, interesting life away from his home, about which he was punctiliously discreet. The household in Kew was suffocating in discretion.

Ros Lord and Peter Lillee sat listening to the wireless, as they often did after dinner. Helen sat with them, reading, tuning in to the news when an item seemed worth her while. Meat rationing was to be introduced on 15 January, and, in a bit of shameless editorialising, doubtless at the behest of the government, the reader embellished the bald announcement with: 'Few people are sufficiently austere or angelic to wish meat rationing, or any kind of rationing, to be introduced for the sake of mortifying the flesh in wartime, but most will be fair-minded enough to recognise that a good case has been established for the rationing of meat. It has been shown by expert authorities that the supply is such and the demands are such that the old system of allowing each consumer to buy as much meat as he or she can afford cannot be continued.'

'It's been as good as rationed anyway for ages,' said Ros. 'Finding a decent cut of meat at the butcher's is a novelty. Most of it goes to the black market, I suppose.'

'You've never bought anything under the counter, Ros?' Peter Lillee raised an eyebrow.

'Your Sunday roast isn't always in the window, Peter, if that's what you mean.'

'There's a confession for you, Helen. Arrest this woman.'

'I've eaten so many Sunday roasts I'd have to arrest myself as an accessory.'

In a stunning breach of protocol, Peter asked, 'How's work, Helen? You don't talk about it much.'

Helen shot her mother a look, and was surprised to see her face open and smiling.

'I like my work,' she said. 'I don't like the other coppers much, but some are all right.'

'I couldn't do your job,' Peter said. 'Too much of a coward, and I suppose you see the very worst of human nature.'

'And not just in criminals.'

Peter laughed.

'Your father used to say that if it wasn't for the uniform, you wouldn't know who were the crooks and who were the coppers,' Ros said. 'He had rather a jaundiced view, of course.'

Helen, usually astute in her readings of conversations, failed to hear in her mother's voice the invitation to talk, and so, in a mild panic, excused herself and went upstairs to her bedroom. Peter and Ros retreated into the familiar pattern of reticence, and said nothing. They gave their attention to the wireless.

Helen picked up the novel she'd been reading, making it to the end of one page without understanding a word she'd read. The incident downstairs — in her head, the sudden mention of her father had become an 'incident' — had unsettled her, and in this mildly discombobulated state her thoughts turned to Joe Sable. She'd been cool to him, and she'd known that he'd felt the coolness, but that he'd been baffled by it, not chastened. Bafflement didn't offer the salve to bruised feelings that successful chastisement offered. Nevertheless, and despite the bleak pleasure to be had from simmering resentment, she acknowledged to herself that Joe's physical suffering might serve as a displaced expiation for his failure to trust her at a critical point in the Ptolemy Jones investigation. Indeed, had she been more worldly, she might have acknowledged that his problematic heart and his physical wounds served to arouse her feelings in ways that threatened to transport her into unruly and unpredictable territory. Should she telephone him? No. If he answered, she'd stumble and stutter her way to an unconvincing explanation for the call; and if he didn't answer, she'd be annoyed by his failure to do so and would speculate pointlessly as to the reason. She picked up the novel and returned to the top of the page she'd already read.

★　★　★

Inspector Titus Lambert was already in his office when Sergeant David Reilly arrived. Reilly had just sat down when Helen Lord came in.

'Constable,' Reilly said, and nodded.

'Sergeant,' she replied. There was nothing in Reilly's manner to suggest that he was doing anything more than adhering to protocol, but Helen suspected that he took pleasure in the daily reminder of the difference in their rank. Joe Sable arrived, and the exchange was identical.

'Constable.'

'Sergeant.' She was at least confident that Joe's use of her rank was un-nuanced protocol. Lambert emerged from his office.

'John Starling was found dead last night on his property.'

Sergeant Reilly, who'd been fully briefed on recent and current investigations, asked, 'Suspicious death, sir?'

If Reilly had seen the expression that fleetingly distorted Helen Lord's face, he'd have realised that the wheels had just fallen off his project to win her over. Reilly was a blow-in — although he'd blown in not long after her own elevation to Homicide — and she felt unreasonably proprietorial (she knew this) about the case that had left Joe Sable wounded and Lambert's brother-in-law near death. Reilly had had nothing to do with this case, had experienced none of its horrors. How dare he presume to ask questions ahead of her?

'There are no indications of violence to his body. The preliminary report suggests that he died of a heart attack; but, given who he was, and the threat issued last night by his son to Sergeant Sable, I think we need to go down to Warrnambool and work from there for a couple of days.'

'Sergeant Sable was threatened?' Helen Lord's voice was as carefully modulated as she could manage. Her internal interrogator hurried to, 'Why didn't he telephone me?' bypassing altogether the more rational, 'Why would he telephone me?'

'George Starling rang me last night from Warrnambool,' Joe said, 'and issued what amounted to a threat. 'You should live every day as if it might be your last, because it might be.' That's what he said, and I don't think he was trying to impress me with some homespun philosophy of living.'

'Did he call himself Fred?'

Joe had come to realise that Helen Lord's thought processes frequently matched, mirrored, or outran those of Inspector Lambert, so a part of him was unsurprised that she'd asked the question Joe was least prepared to answer. Unable to change the version of events he'd given to Lambert, he lied again.

'No. He called himself George Starling.'

Helen was watching his bruised face carefully, sympathetically, and she was shocked by the certainty that he was dissembling.

'Why would he do that?'

'Maybe he figured the game was up. I mean, he's not stupid. He must have known we'd find out his real name.'

'But he is stupid. How could he think that National Socialism was a good idea without a good dollop of stupidity?'

Helen wanted to keep prodding, and Inspector Lambert was inclined to let her do so. He observed Joe with interest.

'Why give us a free kick? Why not at least wait until he was sure his extra layer of anonymity had been breached?'

Joe's eyes darted to Lambert and back to Helen. He was going to brazen this out, despite feeling that his credibility was draining away.

'Maybe you're right. Maybe he is stupid.'

'I don't think we should proceed with this investigation believing that George Starling is a stupid man,' Lambert said. 'That would be a very bad idea.'

Sergeant Reilly wasn't insensitive, or unobservant, and he felt keenly that a storm of some kind was blowing behind the measured calm of this exchange. It unsettled him, because he couldn't determine its implications for him. For the moment, though, he was grateful to be out of the weather as it were.

'You're absolutely right, sir,' Joe said. 'I didn't mean to . . . '

Inspector Lambert raised his hand in a gesture that was both simple and brutal. Joe stopped speaking, and knew immediately that Lambert didn't just suspect that he was lying — he *knew*. How hard would it have been to find the operator who put the trunk call through and ask her if she remembered the name of the person placing the call? 'Fred,' she would have said, because that was the name he'd given her. 'I have a reverse-charge trunk call for Joe Sable from a Fred — no other name.' Would the inspector go to the trouble of checking this? With a sickening recognition of Lambert's distrust that this implied, Joe thought *Yes, yes, he would go to the trouble*.

'Three rooms have been booked at the Warrnambool Hotel for tonight and tomorrow night. I'll be driving down with Constable Lord and Sergeant Reilly in an hour. I'm afraid there's no time to organise a change of clothes. We'll have to make do. Sergeant Reilly, any problems?'

'No, sir. I'll telephone the wife. She'll understand.'

'Constable Lord?'

'No problems at all, sir.' Except that there was

a problem, and it had a name — David Reilly.

Joe said nothing. What was there to say? He wanted to find a toilet and be sick.

'I'm sorry, Sergeant,' Lambert said to him. 'You're not physically well enough.'

In other circumstances, Joe might have protested. But for now, he lacked the will to even nod assent.

2

Selwyn Todd, who always smelled of stale sweat, lived in a shed in a corner of his sister's garden in James Street, Port Fairy. The sister, Aggie, 64, had settled into misandric spinsterhood. People in Port Fairy expressed admiration to her face for the way she looked after simple Selwyn, and proclaimed pity behind her back for the dud cards she'd been dealt in life. No one could remember how old Selwyn was. He'd been sent to Melbourne when he was very young, and had turned up in Aggie's garden some time in his twenties. Aggie had never explained his reappearance, and no one had asked her for an explanation. It was supposed that he was now probably 55 or 56. Initially, people had been afraid of him. He laughed loudly and suddenly, and his speech was incoherent. Giggles and barking laughter were his primary means of communication, making adults uneasy and terrifying children. Gradually, he became a familiar, never-quite-trusted presence in the town. He would sit on an upturned box in Sackville Street, his head lowered, his bottom lip slick with saliva, scratching away on a slate. He'd learned to form a few letters, which he drew over and over. As walkers passed by him, he would raise his eyes and chortle. They found this disconcerting, largely because they experienced an uncomfortable feeling of being judged, of being laughed *at*. To make themselves feel better, they took to referring to Selwyn as 'The Village Idiot'; thus cabined, they took little interest in him.

Aggie Todd didn't have the luxury of complete indifference to Selwyn. She'd inherited him from her brother, Andrew, in Melbourne. Selwyn had taken to frequent and unguarded bouts of masturbation. Aggie's sister-in-law, Phillipa, put her foot down when she entered her living room one morning to find Selwyn pleasuring himself in one corner while her five-year-old son, Matthew, was reading in another. Neither seemed aware of the other, but Phillipa declared that very evening that Selwyn had to go — what if he did this disgusting thing in front of little Rose? There was only one place for him to go to. 'That spoiled sister of yours. She got your parents' house in Port Fairy, and you didn't lift a finger to stop her, and no one's ever going to marry her. There's plenty of room. End of discussion.'

Selwyn had been with Aggie for only a few days when she'd decided that he couldn't live with her in the house. He never willingly bathed himself, as he seemed terrified of water. He stank, and Aggie was certain that the smell was getting into the curtains and the carpet — even into her own bedding. She'd never allowed him into her bedroom, but she could smell him on her sheets. He was therefore banished to the shed. She wasn't cruel to him. She fed him healthy food, withholding it from him only occasionally when she used it as a reward for him allowing her to hose him down. She did this when she believed the smell was creeping from the shed, across the backyard like a viscous ooze, into the house.

When she'd done this for the first time, Selwyn had been with her for perhaps five weeks. She'd explained what she was going to do, that the water would be cold, but that she wouldn't send it at him in a rush. Selwyn whimpered, but understood that Aggie was someone he had to obey — and he was hungry. Aggie told him to take off his clothes. He thought she'd meant all his clothes. She'd thought that modesty was a virtue separate from mental acuity. Selwyn stood before her, naked, not knowing that he should cup his genitals against his sister's sight. He hadn't yet grown podgy, and his pale body quivered in frightened expectation of the hose. Aggie was transfixed. She stared at him, with shame, horror, embarrassment, and something worse, far worse — excitement — jostling for position. She'd never in her life seen a naked adult male, and Selwyn stood there, his arms by his side. As her eyes darted over him, he was a confusion of muscle, hair, and penis. She glanced at it, and quickly looked at his face. She turned on the hose, not fully, so that the water flowed gently, and approached him. She let water fall over his shoulders, and he flinched.

'Hold up your arms, Selwyn.'

He did as he was told, and, with her thumb over the end of the hose, she directed a sharp spray into each armpit. She showed him that she wanted him to rub there with his free hand, to help sluice the filth away. She went behind him and sprayed vigorously between his buttocks. Facing him, she sprayed his chest, and he rubbed there with his hands; averting her eyes, she sprayed his private parts, which, having learned now what to do, he also rubbed. His erection so startled Aggie that she dropped the hose and returned to the house. Two hours later, she came outside to find the hose still running, her precious tank water soaking into the ground where Selwyn had outraged decency.

Aggie waited two months before hosing Selwyn down again. The shock of that first occasion had by now been dulled by Selwyn's frequent bouts of onanism, which he at least confined to the premises. There were times when Aggie watched him, and her disgust mutated, to her guilty dismay, into something that felt disturbingly like desire. Who would know, she allowed herself to think one morning, who would ever know if . . . This was as far as that thought went before a rush of nausea sent her to the bathroom. The thought crept back, and each time it did, the punishing nausea diminished until it wasn't there at all. Eventually, in an astonishing feat of calculated moral and emotional sequestration, Aggie Todd encouraged her brother into her bed — or rather, his bed. She couldn't bear the idea of him touching her sheets. This happened only twice, and each time their fumbling, mutual uncertainty made the experience clumsy and dull. It was too elaborate and confusing for Selwyn, and when Aggie, fully clothed, straddled him and forced him into her,

26

she was barely able to tolerate the smell that came off him. Afterwards, she explained the incident away as having been the consequence of a vague fear she harboured that a mean-spirited mortician might snigger at his discovery that she was, post-mortem, *virgo intacta*, and that he might stand back from her elderly, shrunken corpse and say to himself, or to an assistant, 'Well, after all, who'd want that?' As time passed, Selwyn grew fat, and Aggie mostly managed to expunge the incidents from her memory.

No one in Port Fairy would have called Aggie Todd cheerful, but neither would they have called her unpleasant. Dour perhaps, and a little snobbish. She took great pride in owning a highly polished set of silver apostle spoons. People knew about her apostle spoons — real silver, not plate — because they glittered in the saucers under teacups at the occasional morning tea that Aggie organised for the ladies of St Patrick's. The women who came to these teas did so with some trepidation, knowing, as they did, who lived at the bottom of Aggie's garden. Selwyn, however, never made an appearance, and he was only ever seen at his station in Sackville Street.

* * *

The Todd family had lived for several generations in Port Fairy, and although Selwyn did little for their reputation, it was generally held that old families inevitably threw up a wrong'un at some stage. Father Brennan, a man Aggie had

27

little time for, ludicrously suggested to her once that Selwyn was God's gift to the family.

'God loves his Selwyns,' he'd said. 'They are as innocent as children.'

You wouldn't think that, she'd thought, if you had to hose him down.

Aggie's brother Andrew had married 'out'. Not only was Phillipa a Melbourne girl, she was a Protestant, and when the collective intake of breath in Port Fairy was exhaled, it blew the couple to Melbourne, where standards were lower. Visits after the death of the elder Todds were infrequent, and ceased altogether when travel restrictions were introduced after the outbreak of war. This was hard on Phillipa, because both her children, Matthew and Rose, who'd grown up with the sense, instilled by their father, that the Port Fairy district was a sort of Todd demesne, had chosen to live there. Rose had married a stolid, plain, and incompatibly short dairy farmer. That was Aggie's assessment of John Abbot, at any rate. On the few occasions she'd met him, the impression he'd left had faded quickly. He was stocky, probably reliable, and definitely boring. She didn't have a much higher opinion of her niece. She was pretty, but insufficiently interested in her appearance to do herself justice. Her voice was irremediably awful, beyond surgical help because it wasn't just a question of adenoids. Timbre, tone, and pitch were all off. For Aggie, a conversation with her niece was aural agony.

Her feelings about her nephew, Matthew, were, if not extreme, at least extravagant. She adored him. He was beautiful — others less smitten admitted to his being good-looking, nothing more — and his decision to live within minutes of her had raised her flagging spirits. The adult Selwyn had been a shock to Matthew at first, understandably. His childhood memories of him were vague and insubstantial. When Matthew had next met him, Selwyn had been very substantial indeed. Aggie could tell at this first meeting that Matthew had been repelled by Selwyn. Well, how could someone who looked like Matthew not be repulsed by someone who looked like Selwyn, and the hideous fact of their blood relationship must have been hard to stomach. Nevertheless, as Selwyn became more intractable about being hosed down, Matthew pitched in and helped manage him.

When he'd first seen Selwyn — pale, blubbering, and shivering in expectation of the hose — Matthew had expressed disgust, and then laughed. He'd poked at his uncle with a broom handle, and chortled at how far it sank into the exposed belly. Selwyn had chortled, too, and Aggie had allowed a giggle to escape. There were no more giggles after this. As Matthew became comfortable in his aunt's house, and as he came to understand that she'd formed an attachment to him, his intolerance of and disgust with Selwyn were given free expression. The hosing sessions became brutal exercises in efficiency. When Selwyn was called to the yard, any hesitation was met with a vicious slap from Matthew, and when he tired of stinging his own hand, he used the broom handle and whacked

29

Selwyn about the shoulders. Aggie had been horrified the first time she'd seen Matthew slap Selwyn's face, but he'd explained to her that someone as retarded as Selwyn felt pain like a dog or a cow felt it. It was an effective corrective, but it had to be repeated because the memory of it faded quickly. It was the only way to discipline dumb animals. It was the way he disciplined his dog, and he liked the sensation of raising his hand and watching the animal cower in expectation of a blow. He liked, too, the way the dog came to him, its head lowered, grateful that he'd stayed his hand. It was astonishing how like the border collie Selwyn was. Aggie could see it, too, as Matthew demonstrated by showing Selwyn the broomstick. He smiled triumphantly as his uncle flinched and widened his eyes in fear.

'Now, see,' Matthew said as he put the broomstick behind his back and patted Selwyn's naked shoulder. Selwyn laughed, and relaxed.

'See.'

Aggie saw. She saw as Matthew went behind her brother and swung the broom handle in a wide arc so that it hit Selwyn's buttocks with a sharp 'thwack!' He yowled.

'Turn the hose on him, Aunty. That'll shut him up.'

Aggie turned the hose on Selwyn, and, without her really noticing it, her pity ebbed away.

3

The drive to Warrnambool took six-and-a-half hours. Helen Lord drove. She recognised this as a gesture of Inspector Lambert's confidence in her. Indeed, when they'd approached the car at Russell Street, David Reilly had automatically put his hand on the driver's side-door handle.

'You've got reading to do,' Lambert said. 'Constable Lord will drive. I'll sit in the back. She can answer any questions you might have about George Starling and his cronies.'

He handed Reilly a folder.

'I've read this, sir.'

'Read it again, and ask questions. You need to have a clear understanding of the person we're dealing with.'

Reilly nodded, and wondered how he'd disguise the motion sickness that plagued him whenever he tried to read in a moving vehicle. It was hot, so at least the windows would be down.

In the back seat, Inspector Lambert read through the contents of his own folder. It contained the same notes and photographs he'd given Sergeant Reilly. He pored over these notes, trying to find the point in the initial investigation where he ought to have identified its true nature. He'd sat up in bed with Maude, passing her sheaf after sheaf, but neither of them could say, 'There! That's what we missed.' Maude tried to reassure him that her brother's injuries were

31

unforeseeable, at least by Titus, but she wasn't willing to extend this dispensation to Joe Sable. She knew, after years of sharing the details with him, that Titus's investigations rarely progressed with the logical certainty of a puzzle. The solving of cases depended as much on the carelessness and stupidity of the perpetrators as on the deductive powers of the detectives. There were no master criminals. There were chancers, drunks, mean-spirited losers, and psychopaths, and the thing that bound them all, as far as Maude could determine, was a fatal flaw in their intelligence. However well they presented, however smart they appeared to be, when you got right down to it, they were just plain dumb. The worst of them were dumb and dangerous. Titus didn't entirely agree with her, and frequently cautioned her against confusing moral bankruptcy with intelligence. In return, she cautioned him against confusing intelligence with elusiveness. Titus often ran the conversations he'd had with his wife through his head. He could be unguarded with her in a way that would be unthinkable with a colleague, and he couldn't imagine doing his job effectively without her.

The car made it to Camper down before David Reilly lost his battle with motion sickness. He asked Helen to pull over, almost fell out of the car in his haste, and emptied the contents of his stomach beneath the beautiful, bronze statue of Victory in the avenue of elms. Ashen, sweating, and ashamed, he returned to the car. Helen, who moved around to the passenger side, said, 'You should have said you got car sick.'

32

'I don't if I drive.'

Helen narrowed her eyes slightly. Reilly noticed.

'I didn't mention it because it makes me look like a spoiled little boy who chucks a turn if he doesn't get his own way.'

Inspector Lambert leaned out of the window.

'Are you well enough to drive?'

'Yes, sir.'

'Then perhaps that's what you should do. I'd like to get to Warrnambool before next week.'

Helen and David looked at each other across the roof of the car, and for the briefest of moments they were allied in feeling included in the sweep of Lambert's irritation. David Reilly managed a small smile, and Helen Lord managed to return it.

⋆   ⋆   ⋆

Constable Manton wasn't at his desk when the trio arrived at the Warrnambool police station, so the constable on duty was confused initially when Inspector Lambert identified himself and his colleagues as being from Homicide in Melbourne.

'Never heard of it,' he said, but tidied his response when he was made aware of the rank of the thin, balding man before him. The presence of the woman, who'd inexplicably been intro-duced as 'Constable Helen Lord' — he thought he'd misheard — further confused him. They were rescued from the tedium of more explanations by the emergence of a trim, well-dressed man with short, grey hair. Everything about him was clipped, which lent the moustache he wore drama it hardly needed. It was lush, black, and carefully topiaried into a shape familiar from daguerreotypes, but rarely seen in the flesh. Detective Inspector Greg Halloran looked as if he'd stepped out of the nineteenth century into 1944.

'Titus,' he said, with shocking familiarity.

'Greg,' Titus said, with an equally shocking indifference to protocol.

'One Homicide man might be considered alarming, but three! Pardon me — two and a lady. I know we're a bit out of the way down here, but I think even we would have noticed a mass murder.'

'Detective Inspector Halloran was the outstanding talent in our intake at Detective Training School,' Titus said. 'To everyone's dismay, he chose to exercise those talents in Warrnambool.'

'Where,' Halloran said, 'they have become comfortably flabby through disuse. I presume that's where your homily was headed, Titus?'

'I don't believe that for a minute.'

'Come on through.'

Halloran's office was small, and the order that had been imposed on it was strict. A small cobweb, high in one corner, struck Helen as an undiscovered region of anarchy that was unlikely to flourish. Greg Halloran noticed her eye loiter on the ceiling, and he followed her line of sight to the fluttering web. Its hours were numbered.

The easy camaraderie between Titus and Greg

was curious to Helen. She'd never seen him relax so quickly and so easily in the company of any of the detectives at Russell Street. She'd never thought of him as having friends, or people who were accommodated by him as being equals — apart from his wife, Maude. Detective Inspector Halloran was something of a revelation. She was struck by his acceptance of her presence as uncontroversial and unremarkable. She'd been steeling herself for a sort of blokey repartee that she was expected to hear with good grace, and perhaps compound with a bit of self-deprecation. Halloran seemed to have no interest in playing that game.

'We can't find George Starling,' he said, revealing that he was acquainted with the case, 'and all the indications are that John Starling died of a heart attack, which is disappointing.'

Helen raised her eyebrows.

'If George Starling had murdered his own father, he'd find it very difficult to hide in this community.'

'You mean his Hitlerite sympathies might not make him a pariah on their own?' Helen asked.

'Warrnambool is like everywhere else, Constable. There are good people, and there are bad people, and the full sliding scale in between. Hitlerites? I imagine there are the odd one or two, or three or four, but it would be a brave or stupid man who called himself that out loud these days. Back in the Thirties we were aware of a small group that met out at John Starling's house. He fell out with them, and the group broke up.'

He handed each of his visitors a sheet of paper.

'These are the names and addresses of the members who are still around Warrnambool. As you can see, there are only three. None of them has a criminal record, which doesn't mean they're nice people. I can personally attest to the fact that the last name on the list is a deeply unpleasant man. His name is Stanley Halloran, and he's my brother.'

Helen, in a way that was becoming automatic with her, checked for Titus's reaction. A slight widening of the eyes suggested that this was news to him; she surmised that the familiarity and warmth between him and Halloran had been established long ago, but that they were not in regular contact.

'I've asked around the station, and no one can really remember George Starling. He didn't attract any attention growing up. He left school at 14, and I don't think he hung around here or Mepunga much after that.'

'Was there a Mrs Starling?' David Reilly asked. It struck Helen with some force that Reilly had asked a question she hadn't thought to ask.

'Mrs Starling died when George was an infant. There was an accident with a tractor. If you talk to some of John Starling's detractors — and if you threw a dart at random in Leibig Street, you'd hit one of those — you'd hear that Mrs Starling was often seen in town with a black eye or a swollen lip. It's generally assumed that John Starling went too far one night and then used a

36

tractor to obscure her injuries. There was never any proof. Death by misadventure was the official version.'

'George Starling made his phone call to my sergeant from Warrnambool,' Titus said, 'so we know he's in the area. Someone must have seen him.'

'I imagine a few people have seen him, Titus, but I doubt anyone would recognise him. You told me yourself that the only photograph you have of him was taken when he was, what, 16, and that he was fat? If anyone does remember him, that's what they'd remember — that he was fat. A fat kid looks very different from a lean adult.'

Titus reached into his bag and withdrew a sheaf of papers.

'These are the artist's impression of George Starling. Sergeant Sable gave the description, and he's happy with the likeness.'

Halloran took them and looked closely at the image.

'I don't know him, but I wouldn't want to run into him in a dark alley. I'll get these circulated. Maybe they'll jog someone's memory. It's not a face you'd forget in a hurry. How do you want to proceed, Titus?'

'Those three names need to be visited. It's a long shot, but George Starling might have gone to ground with one of them. Is your brother really worth visiting?'

'If you mean socially, no. In relation to Nazi sympathies, yes. He's been a big fan since the Thirties. I haven't spoken to him since the

37

beginning of the war, and I'd rather not break that habit, so I'd appreciate it if one of your people did the honours there.'

'Of course,' Titus said. 'These other two . . . ' he checked their names ' . . . Hardy Truscott and Maria Pluschow — are they violent people?'

'Neither of them has a record of any kind. Truscott lives in a perversely situated house overlooking the Hopkins River. The house faces away from the view. If you look at it from the far side of the river, where you'd expect a decent window, there's a blank wall. He built the bloody house, so I suppose that tells you a great deal about his style. Maria Pluschow lives out on the road to Port Fairy. She's a widow, and not German herself — she married a German. She used to walk around looking like a storybook frau, but the braids have gone now, and she's stopped raising the swastika on Hitler's birthday. She confines her prejudices to Catholics these days, but that's par for the course here. If you want to live dangerously, walk into the Lutheran church and yell out Daniel Mannix's name.'

In a strategic move, David Reilly suggested that he call on Maria Pluschow.

'You'll need to be driven out there.'

'Sergeant Reilly can use our car. You don't need to deploy one of your men. I imagine you're short-staffed.'

'Well, as a matter of fact, we're not really run off our feet. However, Sergeant Reilly certainly won't require protection. Perhaps Constable Lord can visit my brother. He'll be quietly appalled that policewomen aren't just a nasty rumour. You and I can make a house call on Mr Truscott, Titus. We'll take the coal-burning vehicle. It's slow, but Truscott is close by. By the time we get back here, Constable Manton should have returned, and he can tell you himself what he found out at John Starling's place.'

'We'll need to go out there ourselves and look through the house.'

'Of course.'

Each of them took a picture of George Starling before leaving Halloran's office.

★   ★   ★

Inspector Lambert and Inspector Halloran didn't drive directly to Hardy Truscott's house. Greg wanted to show Titus the view of the house from the opposite side of the Hopkins River.

'I want you to see for yourself,' Greg said, 'the difference between what someone can aspire to and what someone is capable of.'

Truscott's rejection of what would have been a beautiful outlook seemed inexplicable. His house was perched on top of an escarpment, with a mean, narrow set of steps leading to a back door. There was a single small window above this door, but the occupier would need to climb a ladder to look out of it.

'Astonishing,' Titus said.

'He should have been interned on architectural grounds.'

'What do you know about him?'

'Not a great deal. I'm tempted to say he's

harmless, but the material you sent me to read was a bit of an eye-opener. Fortunately, the local fascists tended to be loners. They tried to get the odd meeting going, but, honestly, they couldn't organise a fuck in a brothel, which is why someone like John Starling went to Melbourne to join a group there.'

'I didn't know your brother was attracted to Nazism.'

'He was a bully, and he was stupid, so National Socialism was a comfortable fit. We never got on, even as children. He's a few years older, and he got big very early — not fat, just big, bulky. By the time he was 16 he was an ill-tempered old man. He terrified Mum and me, and dad couldn't do anything. He was all hollowed out when he came back from the first war. He barely spoke. I watched one day as Stanley pushed Mum up against a wall and screamed obscenities at her. Dad sat at the table, and his face was expressionless. He was seeing it happen, but it was as if it didn't register, or maybe it couldn't compete with whatever else was playing behind his eyes. When Dad did nothing the brakes were off, and Stanley got a taste for terrorising us. I can't begin to tell you how much I hated him, Titus.'

'How did you stop him?'

'I was a kid. I didn't stop him. He left home. Anti-climactic, huh? He just left home, and I didn't see him again until I was a copper. By then he'd begun to cultivate people like Starling and Truscott, and he tried to recruit me — can you believe it? We even had earnest conversations

40

about how well Germany was doing. He gave me a copy of *The Protocols of the Elders of Zion*. Christ, have you read that claptrap? If the bastard didn't look so much like me, I'd swear he was a fucking cuckoo in the nest.'

'Hence the moustache?'

'Thank you, Doctor Freud.'

'You sent Constable Lord to confront this man, Greg. Why?'

'Oh, she's in no physical danger. Stanley's in a wheelchair now. He was hit by a car in Melbourne in 1938 — and it was just an accident. He was drunk. The driver was a vicar.'

'The vicar was drunk?'

'No, Stanley was. He just wandered into the road. The poor bloody vicar still hasn't recovered. He sends Stanley money, and Stanley is such a prick that he takes it. I suppose the vicar finds it difficult to accept that he's done everyone a favour.'

'And you're sure Constable Lord will be safe there, on her own?'

'Titus, I wouldn't have sent a woman into a dangerous situation. She has a much better chance of getting information out of him, if there's any information to get. He'll assume she's not worth a cracker. He has a fairly low opinion of women. He'll be unguarded, and she strikes me as the kind of person who'll be able to take advantage of that.'

'He'd be very foolish to underestimate Constable Lord. Shall we find the front door of this abomination and beard Hardy Truscott?'

Hardy Truscott was short, stout, and rather

tweedy, although his tweeds were of an expensive cut. He was myopic, and wore round spectacles that magnified his eyes, which were a dull brown. His bald pate was spattered with age marks. When he saw Greg Halloran on his doorstep he sighed heavily, but invited him in without complaint. The house was surprisingly cheery, and where Titus had expected it to be dark and gloomy, it was light and uncluttered. Hardy Truscott was a fussy man. There were paintings on the wall, mostly landscapes of a European type. Joe Sable would have been able to assess their worth, but Titus had little understanding of art. Greg Halloran wasted no time.

'John Starling is dead. Did you know that?'

'I haven't seen Starling in years. Why would I know whether he'd died or gone to blazes?'

'You used to have a bit to do with him.'

Truscott laughed.

'It was the Thirties, Halloran. We thought we had something in common. It didn't take long to realise that Starling was a dumb thug.'

Titus hadn't intended to speak until he'd been identified, but the image of this carefully groomed little man, all the ugly bits of National Socialism tidied away into comfortable tweed and carefully chosen furniture, was an intolerable strain on his patience.

'I would have thought that dumb thugs were just what Dr Goebbels ordered,' he said.

'This is Inspector Lambert from Homicide in Melbourne.' Halloran spoke quickly. He'd seen Truscott's lip curl in readiness of making a disdainful query as to Titus's identity.

42

'Homicide?' Truscott said. 'You have my full attention, Inspector. John Starling was murdered, was he?'

Neither policeman said anything.

'And you think I might have killed him? Do you seriously think . . . ?'

Titus produced the sketch of George Starling and handed it roughly to Truscott, who looked at it closely.

'Have you had any contact with this man?'

'So is this your chief suspect, then?'

'Do you know him?'

'No. I can't say I do.'

'Did you ever meet John Starling's son, George?' Halloran asked.

'He was at one or two early meetings, before I got the measure of Starling's stupidity. He used to treat his boy like an animal. Disgusting. He was fat, I remember that. His father used to call him 'Fatso'. Surly kid, but I'd be surly, too, if my dad called me Fatso in front of other people.'

'So you haven't seen George Starling for quite some time?'

'Not since then — so not for, what, ten years maybe? Maybe more.' Truscott looked at the sketch again. 'Oh, I see. This is him. This is George. Yes, I can see that. Suck all the fat out of those cheeks and this is what he'd look like. He killed his father?' Truscott laughed. 'Patricide. It couldn't happen to a nicer bloke.'

'Why were you attracted to National Socialism, Mr Truscott?' Titus asked.

Truscott took the question in his stride, showing no irritation or outrage.

43

'Perhaps we should sit down,' he said, 'and I'll be glad to tell you.'

When all three were seated, Truscott reached for a book on the shelf beside him and pulled it out.

'A very great man wrote this book. You won't have heard of him. His name is Alexander Rud Mills.'

Both Lambert and Halloran were startled by the book's cover, the most prominent feature of which was a swastika.

'Don't be dismayed, gentlemen. This is a harmless book of poetry. *Hael, Odin!* Flick through it, by all means.'

He gave the book to Titus.

'I've heard of Mills,' Titus said.

Truscott was impressed.

'Not for reasons you might admire, Mr Truscott. Mills has come to the attention of the authorities on account of his unpleasant politics. They found him too ridiculous to bother with.'

'A.R. Mills is not interested in politics. His quest is a spiritual one.'

Titus opened the book and found its pages heavily underscored, indicating passages that had particularly taken Truscott's fancy. One poem, 'The Jew', was especially heavily decorated, and included marginalia in what Titus presumed was Truscott's own hand. The words 'Jew thought' and 'equality's pit' had been circled.

'What is 'Jew thought', Mr Truscott?'

Truscott leaned forward, unable to resist answering.

44

'Jew thought, Inspector, is at the heart of every rotten principle espoused by lazy Christians. They don't even know that their religion is just a branch of Jew thought. Jewish-Christianity is a disease, and it's not treason to say so. A.R. Mills has the cure, and it's not Nazism, not as you know it, so you needn't bother shopping me to Military Intelligence. I'm no fifth columnist.'

'So what are you?'

'I suppose you'd call me an Odinist.'

'Oh yes,' Titus said. 'A pagan.'

Truscott smiled.

'I wouldn't expect someone of your plodding intelligence — excuse me, but why else would you become a policeman? — to understand.'

'Try me.'

'I'm not interested in National Socialism as a force for political change. That's something I could never drum into the heads of dullards like Starling and his friends. Salvation is to be found among the old gods, not the Jew god, and the way to them lies within us all, not in some man-made construct like Nazism.'

'Salvation from what?' Halloran asked.

'From the equality pit, as Mills calls it. Equality is a Jewish-Christian lie. Blood matters. Blood is everything.' Truscott picked up another book, its title obscured by the brown paper that protected the cover. He read:

The principle of equality is at war with all God's nature — the enforcement of that principle is a war on all vitality and health.

'That's Mills. Democracy doesn't work. Democracy is Jew thought.'

A nation under Democracy moves onward to Bolshevism and comes under the manipulation of soul destroyers and government by Jews. A return to our own Father spirit in God is the only way out. It is our only road to strength. Our own myths, our own heroes and our own holy places point the way. Odinists and Odinists only will preserve our race and someday revive our nation.

He stopped reading. Lambert and Halloran were watching him, their faces composed. Both were experienced enough to deny Truscott a clue as to the effect of his rant.

'You'll see,' Truscott said, in a tone that suggested he was rounding out his argument. 'The Aryan race is the great builder of culture. If the white people in this country turn to Odin, cultural revival is assured. We can't worship the spirit of another race, and Christianity worships the spirit of the Jew. Deliverance will come from our worship of Odin, our own God — not someone else's.'

Halloran had heard enough.

'You'll let us know, won't you, if George Starling makes contact?'

'Why would he?'

'Maybe he's as crazy as you are.'

'I'd have nothing to say to the offspring of John Starling. He wouldn't be welcome in my house.' He thought for a moment. 'Although, if I did run into him, I'd certainly congratulate him on killing his father.'

'John Starling wasn't murdered, Mr Truscott.'

Titus said, 'We'll see ourselves out.'

★　★　★

Helen Lord pulled up outside the address she'd been given by Inspector Halloran. There'd been no time to brief her on what she might expect, but she wasn't bothered by this. It was a routine inquiry, and she preferred making such inquiries without preconceptions imposed by someone else's assessment of a person's character. In truth, of course, Halloran's thumbnail sketch of his brother as 'a deeply unpleasant man' had fixed Stanley Halloran in her mind as someone of whom to be wary. The house, a California bungalow that looked as if it might have been built in the 1920s, was obscured by a garden that had become unruly, its growth checked by desultory clipping of the most vigorous branches that had been left to rot where they'd fallen. Helen opened the gate, which had been oiled sufficiently recently to utter only a small squeal of resistance. She knocked on the door. There was no response. She was about to knock again when a voice called, 'Who is it? What do you want?'

'I want to speak to Mr Stanley Halloran.'

'Who wants to speak to Stanley Halloran?'

'My name is Helen Lord.'

Helen thought it politic to announce her credentials only after she'd gained entry. Nazi admirers, despite the secretiveness of their sympathies, had more than probably been visited by one or another of the state or federal agencies whose job it was to track them. Stanley Halloran, with a brother who was a prominent policeman, would doubtless have been harried by at least one of the special branches — the Commonwealth Investigation Branch, perhaps, or the Commonwealth Security Service.

'So? What do you want?'

'I'm afraid I have some bad news, but I need to speak to Mr Stanley Halloran personally.'

'What kind of bad news?'

'Please, can we stop shouting at each other through the door? This won't take a moment.'

There was silence for a few seconds. The lock was turned, and the door was flung open. In a bar of sunlight, Helen saw a man seated in a wheelchair, his face in shadow. He was wearing a pair of shorts and nothing else — not unseasonable attire on such a hot day, but Helen noticed a crumpled shirt against the skirting board, and knew that he had taken it off in a deliberate attempt to give offence. She stepped into the house quickly, and closed the door behind her — an action that took the man by surprise.

'Hey, who said you could come in?'

Now that she could see his face, the resemblance to his brother was remarkable.

'I'm in, Mr Halloran, so that saves you the bother of asking me.'

She walked away from him, towards the living room, forcing him to follow her.

'You can't just walk into my house.'

'If you have a complaint, call your brother at the station. My name is Constable Helen Lord. Melbourne Homicide.'

'Constable? You're a fucking walloper?'

'Yes, Mr Halloran, I'm a fucking walloper, and I'm the daughter of a fucking walloper.'

'Christ, they must be desperate. A tough-talking sheila — whatever next?'

Helen looked at him. His face had aged well, but his body had given up pretending it was anything other than its 60-odd years. It was thin and wiry, but also somehow slack and fallen, and the hair that grew on it was piebald and dry, like a withered, invasive creeper. Helen had no wish to prolong this encounter. She unfolded the sketch of George Starling and handed it to Stanley Halloran.

'Do you know this person?'

He looked at it.

'What if I do?'

Helen decided not to dance around the subject.

'I'm not here on a social call, Mr Halloran. I'm here as part of an ongoing homicide investigation. Now do you know this man or not?'

'You think this bloke's killed someone?' He laughed. 'If he did, he's grown some balls since I last saw him. That's George Starling. A skinny George Starling, but it's him all right. Last time I saw him, he was a pathetic, whining fat boy. I knew his father.'

'Knew?'

'Haven't seen him for years. Thick as four planks, he is.'

'John Starling is dead, Mr Halloran.'

Again, Stanley Halloran laughed.

'Well, bugger me. And you think his son did it? Or what? You think maybe I wheeled myself out to his place and did it myself?'

'There's no suggestion that John Starling was murdered by anyone.'

'Would you like a cup of tea, lovey? It's not every day a female copper comes a'courtin'.'

The question took Helen by surprise.

'No.' She added, 'Thank you,' and regretted it when she saw the smile creep across Halloran's face.

'You and John Starling shared an interest in politics.'

Helen had expected that bald statement to make Halloran wary. Instead, he clutched the wheel rims of his chair and leaned forward.

'Let me tell you something about politics, lovey, although it'll go over your head. The female mind isn't designed for thinking.'

He paused to give Helen time to object. She didn't give him the satisfaction, beyond a slightly exaggerated expression of ersatz interest.

'I'm glad we're going to win the bloody war.'

'Are we?'

'Germany lost the war at Stalingrad, and the Japs were nongs for involving the Yanks. That's not to say that National Socialism hasn't got something going for it. I presume that's what you're referring to when you say Starling and I shared an interest in politics. I wasn't Robinson Crusoe about the Nazis in the Thirties, you know. Mr Menzies saw its good points, but I'll

50

wager he regrets saying anything these days.'

Helen looked doubtful in spite of herself.

'He's had a change of heart, but back in '38 he was all for abandoning individual liberty. There was something magnificent, he said, about Germany turning its back on everything that was easy and pleasant. Magnificent — that's the word he used, and he was right. I thought for a while that National Socialism was the answer for this dump of a country, but Australians are too dumb to diagnose their own cancer. Are you following me?'

'Unfortunately, yes.'

Halloran snorted.

'The truth is, lovey, that we don't have any leaders — decent leaders. We've got milksops and nancy boys, but we need harsh men — men who are fanatics and who can inspire fanaticism in others. Democracy is weak. A strong leader, that's what will work.'

'Like Hitler, you mean?'

'Sure. Like Hitler, but he's not right for here.'

'Hirohito, then?'

'Don't make me laugh. Wrong race, lovey. Race matters. I've got nothing against the Nips, except that they're Nips and they should stay in Nipland, where everyone is happy to be a Nip, see?'

Helen stepped around Stanley Halloran, obliging him to turn his chair to face her. She did this because she could no longer bear to look at his body in the full light from the windows.

'You're not a Jew, are you?' he asked.

His tone was so blunt that it bruised her in an

inexplicable way — except that it wasn't inexplicable. As soon as his question struck her, she imagined she was Joe Sable, and heard the words as he might have heard them — each syllable a gobbet of bile.

'No,' she said, 'I'm not,' and instantly wished that she'd answered in the affirmative, realising, with some shame, that her answer represented a small act of cowardice.

'I'm not a Jew hater,' Halloran said. 'Like everyone, they're fine in their place. This just isn't their place. This is what's fundamentally wrong with this country. Jews, Italians, Japs, blacks — no one likes them, but they don't dislike them *enough*. They don't want them in their clubs, or next door, but that's about as far as it goes. If you're going to protect white Australia you have to understand what accommodating these people means; you have to understand this at the level of bone and marrow, and you have to be willing to do something about it, see? And you need someone to lead.'

'You were looking for a leader when you met up with Starling and his cronies?'

Halloran moved his wheelchair forward.

'You wouldn't be saying that if I wasn't in this fucking wheelchair, you smug, ugly little bitch. I was the leader *they* were looking for.'

Helen took a step backwards, repressing the urge to retaliate. The priority here was to find George Starling, not to best an old man in a wheelchair. She was close enough to him to lean in and retrieve the sketch of George Starling.

'So, you haven't seen him recently?' she said.

52

He wheeled away from her, towards the front door, which he opened.

'Get out of my house, and tell my prick of a brother if he wants any information from me he should send a real policeman, not some silly slut who should be doing something useful like working on a munitions line, or fucking soldiers for free. If it's dark enough, they mightn't notice how fucking ugly you are.'

If Halloran was expecting to get a rise out of Helen, he was disappointed. She moved past him, onto the porch.

'Thank you for your time, Mr Halloran. I think I've learned everything about you that's worth learning.' She smiled at him. 'It only took ten minutes.'

He slammed the door.

Sitting in the car, Helen looked in the rear-view mirror.

Sticks and stones, she said to herself. What a pious old lie that is.

★   ★   ★

Maria Pluschow's house sat close to the verge, ten minutes out of Warrnambool, on the Port Fairy road. Sergeant David Reilly liked neat houses — a preference catered to by his wife, who picked up after him — and the Pluschow house was a model of neatness. The land behind it, and on either side, was a comparative chaos of ungrazed grass and thistle, leading Reilly to surmise that it wasn't owned by Maria Pluschow.

He was slightly nervous. Having read and re-read

the briefing notes, he'd been appalled by the violence meted out by people of Maria's political persuasion. It had come as an unpleasant shock to him that there were people in his own familiar city who thought seriously, passionately, and dangerously that National Socialism wasn't just a viable alternative to democracy, but a preferable and necessary one. He half expected that Maria Pluschow would be an exaggerated version of Magda Goebbels, whose austere, determinedly maternal visage he'd seen in newsreels. When Maria Pluschow opened the door to him, he found a thin, plainly dressed woman, with grey hair pulled severely into a bun, away from her face. Her skin was lined, making her look older than she perhaps was. Reilly's wife, Barbara, always said that a little plumpness around the face protected it from ageing too quickly, which licensed her fondness for sponge cake — a fondness that had been sorely curtailed by the frequent difficulty in finding fresh eggs.

Reilly took off his hat.

'My name is Sergeant Reilly. I'm a policeman from Melbourne. May I come in?'

Maria Pluschow looked him up and down, thought about closing the door in his face, thought better of it, and said, 'I haven't broken any laws. Why don't you people leave me alone?'

'May I come in?'

'No, you may not.'

Reilly was wrong-footed by her obstinacy. Back in Melbourne he might have insisted and used his foot against the door to demonstrate this insistence. Here, in a strange town, he felt constrained by an uncertainty about how his city manners would be received by Inspector Halloran. He reached into his pocket and withdrew the sketch of George Starling.

'Do you know this person?'

Maria Pluschow glanced at it and said, 'No. Never seen him before in my life. What's he supposed to have done, and why are you asking me?'

'We're asking a few people, Mrs Pluschow.'

'You know my name. Why?'

Reilly was flustered by the aggressiveness of her questions, and afterwards he realised he'd given her too much information too early in the encounter. He should have tested her claim that she didn't recognise the sketch. Instead he said, 'This is George Starling. He grew up around here. His father is — was — John Starling.'

'Was?'

'John Starling died very recently.'

'How recently?'

'Two days ago.'

'And what's that old bloke's death got to do with me?'

By now Reilly was only too aware that he'd lost control of the interview. Maria Pluschow was asking all the questions. He tried to wrest back some control.

'John Starling's death isn't being treated as suspicious. We want to find his son, that man in the sketch, so that we can tell him that his father has passed away.'

Reilly thought this appeal to sentiment was inspired.

'Why would they send a policeman all the way

from Melbourne to look for John Starling's boy just to tell him his dad was dead?'

Reilly was unable to contain his exasperation.

'Do you, or do you not, know George Starling?'

'Well, now, I wouldn't want to lie to you, given the charitable mission you're on. I knew him when he was a boy. I haven't seen him for years, and that sketch looks nothing like him. And I'll tell you this, there was never any love lost between the two of them. I'd bet my bottom dollar that George won't care less when you break the bad news to him.'

'When was the last time you saw John Starling?'

'He lived on the other side of Warrnambool. I wouldn't have seen him for close enough to 10 years.'

'Did you fall out with him?'

She laughed.

'Now you want more than you're entitled to. No, I didn't fall out with him. As a matter of fact, I quite liked him. Now, you've had your fair share of jibber jabber, and I've got things to do.'

'If George Starling contacts you, the Warrnambool police want to know about it.'

'Why on earth would that boy contact me? And just so you know, if on the off chance he did, I won't be running to the coppers.'

She closed the door, leaving Reilly to begin to construct a version of the interview that he hoped would satisfy Inspector Lambert.

4

Matthew Todd looked critically at his fiancée's face. He often did this, just to reassure himself that she really did bear a passing resemblance to Irene Dunne. Matthew loved Irene Dunne. He'd begun courting Dorothy Shipman the day after he'd seen her in Sackville Street. She was unaware of her resemblance to the movie star, and Matthew never mentioned it. This was a private passion. Dorothy rarely went to the movies. Dorothy rarely did anything that might put ideas into her head. She wasn't silly, though — not by a long chalk. She was something of an accounting wizard, and she kept the books for her father's drapery business. She'd been out of Port Fairy only twice in her life. On both occasions she'd travelled to Warrnambool to see a dentist. Consequently, her experience of the world was narrow, and whatever opinions she'd formed had become inflexible to the point of atrophy.

One of these opinions concerned girls who surrendered their virginity before marriage. No marriage could survive such an assault on decency. Matthew discovered, on the night he made an inelegant manual dash for Dorothy's crotch, the limits of the erotic possibilities between him and his fiancée. She'd been horrified that his fingers had slipped under the edge of her bloomers and brushed against her pubic hair. Indeed it was this incident that led to their engagement. Dorothy felt despoiled, but the despoliation was tolerable if it was to be redeemed by marriage. Matthew, who knew perfectly well that he could satisfy his lust elsewhere, agreed to Dorothy's terms. After all, the idea that he would soon take Irene Dunne's virginity was an irresistible attraction.

As he watched her now, poring over the accounts book in the draper's shop, he wondered if this engagement was such a good idea after all. He didn't need whatever money she might bring to the marriage — and it wouldn't be much, as Shipman's Drapery wasn't exactly booming. He had his own quite lucrative source of income, brokering the catch for several of Port Fairy's biggest fishermen. Despite his relative youth, he'd proved a tough negotiator, and the fishermen's income had increased under his brokerage. They'd been particularly impressed when he'd managed to minimise the rorting of the lobster catch by the buyers in Melbourne. It was common practice for the wholesalers to declare that a percentage of the catch had arrived damaged and that they wouldn't pay full price for damaged goods. They would then on-sell the lobsters for a decent price, having bought them cheaply. The fishermen knew perfectly well that they were being diddled, but had had no way of proving it.

Matthew took it upon himself to track a haul of lobsters brought in by the men he represented from the boat deck, to the wharf, to the railway station, and thence all the way to Melbourne. He watched the unloading, and ticked off each lobster as it was passed for inspection. It was tedious, but no lobsters were declared damaged in the batches he supervised. Other batches from Port Fairy wouldn't be so lucky; he was certain of that. There would probably be an unusual number of damaged animals to compensate. Despite the inconvenience and the cost, Matthew accompanied the lobster catch, each time there was one, for several weeks until he'd established a pattern among the buyers of passing his catch without penalty. It would look peculiar if damaged lobsters suddenly started to appear just because Matthew wasn't there. The fishermen he represented, at first reluctant to hire someone so young, were impressed.

People in Port Fairy liked Matthew Todd, and he liked being liked. He attended church, even if it was the wrong church as far as half the town was concerned, and no one ever saw him drunk or disorderly. It was generally agreed that he and Dorothy Shipman were a good match, although it was occasionally noted that the Shipmans occupied a social rung a bit below the Todds. The fact that the village idiot was his uncle helped close that gap a little. Matthew could see Selwyn from Shipman's window.

'Is your uncle in his usual spot?' Dorothy asked. She asked this question almost every day, despite knowing full well what the answer would be. This irritated Matthew intensely, but each day, in a measured tone, he replied, 'Yes, he's there, dribbling and drooling and scratching away like the moron he is.'

There must have been something slightly different in his tone this day, because Dorothy, instead of going back to her figures, said, 'He's harmless, Matthew. You mustn't be so cruel.'

'I hate him. He's repulsive. He's only half human, and that's the half that pisses and shits everywhere.'

Dorothy was shocked. She left the counter and joined Matthew at the window, intending to berate him about his appalling language. The look on his face stopped her.

'He's not hurting anybody,' she said quietly.

'You wouldn't say that if you were related to him.'

'But I will be related to him, when we're married.'

Matthew turned to her and was disappointed to find that the way the light fell across her face obliterated her resemblance to Irene Dunne. He leaned down, kissed her on the forehead, and said, 'He should be put down. If you had a dog as useless and filthy as Uncle Selwyn, you'd have it put down.'

* * *

George Starling had been in Port Fairy for two weeks, and he'd been careful to keep out of the way. He called himself 'Bert' and didn't offer a last name. He knew that the coppers would be asking about a bloke who called himself 'Fred'. Having spoken to that little Sable cunt, he was glad he hadn't gone back to his real name — not that there'd been any chance of that. The last thing he wanted was for anyone to make a connection between him and his lousy father. Port Fairy was the ideal place to retreat to. No one knew him there. Having grown up on the other side of Warrnambool — despite its being only 18 miles away, it might as well have been the far side of the moon — he felt at home here, in the sense that the weather was familiar. The smells, too, calmed his nerves. Even the briny iodine air that frequently settled over Port Fairy was familiar, his father's farm being close to the ocean. He liked the ocean, and he liked it best when it thundered. As a child, he'd escaped his father's tongue and his vicious fists by clambering down the cliffs of Murnane's Bay and sitting for hours on end on the damp sand of the small, private cove. He'd preferred to do this when the weather was wild so that the ocean drew itself up in a rage and broke almost at his feet. It had frightened him, but not in the way that his father frightened him. This was noble fear, and it excited him. As he grew older he would borrow his father's motorcycle, and eventually explored the coast and hinterland from Mepunga to the far side of Port Fairy. Once, he'd made it to Portland. He came to know this area with the precision of an ordinance map.

At the moment, he had no transport, and this, he felt, made him powerless. To do what he wanted to do — to punish Sable — he needed that motorcycle, although he wasn't sure how he'd get the petrol to take him to Melbourne. There was a tank on the farm, but it would be bone dry. Well, he'd find a way. The important thing was to get hold of the motorcycle, and this was within his grasp because Peter Hurley was delivering a catch of couta and trumper to a mate just beyond the Mepunga turn-off. He'd get a lift and walk the rest of the way. He knew that Hurley would have no interest in his reasons for being dropped off in the middle of nowhere, and he'd repay the compliment by not asking why the catch was going to a farmer and not to market.

★ ★ ★

It was almost four o'clock when the detectives gathered at the Warrnambool police station to compare notes. Constable Manton had returned, too, and had told them that he'd seen no evidence of any violent disturbance at Starling's farm.

'It struck me as not a bad way to go. Starling looked calm, as if he'd sat down for a breather and then died. The flies made it bad to look at. They'd been busy — not that it would've bothered Starling.'

Having heard each separate report, the consensus was that George Starling would be unlikely to make contact with any of the people questioned. Halloran was curious about Helen Lord's impressions of his brother.

'I assume,' she said, 'that I can be frank.'

'Yes. You needn't worry about offending me.'

'I thought your brother was a sad, frustrated, angry old man. Is he a widower?'

'A bachelor.'

'That's a relief.'

'A relief?'

'I don't think he'd have made a sympathetic husband. I know it sounds awful, but I'm glad he didn't get to punish a wife for having had the temerity to be born female.'

'Was he abusive to you?'

Helen thought about that.

'Not in any remarkable way. I was glad he was in a wheelchair.'

'I wouldn't have sent you into a dangerous situation — not on your own, anyway.'

'I didn't mean that I might have felt physically threatened. I meant that I was glad he was in a wheelchair.'

It took a moment for this subtly vitriolic remark to sink in.

'All I can say, Constable, is that I'm not surprised that he lived down to my expectations. One doesn't choose one's siblings.'

David Reilly's account of his meeting with Maria Pluschow stressed her detestation of the police, but gave no hint of the way in which he'd bungled it. Inspector Lambert's account of Hardy Truscott's philosophy was succinct and dismissive. No one had seen George Starling for years. The fact that he'd been the butt of his father's jokes and that he'd regularly been on the receiving end of his fists were interesting additions to the little they knew about him.

★ ★ ★

It was close to 5.30 pm when George Starling walked up the driveway of his father's farm in Mepunga. He hadn't seen his father for several years — years during which he'd made his body hard and useful. Even so, he was nervous about meeting him. The memory of his violence and contempt remained raw. Now, though, he was ready to knock the old man down at the slightest provocation. He was going to take the motorbike, and that was that — if his father objected, it wouldn't end well. He noticed that there was fresh hay in the paddock closest to the house (he wasn't to know that Constable Manton had returned briefly and put it there), and that the horses and donkey were hoeing into it. Bypassing the house, he went straight to the shed where the motorbike was kept. If he could get away without having to confront his father, well and good.

While he was in the shed he heard the sound of a car pulling into the driveway. His father didn't own a car, so it wasn't him. He could see the driveway from the door of the shed, and he was shaken when he saw a police car. They'd come looking for him. Why else would they be there? He watched as four people, including a woman, got out. A female copper? Surely not. One of them looked familiar. He might have been there that night a few weeks ago in Belgrave, but Starling couldn't be sure. There was a door in the back of the shed, and he slipped through it, out into the yard, through a gap in the fence, and crouched behind a thick clump of blackberries. He had a good view of the back of his father's property, and he was confident that he couldn't be seen from there.

The four visitors didn't go up to the front door. Instead, they walked to the old cypress, just beyond the back fence. Starling didn't have a clear view of the cypress, but he could see enough to be puzzled by their interest in it. They spent several minutes near the tree before checking the backyard, including the shed holding the motorbike. When they walked in there, Starling quickly raised his forearm to his nose. Did he smell strongly of fish? Could he have left a scent behind that would puzzle the police? No, that was a ridiculous thought. These were plods, not Sherlock Holmes. Anyway, no one would be surprised to smell fish around these parts.

The police entered the house through the back door without so much as knocking. Why would they do that? They mustn't have been looking for him, after all. Were they hoping to take his father by surprise? No. If they'd wanted to do that, they'd make sure both the front and the back were covered. So, either they were expected or . . . George felt a sudden rush of excitement. They knew before they arrived that Starling senior wasn't at home. And what could that mean? His father had either left the district unexpectedly and suspiciously, or he was dead. At any rate, something had happened to him, and George didn't particularly care what. Whatever it was, he wouldn't need his house anymore — George Starling had no intention of claiming it or living in it. What he intended to do was burn it down. After the police left, he'd give them time to get back to Warrnambool, and then he'd cauterise the bloody memories of his childhood with fire.

The police were inside the house for about 20 minutes. Clearly, they were searching it. If they were looking for anything to do with him, they'd be disappointed. They came out, taking nothing away with them, and drove away.

He came out from behind the blackberries and returned to the shed that housed the motorcycle. To his surprise, the petrol tank was almost full, and there were two full tins of petrol hidden under hessian bags. His father must have acquired this fuel illegally. George didn't think that two tins amounted to stockpiling, but John Starling was unlikely to have been constrained by rationing laws, and there were probably more tins of fuel squirreled away on the property. George picked up one of the containers and took it with him to the house. He didn't want to waste it, so he splashed it judiciously, not liberally, at points in the living room and corridor where flames would have something to crawl up. He didn't bother checking any of the rooms — they held nothing of interest for him. The only place he did check was the kitchen, where his father used to hide money in the flour tin. George upended its contents and, sure enough, it wasn't only flour that spilled onto the floor. He gathered up the notes, and to his astonishment found that he was holding close to £5,000. He did something he rarely did: he laughed.

He wasn't yet ready to strike a match, though.

He'd give the police another 15 minutes. He didn't want them seeing smoke and coming back. He wanted a head start on them, but he also wanted them to know that he'd been there, that the house fire had been deliberately lit, and that he, George Starling, had lit it. He wanted them to know that they'd missed him, and that he was smarter than they were. He walked out into the backyard and picked up the wood splitter — the same splitter whose condition Constable Manton had lamented. He took it with him into the paddock where the two horses and the donkey were eating the last of the hay. He opened the gate and called, 'Oi!' The animals looked up and, in expectation of more food, came placidly to him. He swung the splitter with a fierce precision, and broke a front and back leg of each animal. Starling thought for a moment that he might put them out of their misery, but decided against it. He wanted whoever found the creatures to know that the person who did this was pitiless. As he listened to the pathetic whinnying and snorting, he realised with satisfaction that he was indeed pitiless. He felt nothing, except perhaps amusement at the way the donkey tried again and again to stand.

He returned to the house and threw a lit match at each splash of petrol. He waited to make sure that the flames took hold, and then put both fuel tins on the motorcycle and set out for Melbourne. The timing was perfect. He wasn't happy about being in Port Fairy when police from Melbourne were sniffing around in Warrnambool. There was no doubt in his mind

67

that those police were city wallopers — a female copper in the Warrnambool force was unthinkable. Now he had some time up his sleeve. Peter Hurley wasn't going to take his boat out for a few days, so he wouldn't be looking for him to clean the catch. He had money, fuel, and a machine that would take him all the way to Sergeant Joe Sable.

★ ★ ★

Dinner at the Warrnambool Hotel was corned beef with boiled potatoes, leeks, and green beans. It was edible, although it arrived at the table without any sauce to disguise its blandness. The chef's excuse would no doubt have been austerity, although David Reilly, who liked his leeks to swim in a white sauce, supposed its absence had more to do with laziness than patriotism. Inspector Lambert wasn't interested in whether a sauce was white, green, or brindle, or in whether it was there or not. For him, food was fuel; he took no particular pleasure in it. Helen Lord found herself aligned with Reilly on the sauce question — although, as she wasn't paying for the meal, she didn't complain. Not that Reilly complained exactly. When the food was put down in front of him, he simply remarked that the plate looked naked.

'Cook's night off,' he said, and smiled to indicate that he didn't want this observation to be taken as a whinge.

At the end of the meal, all three of them remained in the dining room. Reilly would have preferred to decamp to the bar, but Constable Lord's presence made that impossible. As Homicide's budget didn't run to alcohol, he abstained from ordering a drink on his own account. He wasn't willing to pay the surcharge added to alcohol served in either the dining room or the ladies' lounge.

Conversation over dinner had included speculation about the nature of the threat posed by George Starling. David Reilly wasn't convinced that he was any more dangerous than a common or garden thug, and he felt that Starling's connection to the Hitlerites made him a ludicrous figure, rather than a threatening one.

'You *have* read the case notes?' Helen said.

'Yes,' Reilly replied evenly. 'I've read them, and I've re-read them.'

'And have you understood them?'

Reilly's eyes darted to Inspector Lambert. If he was hoping that he would intervene in what was, at the very least, an expression of insubordination, he was disappointed. Lambert seemed unperturbed by Lord's offensive question. Reilly breathed in, and waited a few seconds. He'd found this a useful technique when dealing with some irrational remark made by his wife. Early in his marriage, he'd flown off the handle, and said things that he'd meant, but which he regretted. So he'd learned to pause and not to say them. This had little to do with protecting his wife's feelings. Rather, he saw losing his temper as a weakness, and he gained great satisfaction from controlling it. His wife no doubt believed that she'd won her point. Reilly knew differently; Barbara Reilly never won any points. Her husband's carefully managed annoyance was a form of condescension that Helen Lord wouldn't respond well to. He knew this, and the situation was novel to him. He wasn't sure how to respond to her question, so he chose to agree with its implication.

'Perhaps I haven't fully appreciated how violent these people can be. I wasn't there to see it.'

'You've seen Joe Sable, and you've seen the other consequences.'

'Yes, you're right. I suppose I was just put off by my meeting with Maria Pluschow. She's the only Hitlerite I've ever met, and she struck me as absurd.'

'How did *The Publicist* strike you?' Titus asked.

'Well, of course I was shocked by all that stuff about Jews, but as I'd never even heard of the magazine, or of Australia First, I just assumed that they were fringe-dwellers and of no more importance than, I don't know, Tarot readers or circus freaks.'

'The friends of these people are killing Jews in Europe in unimaginable numbers,' Titus said. 'We know that. Keep that in mind. Maria Pluschow's absurdity is just a matter of geography.'

Sergeant Reilly, who felt unfairly chastised, was about to offer a response when Inspector Halloran entered the dining room. He wasn't smiling as he walked towards the Homicide officers.

'Starling's house has burned down — or, more correctly, someone's burned it down.'

Titus stood up. Helen Lord followed his example. David Reilly remained seated, caught now between appearing slow to move or being too obstinate to do so.

'George Starling?' Titus asked.

'It was set alight not long after we left, and it was definitely set alight. There were no grassfires or bushfires in the area.'

'He was there, wasn't he, when we were looking over the place?' Helen said.

'He left a message, of sorts,' Halloran said. 'We had to put the horses and the donkey down — their legs had been broken. A wood splitter was leaning against the fence, just in case we were wondering.' He paused, and in the pause Helen shot Reilly a pointed look, as if to suggest that perhaps he might now care to take George Starling seriously.

'The motorcycle that was in the shed is missing.'

'He's on his way to Melbourne,' Titus said. 'We need to telephone Sergeant Sable, and we need to get back there tonight.'

'There are fires around Camperdown,' Halloran said, 'but the last I heard they were under control. Does Starling know where Sergeant Sable lives?'

'Yes, he does,' Reilly said, and hoped that would prove definitively how closely he'd read the case notes.

'He's already paid Sergeant Sable one visit,' Titus said. Helen Lord looked at him, and saw in his face something like fear.

5

Joe Sable wondered whether his almost obsessive scouring of newspapers for news of atrocities in Europe was unhealthy. The massacres had shifted his indifference to his own Jewishness — an indifference that had been encouraged by his parents' belief that they were English first, and Jewish a very poor second. Joe felt no connection to the Jews he saw in Carlton. His father had dismissed these 'ostentatiously Semitic' types as an embarrassment. He'd called them '*shtetl* peasants' who gave Jews a bad name. The Sables were several cuts above, possibly even aristocratic.

Joe had never experienced overt anti-Semitism, which was why he'd been so dismayed when news of what was happening in Europe had begun to find its way into the newspapers. It was a trickle, never a flood, but he cut out whatever he could find, and put the pieces in a folder, as if in marshalling them in this way he could contain the horror. He couldn't. He read and re-read the reports; and, when he did so, outrage, despair, and shame grew and spread like gangrene in the soul. The discovery that National Socialism had local admirers had shocked him. When he'd first read *The Publicist*, a magazine unknown to him before the investigation, he'd been sickened by its brutal certainty that he, as a Jew, represented a threat to everything that was decent about Australia. Two sentences from among thousands decrying the presence of Jews had taken up residence in his mind, and they hummed constantly, like a hovering wasp: 'What is the solution to the Jewish problem? There can be none while a Jew lives.'

He'd kept his feelings to himself, and it disturbed him to think that his contact with Australia First and with the psychopathy of Ptolemy Jones had poisoned him. It had weakened his capacity to trust, and Joe worried that he might never recover from this blight. So he searched the papers looking for proof that optimism was a kind of moral blindness. The past week had been dominated by stories covering the bushfires, which were even more devastating than the fires in 1939. There'd been growing panic that the state would be overwhelmed. The fires had swept into the suburbs: Rosanna, West Heidelberg, and Preston; and Mentone, Beaumaris, and Cheltenham. Beyond the city, in Daylesford, Woodend, Gisborne, Mortlake, Hamilton, Camperdown, Seymour, the whole Western District; Pakenham, Gippsland, the Dandenongs — north, east, and west of Melbourne — the fires burned. Even the air in Princes Hill smelled of smoke. It came in through Joe Sable's windows.

He noted, within the catalogue of destruction reported by the newspapers, that William Dobell had won the Archibald Prize. It was hard to tell what his portrait of Joshua Smith actually looked like. The black-and-white reproduction of it made it look odd. He cut out the image and put it among his other cuttings. He did this because he liked Dobell, and he thought the picture

73

would provide some relief when he hunted through his collection.

The fires had taken up so much space that there'd barely been room in the past week for war news. The Allies were advancing into Italy — that, at least, made it to the front page. But tucked away in *The Argus*, on page 16, was an article that snagged Joe's eye:

Hungarian War Criminals Seek Refuge In Germany

From Our Own Correspondent
LONDON, Friday

Admiral Herthy, Regent of Hungary, has been forced into the extraordinary position of having to demand from Hitler the extradition of three war criminals who were whisked across the frontier into Germany. They are the Hungarian officers Field-Marshal Ferenc Feketehalmy-Czeydner, Gen Joseph Grassy, and Col Lazlo Deak.

They are accused by their own government of mass murders in a Jugoslav town on the Danube which the Hungarians occupied and renamed Novisad. After holes had been knocked in the frozen river, between 1,500 and 3,000 Serbs and Jews were driven at bayonet point to the river and drowned.

The officers now in flight are alleged to have directed the massacres, news of which could not be suppressed. After an official inquiry they escaped with the connivance of the Germans. There has been a storm of protest in the Hungarian press, which demands that they should be punished.

74

Joe looked for more, but there was nothing. This was a strange article, and Joe was wrestling with its meaning when the telephone rang. He looked at his watch. It was just after 10.00 pm. He picked up the receiver, expecting to hear George Starling's voice.

'Person-to-person call for Joe Sable,' the operator said.

'Yes, fine. I'm Joe Sable.'

'Thank you. Go ahead.'

'Joe, this is Inspector Lambert.'

'Sir?'

'I want you to do exactly as I say, without argument, without even thinking about it. George Starling is on his way to you. I'll give you the details later, when I see you. For now, I want you to go to my house immediately. Maude will be expecting you. It's absolutely critical that you leave your house now. We're not sure exactly when Starling left Warrnambool. He's on a motorcycle, and wherever he is, he'll be fairly close to you by now.'

'Mrs Lambert . . .'

'Sergeant! You are to do this *now*. Not in half an hour, not in five minutes. Now!'

The tension in Inspector Lambert's voice was contagious, and Joe felt his heart shiver — it was a sensation he dreaded. He was used to his heart's uncertain rhythms, but its unpredictability terrified him. It was his great weakness, the one thing about him that was utterly unreliable. It had kept him out of the army, and it reminded him — and always at the wrong time — how vulnerable he was. Now, as Inspector Lambert's

75

voice throbbed with urgency, Joe felt his heart begin to let him down.

'I'll go now,' he said, and hoped Lambert didn't detect the wheeze in his voice. Joe hung up the telephone as a wave of nausea swept over him. He took two steps towards the chair he'd been sitting in, and managed to kneel before he lost consciousness.

★　★　★

George Starling had ridden without stopping, except to take a piss just outside Colac. At the precise moment that Joe Sable's telephone had rung, Starling was passing Victoria Market, and was just 15 minutes from Joe's flat. The streets were dark, but not as dark as they'd been in the early years of the war. Lights showed here and there, and cars drove with their headlights dimmed, but without the obscuring shades that allowed only a slit of light to escape. The blackout, which had been relaxed to a brownout, was no longer policed with any rigour. It would require another scare, such as the 1942 attack by Japanese submarines on Sydney Harbour, to encourage the authorities to risk public annoyance by tightening controls. Starling saw this relaxation as complacency, and typical of the undisciplined, lazy Australian public. The men were beer-swipers and the women brummy fowls. He hadn't thought much about National Socialism since Ptolemy Jones' death. He thought its principles were sound; but, in truth, he wasn't really interested in politics. He liked

76

Nazism's certainties, its belief that negotiation was weakness. More than anything else, he liked the way it frightened people. There was a negative side, of course. Politics meant talking to other people about, well, politics, and Starling had no patience for other people. Anyway, he didn't need National Socialism, however much he agreed with it, to settle scores. For now, his only ambition was to do just that, and he had the means and the money. Joe Sable was first on his list, but there were others.

★ ★ ★

Joe was on all fours in his living room, dizzy and trying to marshal his anxiety by telling himself, out loud, that this had happened before, and that his doctor had assured him that his heart was strong enough to survive its irregular beat. There'd been a rider to this diagnosis: he'd been advised that he needed to be careful. He couldn't afford to treat his heart with the cavalier inattention of most young men.

He stood up, steadied himself, and felt his urge to be sick subside. He was sweating, and the smell of burning eucalypts from Melbourne's fringes seemed somehow stronger than it had been before he'd fainted. He turned out the lights, crossed to the window, pulled back the blackouts, and closed it. Pigdon Street was deserted. A motorcycle passed by slowly, heading towards Lygon Street. Inspector Lambert had said that Starling was on a motorcycle. Joe looked at his watch. It was now after 10.15.

Lambert had warned him to leave immediately, and somehow almost 20 minutes had already elapsed. The motorcycle didn't slow further as it passed his window, which he reopened in order to listen, in case it stopped or turned around. It didn't. He heard it turn right at Lygon Street, and then the sound of its engine faded. Joe realised as he strained to hear the engine that he was frightened. This angered him. Surely if he stayed he could set a trap to catch George Starling. His heart fluttered, and he knew he had to leave. Apart from any other consideration, if he didn't go to the Lamberts' house, he'd be disobeying a direct instruction, and his position in Homicide felt tenuous enough as it was. He decided to walk up Sydney Road to the Lamberts' house in Brunswick. This would take 30 minutes — 30 minutes in which he could prepare himself to meet Maude Lambert for the first time since she'd turned her unforgiving back on him in the hospital a few shorts weeks before.

★   ★   ★

George Starling turned into Pigdon Street from Bowen Crescent. He drove slowly with his headlights switched off. He knew Joe Sable's flat, having been there once before. As he approached it, he saw a window on the first floor — Sable's window — close. He couldn't make out the figure who'd closed it, but he knew there was a possibility that the motorcycle had been seen, certainly heard. On the ride from Warrnambool

78

he'd considered the probability that the police who'd visited his father's farm would have either returned to the farm or been told that the motorcycle was missing. He hated them, but he didn't think they were stupid. He wished now that he hadn't torched the house. It would only have taken a phone call to warn Sable. Maybe, though, the house had been razed without having been noticed, although with the current panic about bushfires no plume of smoke would have gone unchecked. The fact that Sable was still in his flat — and who else could it have been closing the window? — meant that Starling had arrived ahead of any warning. Nevertheless, to be sure, he drove on to Lygon Street, and revved his engine to alert any listener that he'd turned towards the city. He rode two blocks south, turned right at the cemetery into Macpherson Street, cut the engine, and dismounted. He pushed the bike to the corner of Macpherson and Arnold streets. Sable's flat sat two blocks north, on the corner of Arnold and Pigdon. He parked the bike and began to walk. He passed a school and might have stopped to smash a few windows if he'd known it was a Jew school. When he reached Sable's block of flats, he stood in the shadows on the opposite side of Arnold Street, and considered his options.

* * *

Joe Sable threw a few personal effects into a small bag. The idea of spending the rest of the night in Inspector Lambert's house was peculiar,

79

even without the added tension of confronting Maude Lambert and her injured brother, Tom Mackenzie. He packed his razor, a comb, and a change of underwear and socks. The thought of that motorcycle bothered him, but if he stuck to Sydney Road it would be difficult for anyone to take him by surprise. He left his flat, and walked downstairs and out into Arnold Street. He didn't notice a slight movement in the deep shadows on the opposite side, and he didn't notice either as the figure in those shadows broke away and began following him from a safe distance.

Joe was alert to all the traffic on Sydney Road. There wasn't much. A motorcycle roared past, but Joe recognised the uniform of an American soldier. Occasionally he looked behind him, and once he ducked into a doorway and waited a few moments. He'd seen someone do this in a film. Unlike the film, no follower caught up and revealed himself. Joe felt slightly silly when he stepped back into Sydney Road. There was someone several blocks back, on the other side. Whoever it was turned into a side street and disappeared.

★   ★   ★

Starling was an instinctive predator. He kept far enough back to make identification of him impossible, and he walked with the loose slouch of a purposeless pedestrian. If Sable looked back, he might see him, but his gait would suggest a person who perhaps had had just enough to drink to dull any urgency in his reason for being

80

in Sydney Road. He saw Sable slip into a doorway and guessed at his reason for doing so. He made a small, derisive noise at the man's inexperience. As if any follower would fall for that! When Sable emerged, he stopped and looked down Sydney Road. Starling noted this, even though the distance between them was considerable, and with unhurried steps he turned into a side street. He waited a few moments and returned to Sydney Road. Sable had drawn further ahead, and Starling now hurried to make up the distance. He kept to the shadows, but Sable had stopped checking behind him. He turned right into Albion Street, where Starling lost sight of him. He ran to catch up, stopped at the corner, and crossed the narrow street. He saw Sable about 100 yards along Albion Street.

★   ★   ★

Albion Street was narrow and dark, and no traffic moved along it. Joe had been to the Lamberts' house once before, on New Year's Eve. So much had happened in the ensuing weeks that it seemed like a lifetime ago. He paused at the corner of Bishop Street to gather his thoughts. Maude Lambert was expecting him.

'Who was that?' Tom Mackenzie had said when Joe had rung Inspector Lambert 48 hours earlier. 'Nobody,' had been Maude's devastating reply.

He breathed deeply, and was aware that his hands were shaking. He walked towards the house, turned in at the gate, and paused yet again.

There was a light on in the front room — Joe could see a seam escaping down one side of the blackout. He knocked.

★　★　★

Starling stood at the end of Bishop Street and watched as Joe opened a front gate. He seemed to hover for a moment and then, in the general quiet, the sound of Sable knocking on the door reached Starling. He hurried along the far side of the street, protected from view by the absence of lighting. There were no trees to obscure him, but he didn't need them. He arrived opposite the house in time to see the front door open and Sable slip inside. It was too dark to get a glimpse of the person who'd let him in. Starling found a place where he could watch the house, and sat down with his back against a picket fence. Whose house was this? Did Sable have a girlfriend? After a few minutes, Starling decided he hadn't walked all this way to just sit and wait. He wasn't a patient man. He counted the houses back to the laneway that gave on to the nightsoil man's laneway that ran behind Bishop Street. Counting back, he found the back fence of the house that Sable had entered. There was a gate, which was carelessly unlocked — perhaps the nightsoil man was due — and Starling opened it and entered the Lamberts' backyard.

★　★　★

Joe had been aware, since his earliest days in Homicide, that Maude Lambert was as important to Inspector Lambert's investigations as any of his detectives were — possibly even more important. He knew that Helen Lord was resentful of this, and suspicious of Mrs Lambert, but he admired her, and her good opinion of him mattered. This was not to gain any professional advantage, but simply because he wanted such a person to note him and to like him. He had, however, fallen from grace, and when Maude opened the front door to him he felt an impulse to simply walk away.

'Sergeant Sable,' she said. 'You're safe. Come in.'

Joe said nothing. No words would come. He nodded and followed Maude down the corridor to the living room. She was wearing a silk dressing gown, and a faint, discreet perfume drifted from her. He noted that the door to the front room was closed. That, he assumed, was Tom Mackenzie's room.

There were two standard lamps, each beside a comfortable armchair. Only one of the lamps was on, and a small book, smaller even than a deck of cards, and much thinner, lay open on a table next to the chair. Maude indicated that Joe should sit in the unilluminated chair.

'Would you like a cup of tea? I can't offer you any alcohol. We drank the last of the whisky at Christmas.'

'A cup of tea would be fine.' Joe was conscious that his voice sounded strangled.

'You'll have to take it black, I'm afraid.

Neither Titus nor I drink milk. There is sugar, though. I'd hate you to think you're among barbarians.'

This small joke caused relief to flood through Joe's body, and he felt himself on the verge of tears. Maude saw this and withdrew to the kitchen, where she called, 'So, how many sugars?'

Joe, who failed to appreciate Maude's discretion, was thankful only that her fortuitous exit gave him time to collect himself.

'No sugar, thank you. I like my tea black.'

Maude returned to the living room and sat down.

'I'm sorry,' Joe said.

Maude looked at his bruised face and his wounded shoulder.

'You know, Sergeant, until just a few hours ago I really did hold you responsible for what happened to Tom. It was unjust — I knew that. I didn't want to talk to you, or see you. I didn't want to find reasons to forgive you. Of course, the idea that I would assume that there was anything that needed forgiving, or that I should be in the position to offer forgiveness from some lofty height, was in itself arrogant and unjust.'

'Please, Mrs Lambert . . . '

She shook her head.

'No, Sergeant, let me finish. Titus tried to change my mind, but every time I looked at Tom I needed to blame someone, and I wasn't willing to blame him. When Titus telephoned to say that you were in danger, I realised properly, absolutely, that blaming you was like blaming the person coming in out of the storm for the storm itself. That's rather clumsily put, I'm afraid.'

The kettle began to whistle, and Maude got up to make the tea.

★ ★ ★

The Lamberts' backyard was small and ordered. Vegetables grew in beds on one side, and shrubs struggled on the other. There were no blackouts on the kitchen window at the rear of the house. A dim light glowed in the room, almost too dim to be of much practical value. Starling watched as a woman came into the kitchen, and supposed she was making a cup of tea for her visitor. There was too little light to make out her features. Was she Sable's girl? His mother? Starling moved cautiously up a side path. There was wood stacked against a fence, and a proliferation of saw-toothed ferns. There was a window halfway down. Its blackouts were up, but it was open at the top. He took the precaution of getting down on all fours, and he moved slowly. There were dried fern fronds, leaves, and bark from the wood stack, and a carelessly placed hand or knee would create a betraying fusillade of crunch and crackle. When he reached the window, he manoeuvred himself into a sitting position. He could hear two voices, although he couldn't make out what was being said. He felt frustrated. It wasn't a feeling he liked, and it wasn't a feeling he could control well. It led to anger, and often to rage. As he strained to hear the conversation, the first churnings of anger began.

85

★ ★ ★

Joe took the full teacup from Maude. To his dismay, it rattled slightly in its saucer.

'You're shaking, Sergeant.'

'Yes, I'm sorry.'

Maude waited.

'It isn't fear. It's . . . '

'I know that, Sergeant.'

'I don't know why I'm shaking.'

'Titus and I don't have any secrets. I think you know that. He told me what happened in that house in Belgrave. Of course, I don't pretend to understand what it must have been like. I suspect what took place there is more than reason enough to make your hand unsteady.'

Joe heard the door of the front room open, and Tom Mackenzie's footsteps coming up the hallway. He thought he saw a subtle, rapid shift away from sympathy in Maude's expression. When she spoke, however, there was no hostility in her voice. Very softly, she said, 'Tom needs time, Sergeant.'

Tom Mackenzie took a couple of steps into the living room and stopped. He looked at Joe, was puzzled for a moment, and then smiled.

'I thought I heard someone come in.'

Joe was startled. He'd been expecting Tom to be an incoherent, shattered man. He was wearing only pyjama bottoms, possibly because of the hot night, but more probably because his torso was bruised, cut, and spot-burned by cigarettes. Several of his fingers were in splints, and his face was swollen. Joe stood up.

'Tom.'

'Yes, I'm Tom.'

'It's good to see you again.'

Tom nodded politely, but gave no indication that he recognised Joe.

'I'm just going to the toilet.'

'Can you manage?' Maude asked.

'Yes. I'm right.'

He walked through into the kitchen, opened the back door, and stepped down into the backyard.

In the living room, Joe sat down, stunned.

'The psychiatrist said it was a kind of shellshock,' Maude said. 'I'm sure he recognises you, but his mind is protecting itself against, well, against any associations with what happened, I suppose. He is getting better, Sergeant. I see that every day, but his physical injuries are always there to . . . '

'Remind him.'

'Yes. He smiled when he saw you.'

'And then he stopped smiling.'

★　★　★

George Starling heard the back door open. He could still hear the murmur of two voices, so a third person was now in the house. Starling stood up awkwardly. His left leg had gone to sleep. He shook it, and waited for the tingle and ache to pass. Stepping carefully, he returned to the backyard. The door to the privy was open. He waited by the side of the house for whoever was using it to emerge. A man coughed. Now was the time to take him, Starling thought, when he had his trousers down around his ankles. Who was in there, though? An attack, even when the attacker had the advantage, was risky, and Starling's advantage was diminished by his uncertainty about this bloke's identity. Not that Starling thought he might be armed. He might, though, be fast and strong, and Starling was not carrying a weapon. While he was pondering this, the person came out of the dunny. The faint spill of light from the kitchen revealed a man wearing pyjama bottoms. With a jolt of surprise, Starling recognised Tom Mackenzie. So he was still alive. It was obvious from the confusion in Mackenzie's face that he wasn't immediately able to account for the presence of the man he knew only as Fred. What he did next took Starling by surprise. Tom turned, calling at the top of his voice, 'Maude! Maude! Maude!', and retreated to the toilet, where he pulled the door shut after him. He continued calling, 'Maude! Maude! Maude!' The peculiar keening quality of his voice unsettled Starling. Unsure how many people might emerge from the house, he decided not to risk a confrontation and left quickly through the back gate.

★   ★   ★

Tom Mackenzie sat where Joe had been sitting before he and Maude had rushed into the backyard.

'He was there, staring at me. Fred — Fred was there.' He was shaking. 'I hid in the toilet,' he said with quiet shame.

'Do you have a torch, Mrs Lambert?'

'On the bench in the kitchen.'

Joe picked up the torch on his way to the backyard. He also picked up a knife, and moved quickly. If he stopped to think about the implications of Starling being so close, he might lose his nerve. He checked the side of the house first and then swept the torchlight over the garden. The only place for Starling to hide was the toilet, but it was empty. Joe checked the back gate, and saw that it was unlocked. He stepped into the laneway and shone the torch to the right and left. The batteries were weak, so he couldn't see far. He switched off the torch, not wishing to run it down, and knowing that batteries were almost impossible to get. He waited. There was no movement that he could discern. Had Starling really been here, or was Tom jumping at shadows? The thought that Starling might have been here made Joe feel sick. It meant that he'd been followed and that he'd brought this monster into Inspector Lambert's home. This could only be seen as more incompetence, more carelessness. But he'd been careful. He'd looked back at regular intervals. No, this had to have been a waking nightmare for Tom.

Joe went back inside. Tom looked at him, and with sudden recognition said, 'Joe — he was here. Fred was here — out there.'

'I searched, Tom. I couldn't find him.' He was reluctant to suggest that Tom might have been mistaken. Tom looked at Joe quizzically, and was about to speak when something in him seemed to collapse. The animation that appeared briefly in his face vanished. He stood up and returned to his bedroom. Joe, unable to hide his distress, said, 'He thinks I don't believe him.'

'And do you believe him?'

'I don't want to believe him.'

'Because that would mean you brought him here.'

'Yes.'

'Sit down, Joe. Nothing's changed. This Fred, or George Starling, or whatever he calls himself — maybe he was here, and maybe he wasn't. If he was here, he followed you. That doesn't mean you brought him here.'

For Joe, this was precisely what it meant. Inspector Lambert would think so, and so would Helen Lord.

'Titus won't be here for a couple of hours. I'm afraid there's no spare bed, just a fold-down camp bed in Tom's room.'

'I don't think I should . . . '

'No, of course. I was intending to bring it up here.'

'I'm just as happy to sleep sitting up in one of these armchairs, Mrs Lambert, although I don't imagine I'll sleep at all tonight.'

'I'll get you some pillows when you're ready.'

'Does your back gate lock?'

'There's a bolt that goes across it. I'll make a fresh pot of tea if you go out and bolt it.'

When Joe bolted the gate he shook it to test its strength, and then unbolted it and stepped again into the laneway. He was afraid as he stood there in the darkness. He had to force himself to stay there. If Starling was nearby, with his eyes accustomed to the night, he could take Joe easily. He swallowed, exquisitely aware that his heart was pounding and that at any moment it might miss a beat. He breathed deeply, concentrating on its rhythm; as he did so, it began to slow. He listened intently. There was a skittering nearby — a possum, or a rat. There were no other sounds. The air was still; so still that not even leaves rubbed together. He began to hear low sounds that must have been in the background always — a late tram rattling down Sydney Road, and, far in the distance, a car's horn. There was, too, the sound of a motorcycle, faint and nowhere near Bishop Street. He was suddenly aware of the sound of breathing, and it took a moment for Joe to realise that it was his own. He went back into the yard, locked the gate, and returned to the living room.

'I checked the lane again. Nothing. I think you should lock the back door. It wouldn't hurt to take precautions, just in case . . . '

'Just in case Starling really was here.'

'Yes.'

'Tell me about him, Joe.'

Joe hesitated.

'Titus has told me a good deal. I'm under no illusions about the type of person Starling is, but he's never met him. You have. Tell me why my brother is so afraid of him. He's never been afraid of anyone before.'

'It wasn't Starling who tortured Tom.'

'Yes, I know.'

'In some ways, though, he's even worse than the man who did.'

'Is he a Nazi, do you think?'

'He could probably spout a few bits of National Socialist philosophy, but I think he's attracted to its ugliness, to the licence it gives him to be violent — not to anything else about it. It's a way to express his hatreds.'

'Titus thinks he'll lose interest in it now that his leader is dead. Would you say that was likely?'

'He's a follower — I know that much.'

'Yes, but will he find someone else to follow?'

'I don't think he will. None of the other people I met — the other sympathisers, those Australia First people — are candidates. Starling had nothing but contempt for them. He thought they were soft, effete little dandies.'

'So politics won't be driving Starling. That leaves what? Grief?'

Joe looked at Maude Lambert, and found that she'd been watching him closely.

'Grief?' he asked.

'Yes. How close was Starling to Ptolemy Jones?'

'Are you asking if Starling is queer? Nazis hate queers almost as much as they hate us. Jews, I mean. I'm Jewish. Did you know that?'

He hadn't meant there to be, but there was a sharpness in the question that somehow implied that he needed to express this fact defiantly.

'Yes, Joe, I knew that,' she said quietly, and was offended that Joe thought he needed to be defiant with her. She wanted to say something, but held fire.

'I was wondering if there'd been some element of homo-eroticism in the relationship between Starling and Jones. It would probably never have

92

been acknowledged, maybe not even recognised as that. That isn't really what I meant, though. What did Jones offer Starling? Just a political direction, or something more?'

Joe felt out of his depth, and was suddenly conscious of how young and inexperienced he was. Homo-eroticism. He wasn't absolutely certain what that was, although he was pretty sure that there weren't many women in Melbourne who could introduce it into a conversation with Maude Lambert's unembarrassed ease.

'I'm sorry, Mrs Lambert. I'm not sure I understand what you mean by Starling feeling grief.'

'His emotions may seem crude to you, Joe. The only emotion you've ascribed to him is hatred.'

'That's the only emotion I saw.'

'Is that what you saw when Starling spoke to Jones, or looked at him?'

'No.'

'So what was that emotion?'

'I don't know.'

'Was it indifference?'

'No.'

'Annoyance? Anger?'

'No. You want me to say 'love', Mrs Lambert, but it didn't look like that either. If you ever met Starling, you wouldn't believe he was capable of love. A shared passion for cruelty isn't love.'

'A shared passion for anything can sometimes feel like love. I don't think George Starling needs National Socialism to feed his anger. I really do think it's fed by grief, and I think that puts him beyond the reach of reason.'

'So, revenge?'

'Revenge, pure and simple. I remember, years ago, probably before you were born, Titus worked on a murder case that just seemed senseless. He couldn't find a motive until he discovered that this was the second victim, not the first. The first had been killed in a fit of vengefulness. I can't recall the details, but I do recall that after the first murder, the killer didn't feel that his thirst for revenge had been satisfied, and so he looked around for people who'd only been peripherally involved in whatever the dispute had been. Titus was convinced that he wouldn't have stopped at two. He would have moved out in widening circles from the centre, finding reasons to punish people.'

Maude paused. Joe understood that she was equating Starling with this earlier killer, and that she could only have formed this view from a close reading of the case notes.

'We don't have evidence that directly implicates Starling in any murders,' Joe said.

'Yes, it's strange, isn't it?'

'Strange?'

'Yes. Because your sense of him, and our sense of him, is that he's at least as violent as Jones was. He's a frightening figure.'

Joe thought about that.

'Is it weak to be afraid of him, Mrs Lambert?'

'It would be foolish not to be. I don't think we're inventing a bogey man, and this might be a bit forthright for you, but I believe that if he gets to you, he won't stop at you.'

'He won't get to me, Mrs Lambert. And I promise you, he won't get to Tom either.'

★   ★   ★

It was 3.00 am when Inspector Lambert made it home to Bishop Street. He'd dropped Helen Lord and David Reilly at their respective houses first. (The first thing Reilly said to his wife on waking her was, 'You should see the house that Helen Lord lives in. It's a mansion. She shouldn't be taking a bloke's job.')

Joe and Maude were still awake when Titus entered the house. Before he'd spoken a word, Joe told him about Tom's encounter, real or imagined, with George Starling. He spoke calmly, but there was a desperate edge to his voice that Titus couldn't miss. It was a strange relief to Joe when Titus suggested that they should proceed on the assumption that Tom had, in fact, seen George Starling. To do otherwise was folly. There must have been some silent exchange between Titus and Maude, Joe thought, because Titus hurried to assure Joe that Starling's being in the backyard didn't represent a failure on his part. Rather, it provided further proof that the man they were dealing with was not to be underestimated. He briefly outlined what they'd learned in Warrnambool, and included the hideous cruelty meted out to John Starling's animals.

'Do you think he killed his father, sir?'

'It doesn't look like it, but I don't think he'll waste time weeping over him. He burned his house to the ground. I presume he would have

95

inherited it. Clearly, he's not the sentimental type.'

Titus suggested that they try to get some sleep. When Maude fetched a couple of pillows for Joe, he assured her again that he could sleep comfortably sitting up.

In the bedroom, Titus held Maude to him, despite the heat. He needed to feel her body against his skin. They spoke softly, conscious of Joe just a few feet from them in the living room.

'Joe is sure he wasn't followed,' Maude said.

'Joe wants to believe that.'

'He shouldn't be back at work, Titus. As soon as I saw him, I wanted to cry.'

'At least if he's at work we can keep an eye on him.'

'How can you do that after hours?'

'We don't have the manpower to post someone at his flat around the clock, and we can't do that here, either.'

'You really believe that this Starling creature was here, don't you?'

'I'm certain of it. However alert Joe thinks he is, he's injured, he's scared, and he's not himself. On top of that, he's inexperienced, and he can't get past feeling guilty about Tom.'

'I didn't help him, did I?'

'Please, darling, don't you start feeling guilty, too.'

'I don't feel guilty. I'm just angry with myself.'

'You and Tom — well, all of us — need to move somewhere safer. I can't protect us here; not now.'

Maude knew that he was right, although her

fears were for Tom, not for herself.

'We can stay at Tom's house. It'll be messy, but it's got two bedrooms. What about Joe?'

'He won't like it, but he can't stay at his flat. I'm not giving him a choice. I'm billeting him with Helen Lord.'

'Does she know this?'

'Not yet, and neither does Joe. I knew she and her mother lived with her uncle in Kew. What I didn't know until this evening is that the house is huge. It's a proper Victorian pile. There must be half-a-dozen bedrooms; more, probably. It's the kind of place that would have a butler's pantry — whatever that is.'

'How did Helen Lord go in Warrnambool?'

Titus elaborated on the sketch he'd given earlier of their investigations. He expressed reservations about David Reilly — reservations he'd spoken of to no one else. As they both began to drift into sleep, Titus said, 'There's something eating away at Joe. Something apart from this case.'

'I think it's Europe,' Maude said, but Titus's breathing had deepened, and he didn't hear her.

6

When Matthew Todd looked at his sister, Rose, he wondered, just as his Aunt Aggie did, why she didn't take more trouble with her appearance. She was a looker, but everything about her was practical. She had a practical haircut, wore practical clothes and shoes, and never wore make-up. Matthew didn't understand people who took no pride in their appearance, unless there was nothing about them that was worthy of pride — and, God knew, there were legions of people like that. Rose's choice of husband had done nothing to raise Matthew's opinion of her. She'd married beneath her; beneath all of them. John Abbot was stocky, stolid and, yes, practical. He was plain as a pikestaff, and when Matthew visited, Abbot thought the occasion was so inconsequential that he wore his singlet indoors. In fact, he'd been known to sit down to lunch in a singlet, and Matthew found his hairy shoulders an affront to etiquette. It didn't seem to bother Rose in the least, which was proof enough for Matthew of how far she'd fallen.

The Abbots ran dairy cattle on a large property outside Port Fairy, on the Portland side. John Abbot had been raised by his father, his mother having died when John was ten years old ('Sensibly died,' Aunt Aggie had said). This explained his staggeringly awful uncouthness, Matthew supposed. Old Mr Abbot had died at the age of just 55. He'd never looked youthful, and most of the mourners at St Patrick's — and the church had been full — were surprised to learn that he was so young. He'd always been referred to in the parish as 'old Mr Abbot'. Father Brennan knew that Abbot could be relied on to leave £5 on the plate each Sunday — a donation that hadn't been continued by his son. John Abbot's view was that you paid money to go to the pictures, but that being bored numb every Sunday should be free.

There was a reason Matthew had taken to visiting his sister. His reason had a name: Johanna Scotney. She wasn't officially a Land Army placement on the Abbot farm, but her employment protected her from being put somewhere out of the district.

Johanna Scotney was 18 years old, the daughter of a fisherman in Port Fairy — not one of Matthew's clients — and she was pretty. Matthew hadn't settled yet as to whom she most closely resembled. He judged all women against their resemblance to someone he'd seen at the pictures. It didn't matter how faint the resemblance, he saw the actress first and the real woman second. Rather than wrestle with a woman's personality, he found it simpler to ascribe to her the traits of the carefully scripted and directed character played by her vague shadow in some film or other. His Aunt Aggie was Judith Anderson — not the severe lesbian, Mrs Danvers, in *Rebecca*, but the less off-putting Ann Treadwell in *Laura*. Rose was Ann Sheridan, stripped back to basics, unmade-up and poorly lit. For Johanna Scotney,

Matthew was tossing up between Deanna Durbin and Ann Baxter. Either way, she needed deflowering, and he'd begun his campaign by making what he believed to be the occasional erotic remark to her. So far, she'd met him with stony, disapproving silence.

★ ★ ★

Rose Abbot suspected that her brother's visits, and his willingness to stay for lunch, had to do with Johanna Scotney, rather than with his having any interest in her, her husband, or the farm. The potatoes and eggs he took away with him weren't sufficient to encourage grateful lingering. She'd watched him follow Johanna with his eyes, and she'd noted with abhorrence the lewd set of his mouth when he did so.

He'd arrived earlier than usual this morning, and Rose hoped he wasn't intending to stretch his stay until lunch. It was just after nine when she heard his bicycle clatter against the front door. She and Johanna were in the kitchen, talking about the boy in Port Fairy who was tentatively courting her. It had become a ritual after the morning milking for Rose and Johanna to repair to the kitchen while John Abbot checked fences and did running repairs on machinery. The intimacy between them was easy, sisterly, but wasn't so deep that Johanna felt able to raise her feelings about Rose's husband or her brother. When she'd first come to the farm, in June the previous year, John Abbot had been cool to her, resentful of her femaleness, because

100

the person he'd wanted was a male. Farm work was for wives and blokes, not young sheilas — especially young sheilas who looked like Johanna Scotney. She pulled her weight, though, so his resentment subsided, and he stopped minding paying her the 40 shillings a week that Rose insisted was fair. After all, the going rate was 30 shillings, and that included food and board. Johanna didn't need three meals provided — lunch was all — and she went home at the end of each day.

Johanna had disliked John Abbot on sight. He was short, and she didn't like short men, and he could only be bothered shaving a couple of times a week, so his already ugly face was made uglier by dark bristles. Still, Rose and John Abbot seemed solid, reliable, and hardworking, so she didn't mind that her feelings for John were unpleasant. They would gradually calm into indifference, or they might have done if, about three months after her arrival, John Abbot hadn't made an obscene remark to her. They'd been repairing a fence, refitting a strainer, when Abbot had said, out of the blue, 'You've got a bloody good set of breasts on you. Anyone ever tell you that before?'

Johanna hadn't known what to say. She blushed and turned away from him.

'Didn't mean to offend,' he said. 'I was just saying. Do us a favour and don't tell the wife I mentioned your knockers.' He laughed. 'She might get jealous.'

She said nothing to Rose — partly because she liked her, and partly because she felt sorry for her having to crawl into bed each night beside that hairy-shouldered gnome. Was she also worried that Rose might believe that she'd encouraged John to speak to her like that? Her mother had warned her to be careful around Catholics. They knew no restraint. Johanna hadn't understood what she'd meant by this. As if it cleared the matter up, Mrs Scotney had said, 'Well, you only have to look in their churches and at the number of children they have.' What one had to do with the other wasn't enlarged upon, but John Abbot's obscenity confirmed for Johanna what her mother had hinted at.

Somehow it didn't seem odd to Johanna that she felt comfortable in Rose Abbot's presence. Although Johanna couldn't understand how she could bear to be physically intimate with her husband, she saw no evidence in Rose's gaze of the revulsion that she, Johanna, felt when looking at John Abbot. Catholics, of course, never divorced, so perhaps Rose was making the best of a bad situation. But, no; there was nothing of the martyr about Rose. The only conclusion that Johanna could reasonably come to was that, inexplicably, Rose loved her husband. It was this, really, that prevented her from voicing any complaint about him. Johanna couldn't put Rose in the position of having to take sides. Besides, Rose was the only woman, apart from her mother, in whom she could confide, and she rarely confided in her mother. Not that she didn't get on with her mother. It was just that she didn't want her interfering in her budding romance.

The boy would soon be 18, but he was mature

for his age — he could, he'd told her, grow a moustache if he chose to. His name was Timothy Harrison. He was tall, and not yet settled into the long arms and legs that seemed to have grown overnight. He knew nothing about fish or fishing. His father, whose health had been compromised by mustard gas in the first war, was an invalid. Fortunately, his mother's people had money, so the Harrison family — his older brother was somewhere in Italy, fighting — was able to live comfortably in town. Timothy planned to join up the minute he turned 18.

Johanna had sketched all this information for Rose during their first talk about Timothy. She'd withheld a couple of things, though. Chief among these was that Timothy was an Anglican. She didn't think Rose would really care — although the crucifix in the living room and the framed picture of Our Lady of Perpetual Succour (Rose had identified it for her) in the kitchen silenced any talk of religion, however inconsequential. Timothy's religious affiliation was one of the reasons she'd kept him a secret from her mother. At least he was a Protestant, but he wasn't Presbyterian, and the Anglicans were pale imitations of the Catholics, according to Mrs Scotney. They didn't go in for popery, though, and their churches weren't quite so gaudy and pagan. The Harrisons were respectable people, so Johanna was confident that she could talk her mother round about Timothy. This wouldn't have been possible if the Harrisons had been Catholic. Nothing would induce Mrs Scotney to welcome a papist into her home. She tolerated them in shops and had a nodding acquaintance with one or two of them when she passed them in Sackville Street. After all, she was fond of saying, she wasn't an intolerant woman. She hoped she had enough Christian charity in her to disguise her contempt. She wasn't in the business of hurting people's feelings.

The sound of Matthew's bicycle annoyed both Rose and Johanna. This morning time together had become the favourite part of the day for each of them. Rose enjoyed being Johanna's confidante. She'd never been in such a position before, having found female company of little interest while she was growing up. Now, as a married woman who'd been inducted into the mysteries and miseries of sex, she felt wise, and able to offer Johanna counsel. Not that sex was ever overtly discussed. Timothy Harrison had made no physical overtures, beyond holding Johanna's hand at the pictures.

'How would you feel if he kissed you?' Rose asked. Johanna was about to reply when Matthew Todd's arrival brought the conversation to an end.

He entered the house without knocking — a habit he had that set Rose's nerves on edge. It wasn't just that it was rude, which it was; it was the proprietorial air he brought with him, as if the Abbot house somehow belonged to him.

'Morning,' he said. 'A cup of tea seems essential. Would you mind, Johanna?'

'I'll make it,' Rose said. 'Johanna's got more important things to do than make you cups of tea.'

Matthew, who hadn't taken his eyes off

Johanna since entering the kitchen, decided she was much more like Ann Baxter than Deanna Durbin, and he was relieved. Deanna Durbin was too impossibly prim and sweet to excite him. Ann Baxter had some spark. Johanna put the tea cup she'd been drinking from in the sink.

'Good day, Mr Todd,' she said as she moved past him. Despite being only a few years older than Johanna, Matthew had never suggested that she call him by his first name. It pleased him to be called 'Mr Todd'. When Johanna had left, Rose said, 'You have a fiancée, Matthew.'

'And what exactly is that supposed to mean?'

'It means I've seen the way you look at her.'

Matthew didn't bother denying it. Instead he said, 'You should do something with your hair. You look like a frump.'

'It's so lovely when you visit, Matthew.'

He laughed. 'Don't take it personally, Rosie. I'm just trying to be helpful.'

'You can be helpful by staying away from Johanna. She's spoken for, and so are you.'

'Is she? Who's the lucky bloke?'

'None of your business.'

'A Port Fairy boy? Or a farming yokel? Not a fisherman, surely? They stink.'

'They're your bread and butter. Do they know what you really think of them?'

'I didn't say I didn't like them. I just said they stink, which they do. Get up close to one of them sometime. How's that cup of tea coming along?'

Rose was sorely tempted to tell her brother to make it himself, but she thought that the longer she kept him in the kitchen the less likely he was to pursue Johanna into the yard.

'How's Aunt Aggie?' she asked.

'She's fine. You should visit her more often.'

'I send her eggs and vegetables. She thinks I've let the Todd family down. I married beneath myself, apparently. I know that's what she thinks, Matthew.'

He shrugged as if this was, after all, an indisputable fact.

'Still, you should visit her. Family is important.'

'That includes Uncle Selwyn, does it?'

'Don't call him 'Uncle Selwyn'. It makes him sound normal.'

'He is family.'

Matthew looked at his sister, and marvelled yet again at her indifference to her looks. An absence of vanity in someone with her face was little short of perverse, he thought.

'Perhaps you'd like to take over looking after him. Maybe he could be housed here. Aunt Aggie would be glad to see the back of him. You could put him in one of your sheds. That'd keep him off the main street, too.'

'He needs to be somewhere familiar. He'd wander off here, and I can't keep an eye on him. Besides, I don't want him here. He scares me. I hated it when he was in our house in Melbourne. That laugh of his gives me the creeps.'

'He didn't ever fiddle with you, did he?'

'No, Matthew, he didn't. You know when Aunt Aggie gets too old to look after him, it'd make sense for you and Dorothy to take over.'

Matthew snorted.

'Well, it's you who's been bleating about family, not me. And you'll be living in town. Aunt Aggie will leave the house to you, I imagine.'

'You think inheriting the house means inheriting Selwyn? He's not really a chattel, is he? He's more of a pointless, dumb animal. I'll tell you this; if Aunt Aggie dies, I will *not* be looking after that great lump of a moron. He can starve to death, for all I care.'

Rose put a cup of tea down in front of him. She considered his face. He was a handsome man, if sisters could ever allow that their brothers looked handsome, but there was something under the skin that made him look cruel, or maybe just calculating. Whichever it was, Rose thought, it made him unattractive.

'Milk?' he asked.

'There's plenty of that, but there's no sugar.'

As she said this, John Abbot came into the kitchen. He brought with him a cattle smell of milk, manure, and piss, which did little to mask the smell of his sweat. Matthew's nose wrinkled in distaste — an action that John Abbot noticed. He said nothing, but pulled a chair as close to Matthew as he could and sat on it. Matthew drew away and stood up.

'Christ,' he said. 'You smell like you've just crawled out of a cow's arse.'

'It's called working for a living. If you don't like the smell, stop coming here. Go and join the bloody army. Make yourself useful.'

Abbot had long ago dropped the social grace of engaging in initial pleasantries with his brother-in-law. Whenever they met, they simply resumed their hostilities from the previous meeting.

'I think I'll go for a walk,' Matthew said, and managed to convey the sense that he was being inconvenienced.

'Make yourself useful and help Johanna sluice out the milking shed — unless you're worried about getting your precious shoes dirty.'

Rose shot her husband a look, incredulous that he'd failed to notice Matthew's interest in Johanna. She moved to open the kitchen door for Matthew, and as she did so she said quietly, 'Stay out of the milking shed, Matthew.'

'Don't worry, Rose, I've got no intention of ending up smelling like your husband.'

* * *

Johanna didn't mind cleaning out the milking shed. More often than not, John Abbot left most of the work to her. He cleaned the equipment, but mopping up the splashed milk and shovelling the cow shit had become one of her daily chores. At least she was alone, and didn't have to endure his looks. This time, she heard a small noise and turned around. Matthew Todd was standing there, just inside the door of the shed, watching her.

'Mr Todd.'

He didn't look away or show the slightest embarrassment. It was she who was embarrassed. She was glad to be wearing the grubby bandana that tidied her hair away from her face, and the shapeless overalls that she'd pulled on after leaving the kitchen.

'What's a nice girl like you doing in a place like this?'

She couldn't think of a witty rejoinder, so she said, 'Well, you know, the war and that.'

Christ, Matthew thought. *She's pretty, but she's pretty dumb.* That was all right. Smart women were trouble.

'What do you know about the war? How are we going, do you think?'

'I don't read the papers much. I see it at the pictures, in the newsreels.'

'You think that's the truth of it?'

'You think we're being lied to?'

'What would you do if the Japs came?'

'What would *you* do if the Japs came?'

Matthew reassessed Johanna. Perhaps she wasn't so dumb after all. He didn't like being criticised by a girl holding a shovel load of cow dung. He was tempted to put her in her place, but smiled at her instead. Emboldened by his anger, he said, 'Who's the lucky bloke who gets to see what's under the overalls?'

Johanna turned away from him and went back to her work.

'Oh, don't be like that. I meant no harm. I just meant that whoever the bloke is, he's a lucky bastard.'

Johanna's face reddened. She said nothing because she was both embarrassed and afraid. Matthew took a step into the shed, and, ignoring the claggy ground, he came up behind her and wrapped his arms around her. His hands found the opening in her overalls, and he forced his fingers behind the cloth and onto her skin. She was paralysed with fear. He cupped her breasts and tried to slip one hand lower. She pulled away and drew the front of her overalls together. She was shaking, and Matthew could see that she was about to cry out. He placed one hand over her mouth and breathed hotly into her ear.

'Come on. Don't be like that. Don't play hard to get. I've seen the way you look at me.'

With his free hand, he grabbed her wrist and pulled her palm to the front of his trousers.

'See. That's what you've done to me. You can't . . . '

The sound of the kitchen door opening made Matthew release her. He pointed a finger at her. 'You say anything, and you're fucking finished. I can make sure your stinking father never sells another fish. We have unfinished business. You can't go around getting a man hard and leaving him with it.'

He walked back to the entrance of the shed and called sunnily, for the benefit of John Abbot, who'd left the kitchen, 'Nice to see you, Johanna. See you again soon.' Abbot paid no attention to him, and wandered off to check his fences.

Matthew returned to the kitchen, and found it empty. He checked the pantry, helped himself to a few items, and walked through the house to the front porch. He got on his bicycle and headed back to Port Fairy. Johanna Scotney, he thought, needed to be taken down a peg or two, and he was just the man to do it. He felt agitated. He'd organise with his Aunt Aggie to hose Selwyn down that afternoon, and he'd have his fun with that great lump of doughy pointlessness.

7

George Starling had left the house in Brunswick with some regret. He should have dealt with Tom Mackenzie when he had the chance. What a whimpering little Nancy-boy Mackenzie was, barricading himself in the dunny and calling for a woman to rescue him. What was her name? Margaret? No. Mary? No. Maude. Yes, Maude. Probably his wife. He should've done it. He should've just pulled the dunny door off its hinges and laid into Mackenzie. He'd thought all this as he'd walked back down Sydney Road, towards his motorcycle. When he reached it, he rode it back to Joe Sable's flat. It seemed a shame not to leave Sable a reminder of who he was dealing with. He broke into the flat — the lock gave way with surprising ease, and with very little noise. He turned on the lights. The place was tidy, and the air carried the faint smell of some sort of cologne. That'd be right. He'd picked Sable right away as soft. He looked around, opening cupboards and drawers. He'd been here once before, of course, but only for a matter of seconds — long enough to knock Sable out. He and Ptolemy Jones had carried Sable downstairs to a car, which they'd driven to a house in Belgrave. That was the night Jones had died.

Starling stood in the bedroom. The smell of cologne was strongest here, and it infuriated him to think of Sable resting his perfumed Jew head on those pillows while Jones was dead. He went to the kitchen, picked up a sharp knife, returned to the bedroom, and slashed the pillows so that feathers floated everywhere. Then he stripped back the sheets and hacked at the mattress, slashing with such force that the blade snapped. He was breathing heavily, but his need to hurt Sable was nowhere near sated. He didn't want to make a noise. There were three other flats in this block, and he didn't want to wake their occupants.

On a table in the living room there was a thick folder. He picked it up and flicked through it. All he could see were newspaper clippings: 'Massacre in Forest' read one headline. He closed the folder and took it with him, along with Joe's ration book, down the stairs to where he had parked the motorcycle. He grabbed one of the spare cans of petrol and went back upstairs. He wasn't going to waste any — a cupful would do. He splashed some on the ripped mattress in the bedroom, and a small amount on the armchair in the living room. He took a box of matches from the kitchen, struck a match, dropped it on the mattress, struck another, and dropped it onto the chair. He opened a window, waited to see that the flames were catching hold, and left. As he pulled away on the motorcycle, he could see the satisfying flickering of light in Sable's flat. It was alight. So what if the whole block went up? They were probably all Jews.

★ ★ ★

The look on the doorman's face at the Windsor was sour, but it sweetened when Starling slipped him a pound note. He hated handing money over to the supercilious bastard, but he reasoned that he'd make sure he got it back somehow, with interest. And he'd wipe that smirk off the doorman's face while he was at it.

He paid for his suite up front, in cash. Money guaranteed all sorts of things at the Windsor — discretion, privacy, and incuriosity chief among them. He registered under his own name. Since the beginning of the war, everybody had been obliged to carry identity papers, and even this fancy hotel would ask to see them. He wasn't worried by this. The police wouldn't be looking for him at a place like the Windsor. No questions were asked as to the absence of sir's luggage. All they wanted to know, given the time of morning, was whether sir would like his breakfast sent to his room. Sir would like that very much, but he'd appreciate it if they'd deliver the breakfast not immediately, but in an hour's time. Certainly, sir.

George Starling wasn't used to luxury. He'd never craved it. Elegant places and elegant people didn't excite envy in him — they provoked rage, and an urge to smash them up and tear them down. Now, though, he was taking perverse pleasure in standing under the hot shower in the bathroom of a suite in the Windsor Hotel. He'd heard about this place, and he'd seen it from the outside, but until this morning he'd never been ushered into the foyer by the absurdly liveried doorman.

When Starling stepped from the shower, the smell of fish had been washed from his hair and body. He raised his forearm to his nose and breathed in the odour of rose-scented soap. He looked at himself in the full-length mirror. He was lean and strong, with no hint of a slack belly. His beard shadow was dark. He'd go to a barber and pay for a close shave. He might even ape Joe Sable and ask for a splash of cologne. He put his clothes back on, and was aware of the smell of fish and sweat that clung to them. He looked around the room and thought, *I'm in no hurry, and there could be no better hiding place than this.* A week at the Windsor would hardly put a dent in his father's £5,000. He'd grow a gentleman's moustache, buy a hat and new clothes — good clothes, too. He had two extra ration books to raid, and more than enough money to silence the toffs in Henry Bucks. A good store like that would be more interested in his money than in his coupons. By this afternoon, he, George Starling, would be able to come and go from the Windsor without anybody casting him a sideways glance. As he waited for his breakfast, he began to flip through the folder he'd taken from Sable's flat. He began to laugh. *My God*, he thought, *they're really doing it.* Jones had been right — Herr Hitler was culling the European Jews. Well, he was doing his bit at this end. George Starling felt absurdly happy.

★　★　★

Joe Sable and Inspector Lambert stood opposite the ruins of 'Rosh Pinah', the building that had housed Joe's flat. Two of the four flats had been damaged by smoke and water; the other two, including Joe's, had been gutted. The occupants of the surviving flats — two sisters, and a widower in his fifties — stood near them. A crowd of locals had gathered as well. A retired schoolteacher who lived in the remaining flat had died in the blaze. There was uncertainty about where the fire had started; perhaps the schoolteacher had fallen asleep with a lit cigarette. An investigation would determine the seat of the fire, but both Inspector Lambert and Joe had no doubt about who'd set 'Rosh Pinah' alight.

The fire seemed to have started some time after 4.00 am. By the time the other residents had become aware of it, it had taken hold, and they'd been lucky to get out in time. If the air hadn't been so full of the smell of smoke from the fires on Melbourne's fringes, they might have noticed it sooner. But it wouldn't have saved the building, as the metropolitan fire brigade was stretched trying to contain blazes in the outer suburbs. A fire truck had to be diverted from Beaumaris, and it took more than an hour to reach Princes Hill. By then it was hopeless.

Lambert's telephone had rung just after 7.00 am, it having taken this long for Joe's identity as the owner of one of the flats to be established. His neighbours knew that he was a detective, and that he was 'in that new branch — Homicide, is it?' It had been assumed that he'd been in his flat, so the policeman who'd attended and who'd rung Russell Street wasn't sure if he was reporting a death or not. The auxiliary policewoman who'd answered the call had been reluctant to give him Inspector Lambert's home number.

'One of his detectives may have been burned to ashes,' he'd said. 'Inspector Lambert might just be interested in that.'

After checking with someone in Homicide, she gave him the number. She never liked to ring the Homicide department, in case that Helen Lord creature answered. What kind of uppity woman would want to work in Homicide?

In Arnold Street, Joe squinted at the ruins of 'Rosh Pinah'. 'He's killed someone now,' Joe said. 'Mr Goldman.'

'I don't think there's any doubt that Starling did this. He'd just come from burning down his father's place. I think he must have followed you to Bishop Street, and then come here. I imagine he broke into your flat.'

'Everything I own was in that flat,' Joe said. 'Everything. It feels strange. I have the clothes I'm wearing, and that's all. That is literally, actually, all.' He thought for a moment, and laughed. 'No. It's not quite that bad — I packed a razor, a toothbrush, and a change of underwear and socks to take to your house.'

'I'm so sorry, Joe. We'll find him.'

Joe nodded, but said nothing. What, after all, was there to say? He was surprised that his reaction to the destruction of everything he owned was so muted. This didn't feel like shock. It felt strangely calm. What of value did he own? He'd inherited good pieces of furniture from his

116

parents, but furniture could be replaced. He was fully insured, so rebuilding wouldn't bankrupt him — not that he'd be rebuilding in a hurry, as building materials were scarce. There were photographs of his parents, but he hadn't looked at them in years, and David and Judith Sable had put such a distance between each other and him that a few snapshots couldn't hope to bridge it so long after their deaths. He'd given up pondering the silent hostilities between his mother and his father. The silence had enveloped him as well. There was never any shouting in the Sable household — just a vast, savage silence. Raised voices would have been vulgar and unworthy of the aristocratic, English, Jewish blood that flowed through Sable veins. He'd grown used to the nasty quiet, he'd adapted to it, and, in his general reluctance to express his own fears, he'd adopted it.

Standing near Titus and Joe, the surviving three occupants of 'Rosh Pinah' seemed stunned. Joe knew very little about them. The two sisters shared the flat below his, and the widower was something quite high-up in one of the war ministries. Their flats were now uninhabitable. Joe looked at the trio, standing close to one another. One of the sisters was weeping. The other caught his eye, and instead of some indication of sympathy, there was a spark of anger. They supposed that the fire had started in Joe's flat, and they no doubt thought it was the result of some carelessness on his part. Their lives had been turned upside down because he smoked in bed, or had left his stove unattended.

Well, he didn't smoke, and he'd replaced the wood-burning stove with an expensive electric one when he'd moved in. Would the fact that the fire had been the result of arson quell their anger? Probably not. Whatever its cause, it had started in *his* flat, and that was that.

'Perhaps you should speak to them,' Inspector Lambert said.

'No.' The word was said quietly, but there was a finality about it that struck Lambert forcefully.

'Maude and Tom are moving to Tom's place in South Melbourne. I'll be with them there as well. You — '

'I can stay with a friend until I find a place to let.'

'You'll be staying with Constable Lord and her family. And before you object, the house she shares with her mother and uncle is enormous. I'm surprised it hasn't been requisitioned. You don't have a choice in this, Sergeant. I'm not giving you a choice.'

'How does Constable Lord feel about this?'

'She doesn't know about it yet, but how she feels about it isn't relevant. This is an emergency. Is there some reason you think she'd object?'

'Well, suddenly having a work colleague living with you is . . . well, I know I wouldn't like it.'

'You need to be safe, and until George Starling is in custody, the house in Kew is the safest place I can think of.'

Without thinking, Joe said, 'I need to come in to work, sir. I can't sit around in a strange house all day.' He hadn't intended to say this. He'd spent the restless night determining that he should tender his resignation, however much it might appear to others that he was running away. They'd think he was a coward. So what? Maybe he was a coward. A brave man surely wouldn't have felt as afraid as he'd felt in the Lamberts' back garden. Now though, with the smell of burnt timbers and wet ash in his nostrils, his instinct was to work. To not pursue George Starling was suddenly inconceivable.

'I would expect you to come in to work, Sergeant, but until your wounds have healed fully you'll have to accept the limitations I set.'

'I hope you know, sir, that you can use me as bait.'

To Joe's astonishment, Lambert said, 'I'm afraid it may come to that.'

He'd said what Joe had wanted to hear, and yet the words created in Joe an awful ambivalence. He was expendable. Lambert would sacrifice him if it meant protecting his family.

'What do I do now, sir?'

'All this will have to be sorted out with the relevant authorities.' Inspector Lambert waved his hand at the burnt-out flats. 'I don't think Starling will make a move against you in broad daylight, and certainly not with so many people about. He may be watching from somewhere, but I doubt it. When you've done all you need to do, I'd like you to come in to Homicide, where we can discuss the temporary arrangements with Constable Lord.'

★ ★ ★

When Joe arrived at Russell Street two hours later, he was met with expressions of shock and sympathy from every person he saw. News had travelled fast. His colleagues in Homicide, all of whom were older and more experienced than he, and who had paid him scant attention previously — except perhaps to wonder, resentfully, at his closeness to Inspector Lambert — nodded meaningfully at him. For them, this counted as an acknowledgement of his predicament. It was quickly obvious that both Helen Lord and David Reilly had been fully briefed. Reilly, unhelpfully, wondered out loud how Joe could have missed being followed; realising too late that this was the wrong thing to say, he tried to mollify Joe by adding that Starling was a crafty bastard and that it was probably very dark along Sydney Road. Helen's mouth tightened, which was sufficiently eloquent for Reilly to feel her disapproval. She told Joe that she'd telephoned her mother and that a room would be ready for him that evening, and that he was welcome to stay as long as he needed to. She was sure, too, that her uncle would be happy to lend him some clothes.

'He's about your size, and he's got wardrobes full. He's got good taste, so you'll be the best-dressed copper in Melbourne.'

'What's he do, your uncle?' Reilly asked.

'He's a businessman.'

'He must do a lot of business.'

'He's successful because he's good at what he does.' Helen's voice was uninflected, but the implication of that repeated 'he' went home to Reilly, and his feelings about Helen Lord, already uncertain, soured. Helen knew that Reilly would have added envy to his catalogue of reasons to dislike her, so she would have to be wary of him and any attempt to undermine her.

With the death of Joe's neighbour, the fire at 'Rosh Pinah' had been shifted from a case of arson to one of murder. Inspector Lambert hadn't taken any measures to prevent the newspapers from reporting this. If Starling read that the person responsible for the fire was now wanted on the much more serious charge — and Starling would know that he'd be the main suspect — perhaps he would go to ground and not risk an attack on Joe Sable. It was probably a vain hope, but it was better than no hope.

By lunchtime it had been established that 'Rosh Pinah' had indeed been the subject of arson, and investigators were fairly certain that the seat of the fire had been in Joe's flat. They were confident that a small amount of petrol had been used as an accelerant. Bizarrely, enough of the mattress and pillows remained to indicate that they'd been slashed and hacked. Joe, when he'd been told this, found the violent intimacy of the act disturbing. He imagined the frantic motion of Starling's hairy arms as they attacked his bed, and, strangely, Joe's fear of him diminished, and was replaced by disgust and anger. He would find him and put a stop to him, even if it meant working outside the protection and auspices of Homicide. It was as if a switch had been flicked: all thoughts of resignation, already fading, vanished. He moved his shoulder to test the tenderness of the knife wound he'd sustained two weeks previously. It ached, but it was well on the way to healing. When Helen Lord spoke to him just after 1.00 pm, she found him buoyant. She was taken aback by this, but didn't press for an explanation. Perhaps his temporary accommodation in Kew wouldn't be as fraught as he expected it to be.

★ ★ ★

Inspector Lambert had telephoned Ros Lord to request a room for Sergeant Sable. He'd briefly outlined the situation, and she'd agreed without a single question. He'd been surprised that she'd never heard Joe Sable's name — he'd asked her if she was aware that he was a work colleague of her daughter's. She was certain, she'd said, that her brother, Peter Lillee, would be more than happy to make space available, especially under these circumstances. Helen rang her mother in the late afternoon and asked her to choose a few shirts, a jacket, trousers, and perhaps even a suit, and put them in Joe's room. Uncle Peter surely wouldn't mind. Ros wasn't so sure about her brother's response to Helen's largesse. The reason he had so many beautiful clothes, she said, was because he loved well-made clothes.

'I've seen inside his wardrobe, Mum. There are shirts in there I've never seen him wear. I can't believe he'd begrudge Sergeant Sable a few cast-offs.'

'They might not even fit Sergeant Sable.'

'They're the same build and the same height.'

'But darling, everything your uncle owns is tailored for him.'

'I don't think Joe — Sergeant Sable — is going to mind if a shirt doesn't sit as precisely as it would on Uncle Peter. He has absolutely nothing.'

'What I really meant, Helen, is that your uncle has been extraordinarily generous to us, and I really can't bear him thinking that he has no say in the requisitioning of his clothes, even his cast-offs.'

Helen felt the reproof keenly, and felt too that it was justified. She hoped that her ridiculous request, and the unguarded enthusiasm with which she'd made it, hadn't exposed to her mother her feelings for Joe Sable. She didn't like admitting these feelings to herself, and she didn't want them running off the leash where anybody might encounter them.

At 5.30 pm, Sergeant David Reilly left the Homicide office to head home. There was a spare room in the Reilly house, and he'd have offered it willingly if the opportunity to do so had arisen. However, Inspector Lambert had made it clear that the house in Kew was where Sable was to be billeted. This was probably just as well. Mrs Reilly was particular about house guests, and Sable still looked a sight. Besides, he was a Jew, and although he had no problem with Jews, Mrs Reilly was regularly uncomplimentary about an elderly Jewish couple who passed the house from time to time. Not that she'd ever be rude to their faces. She was a charitable woman. It was just that they didn't try to fit in, did they?

'See you on Monday,' he said to Joe. He said nothing to Helen. It was a pointed omission, but it was blunted by the sudden ringing of the telephone. Helen stood up to answer it, relieving her of the need to acknowledge Reilly's departure.

★ ★ ★

Peter Lillee, Ros Lord, Helen Lord, and Joe Sable sat down to a dinner of vegetable soup ('Don't expect potatoes,' Ros said. 'There aren't any in the shops.'), followed by beef stew. It was good, unfussy cooking. Ros had mastered the art of austerity meals. It was a mastery that wasn't entirely necessary, given the security of her brother's wealth, but they'd decided as long ago as 1940, when the outcome of the war had been uncertain, that the Lillee house would run as much as possible according to government guidelines. A Plimsoll line had been drawn around each of the baths — although, if truth be told, it was somewhat higher than the recommended height, and there were sacrifices that Peter Lillee simply wasn't prepared to make. He would rather go naked than wear a Dedman suit, and good brandy wasn't a luxury; it was a necessity.

Joe felt awkward and clumsy. His parents had been well off, but he'd never sat down to eat in a room like this one. Everything in it was the best that the Edwardians had had to offer. The furnishings, the mouldings, the window dressings, the light fittings, and the fireplace — all were frozen in Edwardian splendour. They were not, however, in the least exhausted-looking. Peter Lillee maintained, repaired, and indeed curated his house with obsessive care.

Above the fireplace, and in the direct line of Joe's sight, was an oil portrait of Lillee. It was full length, and although it had been done by someone with great skill, it struck the only false note in the room. Joe recognised its origins. It was a copy, with Lillee's head on the body of a man Joe knew as Dr Pozzi, and the painter of the original was John Singer Sargent. In Sargent's picture, as here, the subject stood, dressed in a floor-length, bright red robe, one hand on his hip, the other pulling the gown together at the chest. It was the last word in swagger portraits, and Joe could see why Lillee had been tempted to have it copied. Dr Pozzi wore a beard, while Peter Lillee was clean-shaven, but there was a remarkable resemblance between the two faces. The artist, whoever he was, appeared at a distance to have done a superb job of reproducing Sargent's virtuoso paint strokes. The hands, in particular, had been brilliantly realised. Still, Joe found vulgar the conceit of borrowing so blatantly from another artist. Nevertheless, throughout the meal, during which the conversation stayed resolutely on the Burma campaign, the best and worst of Melbourne radio, the outrageous price of peas, and the implications of meat rationing, Joe's eyes kept lifting to the portrait. For a split second, Joe wondered if he'd spoken his thought out loud, because Peter said, 'It's rather brash, don't you think?'

'Brash?', Joe replied, buying time.

'Yes.'

'It's loud, Peter,' Ros said, 'but I think it's rather wonderful.'

'I suspect Sergeant Sable knows what I mean.' He smiled. 'I noticed that every time you look at it, you look at a different part of it.'

'It's very well done.'

Peter laughed. Helen looked at her uncle. She was lost. Was he attacking Joe, goading him? No — there was nothing in his expression to suggest this. The smile was warm.

'I've seen the original,' Peter said. 'I saw it in 1934, in Los Angeles.'

'But it's a portrait of you,' Ros said. 'What do you mean you saw the original?'

Peter indicated to Joe that he should reveal the painting's origins. How had he surmised so quickly, Joe wondered, that he had an interest in art?

'There's a famous portrait of a man named Dr Pozzi, by John Singer Sargent. Mr Lillee's portrait . . . '

'Please, call me Peter.'

'Peter's portrait is based on it.'

Again, Peter laughed.

'Based on? You're the first person to come into this house and get the joke.'

'Who painted it?'

'A friend of mine — a fellow named Forbes Carlisle. He should be much better known than he is. He's easily the equal of William Dargie, whose mother's maiden name, by the way, was Sargent. As soon as this war's done with, I'm determined to back him. A few really decent commissions would set him up. Do you know what he's doing at the moment? He's camouflaging Jeeps. Not that he minds. I think he rather likes it.'

For the remainder of the meal, the talk was about art. Peter had strong views on Dobell's portrait of Joshua Smith. He loved it, and thought the controversy about it was absurd.

'Smith doesn't like it because it looks just like him. But it has much more energy than Dargie's last two Archibald winners.'

Ros pointed out that Dobell was a friend of Peter's, and that this might have had something to do with his enthusiasm for the Smith portrait. Two hours passed, and the four of them settled into the library for a glass of brandy. It wasn't a misnomer, or a pomposity, to call this room a library. It was lined with books, and the one wall available for pictures was hung in the salon style with a gallimaufry of small paintings, etchings, lithographs, and drawings.

'There's nothing really valuable here,' Peter said. 'Just bibs and bobs I inherited or picked up at auctions. There's one decent Goya drawing.'

Helen, who'd heard enough talk of art to last her the rest of the war, asked her mother if there was a pudding.

'I hadn't planned one,' Ros said, 'but I bought something recently that I've been wanting to try. I'm ashamed to say I fell for an advertisement in one of the papers.'

'That's not like you, Ros,' Peter said. 'You're usually sniffy about that sort of thing.'

127

'It only cost sixpence, and it promises to make us smack our lips.'

'What is it?' Helen asked. 'I'm not sure I want my lips smacked.'

'It's called 'Mary Baker Butterscotch Dessert', and it can be made in three minutes. All you need is milk, and we have milk.'

'Oh, I have to see this.' Helen stood up and left the library with her mother. In the kitchen, before examining the Mary Baker box, Helen expressed her gratitude for her mother's discretion in not asking Joe any questions.

'I didn't need to ask him any questions, darling. Your Inspector Lambert explained the situation to me.'

Helen looked apprehensive, as if Lambert had broken the rules by which the Kew house functioned.

'What did he tell you?'

'He told me enough to know that Sergeant Sable needs a safe place. I assured him that our house is such a place.'

'How much does Uncle Peter know?'

'He knows as much as I do.' She didn't elaborate on how much that was. 'You only have to look at him to know that whatever he's been through, apart from his flat burning down, is still raw and painful.'

Helen was caught off guard by a rush of emotion. Left to run free, it would have produced an incoherent sound, but she caught it in time to camouflage it as a cough. However, she couldn't disguise the tears that flooded her eyes. She turned away, knowing that her mother had seen this, but knowing too that she could rely on her to leave her be. This time, though, Ros Lord confounded her daughter, and wrapped her arms around her.

'I wish sometimes that you'd talk to me, Helen. I wait and wait, but you never do.'

Without knowing how to respond, and without knowing why, Helen said, 'Dad . . . ' and stopped, appalled.

'Your father always talked. Always.'

Helen drew gently away from her mother's embrace. She gathered herself, forced a smile, and took one of Ros's hands and squeezed it.

'Let's make that pudding,' she said. Her usual astuteness failed her, as it always did where her mother was concerned, and she was unable to see the deep hurt she'd inflicted with those banal words.

⋆   ⋆   ⋆

Peter had taken the Goya drawing down from the wall, and handed it to Joe. He held it reverently. It was a quick, gestural ink sketch of a prisoner bent double, his arms pinned behind him, secured by a chain that rose to a bolted ring on the wall. The face couldn't be seen, but it didn't need to be. The agony was contained in the twist of the shoulder and the cruel curve of the back.

'It's not a cheery drawing,' Peter said, 'but no one notices it, tucked away among the others.'

'But it's Goya. His hand actually made these lines. It's wonderful.'

'It was surprisingly inexpensive.'

Joe handed the picture back to Peter and watched him as he replaced it on the wall. He was the land of man who changed his clothes at the end of a working day. Joe hardly ever did this. He would take off his suit jacket and tie, but he rarely bothered with a complete change. Peter Lillee probably enjoyed getting into and out of clothes, and Joe suspected that having really good clothes to get into and out of probably made a difference. There was a family resemblance to both his sister and his niece, although in Helen's case it was only vague. Joe was suddenly conscious of the fact that he hadn't thought about the fire, or George Starling, for several hours. When this struck him, it did so with some force; on turning from hanging the Goya, Peter saw that the colour had drained from Joe's face.

'You look ill, Joe.'

'I'm sorry.'

'Why on earth would you apologise for being ill? We've all been carrying on as if everything is perfectly normal. Having your flat burn to the ground isn't normal. I can't imagine how that must feel.'

'At the moment, I don't feel anything very much. A neighbour was killed. All the flats are ruined — not just mine. I wasn't even there, and it wouldn't have happened if I'd been better at my job.'

Peter wasn't good at confidences. They embarrassed him. He dealt with the world glancingly, and was unskilled at wrangling other people's emotions.

'I'm sure you shouldn't blame yourself. I understand that the fire was started by some criminal.'

'Yes, yes, it was.' Joe felt unable to say any more. He was close to crying in front of this elegant man. He made to say something, but his voice caught. Peter, because he didn't know what else to say, suggested that Joe might like to see his room. Joe nodded, and hoped that Peter hadn't seen his distress.

Peter walked ahead of Joe, thereby avoiding eye contact. In another man, this might have been the result of natural discretion. For Peter, it was social squeamishness in the presence of another man's fragility. They mounted a perfectly pitched staircase, and reached a bedroom on the left-hand side of the divide at the top. The room was sparsely furnished, a situation for which Peter immediately apologised.

'I sold a lot of stuff — a tallboy, and a chair, and so forth. You have your own bathroom. Just a bath, no shower. There's a boiler downstairs, so there's hot water at the tap.'

'A bath would be wonderful.'

Joe had regained control of his voice, and Peter Lillee turned toward him with relief.

'Just ignore the bloody Plimsoll line, by the way. Now, I understand you have only the clothes you're wearing.'

'I have spare underwear and socks.'

Peter laughed.

'And you're hoping they'll see you through to the end of the war, are you?'

'You don't need coupons for socks, so I'll be

right until I get a new ration book.'

'If you look in that wardrobe, you'll find a couple of shirts, two pairs of trousers, a suit coat, and a sports coat. I won't miss them, believe me. You're welcome to them. There's also some underwear and socks — new, I hasten to add — in the bureau drawer. We can't have our policemen wandering around in dirty underwear. Think what that would do to morale. Are you right for a razor?'

'Yes. And I have a toothbrush.'

'Excellent. I don't want you to feel like you're camping out.'

'This is very good of you, Peter.'

'Nonsense. This place needs more people in it.'

'Didn't they billet anyone with you when the Americans were here in full force?'

'Oh no. I didn't want that.'

He said this so emphatically that Joe wondered how much influence Peter Lillee wielded. Helen's explanation that he was a businessman was too vague to account for either his wealth or his ability to keep the world at bay. Inspector Lambert might have believed that Peter Lillee would have had no choice in accepting him as a guest. But, having met him, Joe suspected that the agreement had more to do with loyalty to his niece than with an inability to resist a demand from Homicide. If he'd been able to bat military billets elsewhere, blocking Victoria Police would have been a small matter. He wasn't with Military Intelligence. Joe had had experience with them, and they lacked Lillee's finish. His influence was doubtless directly related to his wealth.

'I'll leave you to your bath.'

'Mrs Lord's gone to the trouble of making a pudding.'

'Don't worry about that. I'll tell you tomorrow how ghastly it was. 'Instant pudding' — two words designed to strike terror into the heart of anyone with a decent palate. I blame the Americans. I bet it's one of their exciting innovations. I'll tell Ros and Helen that you were simply exhausted and needed to get to bed. They'll understand. I'll see you in the morning. If you need anything, just help yourself. It would be nice to have staff to call on, but I'm afraid I couldn't get around that restriction. No domestic servants — what a world we live in.'

★ ★ ★

Helen lay wide awake in her room. It was well after midnight, but her mind was alive with competing thoughts. The most worrying of these was an inchoate feeling of jealousy. She dared not consider this too closely, just as she'd never dared inquire into her uncle's private life. She had suspicions, but she loved him and she really believed that his affairs — both professional and personal — were none of her business. She envied Joe's knowledge of art. She would love to be able to talk to Peter with that facility, and she'd tried to educate herself. The truth was, she just wasn't interested. This wasn't the source of her disturbed feelings, though. She'd occasionally looked at her uncle in the course of the evening, and she'd thought that the intensity of his gaze when he looked at Joe wasn't just because the conversation was lively. She wasn't sure. She didn't want to be sure. Was Uncle Peter looking at Joe with . . . ? She slammed the door shut on the thought. She thought instead of the repulsive Stanley Halloran and George Starling. Starling existed for her only as a sketch and an uncertain threat. These thoughts were preferable to any others, and she took them with her into sleep.

8

Saturday 15 January 1944

George Starling took stock of himself in the
full-length mirror in his room at the Windsor
Hotel. He'd just returned from the hotel's
barber, where he'd been closely shaved and had
his hair washed, cut, and Brilliantined into
disciplined shape. He was wearing a new suit,
shirt, and shoes that had cost him a lot in
coupons and cash. He leaned into the mirror,
and thought he might encourage a neat
moustache. It would grow in a matter of days. As
it was, he needed to shave morning and night to
keep his beard shadow in order. He turned
sideways. He'd pass for a gentleman — no
worries. He thought he might actually be quite
good-looking. He'd never really thought about
his looks before. He'd been told so often by his
father that he was ugly and stupid that he'd
spent most of his life avoiding mirrors. No girl
had ever complimented him on his looks; not
that there'd been very many girls — a couple of
rough slappers, and a prostitute who'd paid with
a bloody nose for calling him a hairy ape. Now,
though, he thought he scrubbed up pretty well.
The police wouldn't be looking for someone who
dressed like a fucking movie star and who
smelled like one, too.

He picked up his new hat — a beautiful, soft

grey fedora — put it on, and tilted it. A good brothel would be more than happy to admit the man he saw in the mirror, and he intended visiting one that evening. For now, though, he'd go down to the dining room, order breakfast, and read the papers. The fire in Princes Hill would surely be reported, and that would be a good start to the day.

In the dining room, he was subject to a deference he'd never experienced before. It gave him pleasure, but the pleasure was tempered with anger. All it took was tailoring, a good barber, and a splash of cologne, and the lickspittles buckled under. His waiter, an effeminate young man — rejected, no doubt, if he'd ever applied, by the army on the basis of deviant tendencies — made obsequious enquiries as to whether sir would care for a pot of tea. It took considerable self-discipline to subdue the malevolence in Starling's eyes, and even more not to slam his fist into the nance's face. He wondered idly if the boy had ever taken a beating by someone as well dressed as Starling. Maybe he'd surprise him later and smash those pursed lips into the back of his throat.

A copy of that day's *Argus* was folded on the table. He ran his eyes over its pages quickly. Where was the good news about Sable's flat? There was plenty about the bushfires. Cheltenham, Mentone, and Beaumaris had been hit. As many as 100 homes had been razed, but this was of no interest to Starling. Still, there was enough in the articles to make him laugh:

When the fire in the Beaumaris district was found to be out of control of the regular firemen, appeals for volunteers were broadcast. Among the first to respond were batches of soldiers from a general transport company who hastened out in trucks from their headquarters near the city with supplies of fire beaters made of uppers from old army boots attached to broom handles.

How ridiculous they must have looked.

Hundreds of women and children were evacuated to the safety of Beaumaris Beach and Ricketts Point. Many assisted to carry furniture and other household belongings from homes threatened by fire.

Starling closed his eyes. What a sight that must have been — tables, chairs, sideboards, and counches, standing in the sand with the sea behind them, and a wall of flames before them.

'Your tea, sir.'

Starling opened his eyes. He cocked his head on one side and smiled. The waiter made the mistake of smiling back.

'Maybe you'd like a drink after work,' Starling said.

'That would be very nice.'

I don't think you'll find it very nice at all, Starling thought, and an involuntary laugh escaped him.

'I finish at five,' the waiter said.

'I'll meet you out the front, but down the

street a bit. Maybe you know a place we could get a decent drink.'

'I know a place.'

Starling ran his eye over the menu.

'I'll just have the toast. Is there butter?'

'Of course. The sausage is very good.'

'Just toast. I don't like sausage.'

'I'll see you at five,' the waiter said, and headed towards the kitchen. Starling was filled with loathing and disgust. It felt right, and it felt good.

★ ★ ★

Matthew Todd sat in the shade in the backyard of his Aunt Aggie's house in Port Fairy. She'd brought him the paper, a pot of tea, and a plate of scones. He'd brought some cream, eggs, new potatoes, leeks, and carrots, all from Rose's farm. He'd taken them without asking. Aggie was suitably grateful — not to Rose, but to Matthew. Selwyn hadn't come out of his shed. Normally, he'd have already left to take up his position in Sackville Street, but Matthew had arrived just as he was about to leave. He'd become wary of Matthew, so rather than risk the blow he'd receive on walking past him, he'd remained in the sweltering heat of the shed.

'He's scared of me,' Matthew said. 'He should be scared of you, too, Aunt Aggie. You could control him better.'

'I can control him all right. All I have to do is say your name and he does as he's told. 'Don't make me get Matthew round here,' I say to him.

138

It works like a charm.'

Matthew liked his Aunt Aggie. She was a dry old thing, definitely a virgin, and he couldn't recall her ever saying anything amusing. Still, she doted on him, and Matthew loved being doted on. Dorothy was in love with him. She'd said so, and he supposed that he might be in love with her, although he might not be, too. He didn't really know. She annoyed him, and she argued with him. That would have to stop. Aunt Aggie never argued with him. She agreed with everything he said, and she was interested enough to listen as well. Dorothy had been known to criticise him for going on about some things. He wanted to be married, though. Marriage was a kind of arrival into adult life. Dorothy would do — that's what it came down to. After they were married he'd be less patient with her. No wife of his was going to turn away when he was speaking, like she did sometimes. Not after they were married, she wouldn't.

'The paper's there for you,' Aggie said. It was the previous day's — Friday's — *Argus*. Melbourne papers never made it to Port Fairy on the same day. 'There's nothing in it.'

'That saves me the trouble of reading it.' He laughed. Matthew rarely read a newspaper. They reminded him that a war was being fought, and that there was more to it than rationing, austerity, and inconvenience. They reminded him that he wasn't in it. He did an important job, of course, as his aunt frequently told him. She had the idea that he was ultimately responsible for the success of the Port Fairy catch. 'Where would all those fishermen be without you to sell their catch?' she often said.

'Dorothy should be here in a minute, Aunt Aggie. Can we shift Selwyn before she gets here? I don't like her having anything to do with him.'

Aggie had long ago stopped feeling any need to defend her simple brother. She agreed with Matthew that he was little more than an unruly domestic animal. He was toilet trained; but, as Matthew rightly said, you could teach a cat to use a sandbox, so teaching Selwyn to shit in the toilet wasn't exactly evidence of high intelligence. She'd gone beyond being disgusted by Selwyn. She'd become inured to even the worst of his physical habits.

'You know,' she said, 'Father Brennan's always at me to bring Selwyn to Mass. Can you imagine it? He knows perfectly well it's impossible.'

'Has he ever actually met Selwyn?'

'Oh, only in Sackville Street, and Selwyn just scratched away on his slate and giggled and drooled. You'd think they'd had some sort of conversation, from the way Father Brennan talks about it.'

'I'm sorry, Aunt Aggie. I know he's a priest and all, but the man's a fool.'

'I think he drinks. He's often rather florid.'

'Maybe it's all those sins he hears in Confession. Maybe he gets overheated.'

Only Matthew could get away with that sort of talk. Aggie would have felt compelled to express strong disapproval at any aspersions cast upon the priest by anybody else. Conversation with Matthew was a delicious conspiracy. She lied to

140

Father Brennan in Confession — she'd never confessed her feelings about Selwyn — but she never lied to Matthew.

'Father Brennan must know a lot of dark secrets, don't you think?' she said.

'If people are silly enough to tell him things.'

'Oh yes. People want absolution, Matthew.'

'Would it shock you to know how long it's been since my last Confession, Aunt Aggie?'

'No, don't tell me. I'd worry.'

And Aggie would worry because, despite her low opinion of the priest at St Patrick's, she believed absolutely in the power of Confession. She was an obfuscatory penitent, but she never took communion without absolution.

'You should go to Confession, Matthew. An eternity in Hell is a very long time.'

'Where will Selwyn go when he dies, do you think? All that self-abuse must be racking up the mortal sins.'

'Father Brennan seems to think he'll go straight to Heaven, without even a short stay in Purgatory. Imagine that, if you please. He commits a mortal sin every day of his life, sometimes twice a day, and he'll get a free ride to Heaven.'

'While you suffer in Purgatory. It seems unfair, and somehow typical of the Catholic Church.'

'Matthew! Besides, my dear, I have no intention of spending any time in Purgatory. I'll have a priest at my bedside to administer Extreme Unction.'

'If it's the last thing you do?'

Aggie laughed. She didn't laugh often, and it

was usually Matthew who provoked it. It was Matthew who brought a quantum of joy into her life.

'If you slip into the house for a moment, I'll get Selwyn out through the back gate.'

'I could just drag him out, if you like.'

'No. I couldn't bear the noise. I have a bit of a headache.'

* * *

Johanna Scotney didn't like snakes. She didn't have a horror of them; she just didn't like them, which was why she said no when Timothy Harrison suggested they take a walk through the mutton-bird rookery on Griffiths Island. She said that she'd prefer to walk the other way, go over the bridge across the Moyne River and saunter through the Botanical Gardens, or the remnants of them. The gardens had fallen on hard times, without a full-time gardener available to tend them. They'd been damaged, too, by floods. And yet, somehow, the presence of many trees — the almost ubiquitous Norfolk Pines mainly, and even ragged hedges — managed to create the illusion of a garden. Johanna's mother had told her that there'd once been a lover's walk in the Botanicals, and that proposals for several marriages, including her own, had been made there.

Johanna and Timothy met as arranged at lunchtime outside the courthouse in Gipps Street. The wharf opposite wasn't as busy as it had been before the war. Many of the boats had

142

been requisitioned by the armed forces, and now, instead of dropping lines for sharks, they moved supplies and ammunition along the New Guinea coast. There weren't as many fishermen either. Even though sharking was a reserved industry, many men had enlisted. The army was a break from the gruelling, dangerous, and poorly paid life of a fisherman. Her father's couta boat, old and too small for military use — it was barely a 20 footer — wouldn't be tied up at the wharf now. He'd left at his usual time of 3.00 am to drop lines ten miles out from shore. Shark numbers had fallen, and Mr Scotney added to his meagre income by smoking a portion of his barracouta catch in a smoker he'd made himself in the backyard of their house in Corbett Street. He had steady orders from locals for his smoked couta.

Timothy knew nothing of this world. Like most people in Port Fairy who weren't fishermen, he had a fairly low opinion of them. They kept to themselves mostly, because townspeople thought them crude and rough. No one doubted their courage, or that the work they did was dirty, hard, and perilous, but they weren't welcome in clean parlours. Most people ate fish only occasionally, even reluctantly — Catholics ate fish on a Friday, of course — and they weren't particularly interested in the lives of the men who toiled to provide for them. If push came to shove, they could do without fish altogether. This certainly couldn't be said of lamb or beef. Johanna was, by degrees, changing Timothy's mind about fishing. She tried to convey to him what life was like on a fishing boat, although she'd never been far beyond the mouth of the Moyne in her father's couta boat. Tom Scotney wasn't willing to expose his daughter to the open sea, not even on the calmest of days. Freak waves had overwhelmed couta boats before, and had drowned the most experienced of men. Fishing was not for women; he wouldn't budge on that.

'Did you know,' she said as they walked towards the bridge, 'that the fish you get at the fish-and-chip shop in town is shark?'

'It's Sweet William, isn't it?'

'Sweet William's just a nice name for shark.'

'Ugh. I'm not sure I like the idea of eating shark.'

'It tastes nice, doesn't it, and it's got no bones.'

'No bones, that's true. I've never really thought about it.'

'Dad catches shark mostly. He gets a better price for it than couta.'

'How do you get a shark into one of those boats?'

Johanna hit him playfully on his shoulder.

'They're not huge man-eaters. They're gummy sharks. Dad says the worst thing about them is that when you cut them open you breathe in a whole lot of ammonia, and it makes your face go bright red. Imagine breathing that in all day.'

'My dad was gassed.'

'Yes, I know.' Johanna was embarrassed, and felt as if she'd done something wrong. 'I didn't mean to compare . . . '

'No,' Timothy said quickly. He was now embarrassed in return, and neither of them could find a way out of the clumsy moment. They walked in silence.

'I'd like to meet your mum and dad,' Johanna said.

'Dad doesn't say much.'

'My dad doesn't say much either, and when he does talk it's always about fish.'

Johanna stole a sidelong glance at Timothy. He was just a few months younger than she was, but she felt so much older, and it wasn't just that the boy wasn't quite yet the man. Her life had been protected, but not sheltered. A childhood spent on the wharf, surrounded by the unguarded conversation of men, had ensured that there wasn't an obscenity or blasphemy she hadn't heard. No one had ever turned abuse on her or done anything as vile as Matthew Todd, though. Tom Scotney would have killed the man who outraged his daughter. This was partly why she hadn't told him about Matthew's actions. Tom Scotney would go to Todd's house, and God help Matthew then. He'd gut and fillet him. Timothy's life had been sheltered. Johanna had never heard him utter a curse. He looked unused. Yes, that was the word — unused, as if he was yet to know how ugly the world could be. He'd grown up with an invalid father, but perhaps Mr Harrison was one of those men who never spoke of the horrors he'd seen. Timothy turned his head, caught her eye, and smiled. Johanna felt a rush of affection for him, and as if he'd sensed it, he did something extraordinary.

He kissed her, right there in Gipps Street, just before the bridge. He leaned down and put his mouth on hers, and she didn't pull away. To the astonishment of each of them, the kiss was warm and smooth, with no hint of clumsiness. They drew apart and began to walk across the bridge towards the Botanical Gardens.

★　★　★

'Kissing in public like that, really, it's disgusting,' said Dorothy Shipman. She and Matthew Todd, having left his aunt's house after a cup of tea, had decided to walk to East Beach, where Matthew thought he might have a swim. When they'd turned into Gipps Street, he'd seen the couple ahead of them and recognised Johanna Scotney at once. He slowed their pace so as to avoid catching up with the couple, and gave no indication to Dorothy that he knew the girl. So that gangly, gormless youth was the beau that Rose mentioned. Matthew chortled.

'What's funny?'

'Nothing.'

'You never tell me what you're thinking.'

'I'm not thinking anything at all, Dotty. My mind is blank.'

'I wish you'd tell me things.'

You wouldn't like the things I could tell you, he thought. When Johanna and Timothy kissed, he experienced a thrill. It wasn't jealousy. It was more visceral than that — it was the thrill of the chase. *Whoever you are,* he thought as he watched the young man put his arm around

Johanna's waist, *you're not going to get there first*. Dorothy, having expressed her disappointment at the lewd display, looked to Matthew for his reaction. She couldn't make sense of the expression on his face.

'Really, Matthew, I insist that you tell me what you're thinking.'

'I was thinking how lucky I am, Dot — how very, very lucky.'

'Lucky to have me, you mean,' she said and laughed.

'Yes,' he said. 'That, too.'

She had no idea what he meant, but she was pleased to be walking beside him. He was a good man — reliable, honest, respectful. Once she'd nominated the boundaries of their physical relationship, he hadn't gone beyond them. She wished he was more mindful of his faith. That was something she could work on after they were married. It wasn't something she wanted to argue about now. The sacrament of marriage and the gift of children would bring Matthew back to the Church. Dorothy was praying for this, saying the Rosary every day, and she believed in the power of prayer. After all, even before she'd met Matthew she'd prayed that someone like him would come along. And hadn't God answered that prayer? Luck, she told herself, had had nothing to do with it.

⋆   ⋆   ⋆

It had become a scheduled part of every week on the Abbot farm that Saturday lunch would be followed by sex. They had the house to themselves. They never took their lovemaking out of the bedroom, even though there was no danger of being caught by anyone. Rose had tried to encourage her husband into other rooms, or outside. He said he couldn't relax and enjoy himself in odd places. Rose lay on the bed in her nightdress, waiting for John to finish cleaning himself in the bathroom. He liked to approach their lovemaking feeling freshly bathed and smelling of Bornns Bay Rum. He also liked to begin matters with his wife modestly covered. Early in their marriage he'd found her lying naked on the bed, and he'd said that the sight of his wife disporting herself was unseemly. He, however, always approached the task naked. He had no personal modesty. Why would a man need to be modest? Modesty was the domain and responsibility of women.

Rose had become used to her husband's contradictory notions about sex. He wasn't a particularly thoughtful lover, but he wasn't rough or nasty either. She'd come to accept that he was a tad boring. It was always the same. He whispered endearments, fiddled about a bit, manoeuvred her into position, pushed himself inside her, and, trying not to lie too heavily on her, began to move back and forth with the monotonous regularity of an underpowered piston. Rose closed her eyes and tried to extract as much pleasure as she could from the exercise. Sometimes this worked, but she had to be careful not to be too expressive. John believed that his wife should enjoy sex, no question about

148

it. There was a difference, though, between enjoyment and wanton abandonment. His wife moaning with pleasure frightened him.

In the kitchen, after each of them had sponged the evidence of their lovemaking away, Rose said that she'd like to drive into Port Fairy, visit her Aunt Aggie, and maybe go for a swim at East Beach. John said that he'd be happy to drive her in, but that he'd go to the pub while she was at Aggie's.

'She doesn't like me anyway, so it's not like she'd care.'

Afterwards they could both go for a swim. That was fine by Rose. She was never comfortable when John and Aggie were together. Aggie made no secret of the fact that she thought him coarse — which he was. Visiting Aggie was a chore, not a pleasure. She couldn't make her laugh the way Matthew could, and she lacked his knack of easy conversation with her. Even though they saw each other irregularly, there never seemed to be anything to say. Aggie would ask if Rose had heard from her parents. The answer was usually no, although occasionally there might have been a recent phone call. Rose knew not to ask after Uncle Selwyn, and she wouldn't have done so anyway. She didn't loathe Selwyn the way Matthew did, yet she felt no connection with him. She avoided Sackville Street, and if she had to shop there, she never acknowledged him.

John parked the truck outside the Caledonian Hotel, and Rose walked from there to Aggie's house. It wasn't far. Nothing was far in Port Fairy. She had a nodding acquaintance with almost every person she passed. Strange faces were a rare sight in town. There was the odd itinerant who came looking for work on the wharf, but generally people were familiar to one another through church, ladies' auxiliaries, or the pubs. Rose met Mrs Hardiman, with two of her seven children in tow. Mr Hardiman was stationed somewhere in the Northern Territory, and Mrs Hardiman had no help with the children. Nevertheless, they were turned out beautifully each Sunday at Mass, and Mrs Hardiman never looked harried. While they were chatting, Mr Butler walked by. He touched his hat politely, but didn't stop.

'He's a Mason,' Mrs Hardiman said.

'Really?' Rose watched his retreating back. 'You just don't know about people, do you? I had no idea.'

'He's nice enough, and his wife's been good to us. They live next door.'

'Still, a Mason.'

'Yes, it's a real shame.'

Aggie was pleased to see, when she opened the door to Rose's knock, that John Abbot wasn't with her. It was bad enough that Rose seemed to have caught some of his uncouthness. Her hair, for example, was either pulled back unflatteringly or was a rat's nest of untidiness.

'I didn't bring any eggs, but I think Matthew probably brought some yesterday.' Rose had noticed that her pantry had been raided.

'Yes, he did,' Aggie said, and managed to convey her disappointment that her niece wasn't as thoughtful or generous as her nephew. Rose thought that reminding her aunt that the eggs and vegetables were in fact hers, and not Matthew's, would be viewed as petty, so she said nothing.

Aggie made a pot of tea, and produced shortbread biscuits that she'd made with butter from the Abbot's farm. She made no mention of this gift, and Rose didn't fail to notice that the teaspoon next to her cup wasn't one of the silver apostle spoons. Matthew, no doubt, would always be favoured with an apostle spoon.

'You look well, Aunty,' she said.

'I just try to look neat, Rose. It doesn't take *that* much of an effort.'

Rose ignored the implied criticism. She had no desire to squabble with her aunt, who was well practised in withering rejoinders. She used them sparingly in company, not wishing to get a reputation in the parish for shrewishness. A well-timed, well-aimed remark, however, helped create an impression of intelligence, and it was generally agreed that Aggie Todd, while dour, had a sharp wit, and she was never short of invitations to elevenses and tiffin.

After some dull remarks about the fires and the weather, Rose asked her aunt what she thought of Dorothy Shipman.

'She was here this morning. She seems a sensible-enough girl. She's a draper's daughter, which I suppose is what passes for society in Port Fairy. Matthew is fond of her, so that's all well and good.'

'I've only met her once.'

'Well, you're out on that farm, aren't you? I

can't see Dorothy traipsing about in cow pats.'

Rose didn't bite.

'No, I suppose not. I'd like to get to know her better. What does she see in Matthew, do you think?'

Aggie looked incredulous.

'What an extraordinary question, Rose. Your brother is the most successful forwarding agent in this town. He's done more for the fishermen here than the Co-operative has ever managed to do.'

'I don't think the Co-op would agree with you, Aunty.'

All of Rose's knowledge of the lives of Port Fairy's fishermen had been gleaned from Johanna's conversation about her father, and her father was a member of the Co-operative.

'You don't live in the town, Rose. If you did, you'd know how well respected your brother is.'

'Is she a Catholic girl, or is Matthew following in Dad's footsteps?'

'The Shipmans are very much a Catholic family. If you came to Mass more regularly, you'd see Dorothy there.'

'Father Brennan understands that it's not always easy for John to leave the farm.'

'It's a mortal sin. Imagine if you fell under the tractor on a Monday, having missed Mass on Sunday. John should make more of an effort. It wouldn't hurt him to be a little more self-sacrificing.'

Rose had no appetite for allowing the conversation to slide into an attack on her husband.

'Be that as it may, Aunty, I'd like to get to know Dorothy better. I'm sure she's a lovely person.'

Rose wasn't at all sure of this. She was curious about the kind of woman who was willing to overlook what Rose believed were Matthew's ostentatious flaws.

Aggie, whose face assumed a little moue when Rose dunked a piece of shortbread in her tea, said that if Rose was serious she could invite the couple out to the farm for dinner.

'Yes, I'll do that. Perhaps you'd come, too.'

'Oh no, dear. Someone has to be here to keep an eye on Selwyn at night.'

This wasn't true. Often, Aggie locked Selwyn in the shed and spent an evening at someone's house.

'If you're serious about meeting Dorothy, you could start this afternoon. She and Matthew were planning to have a swim at East Beach. They'll be there now, I suspect.'

There was no doubting that this was a dismissal, and Rose was happy to take advantage of it. She finished her tea, surreptitiously put a shortbread in her pocket — it was her butter, after all — and effected her departure.

In the Caledonian Hotel, John Abbot was deep in conversation with another farmer. Rose knew these conversations were important to John, infrequent though they were. They were an opportunity to vent frustrations and share information. What she didn't know was that at the moment she walked into the bar — a place she wouldn't normally have entered — John Abbot was telling

153

his friend that Johanna Scotney was a ripe little peach and that she might be up for a bit of how's your father. His friend, a much older man, laughed, but cautioned John that Johanna's father would wreak havoc if he ever found out.

'Nah,' John said. 'She's playing hard-to-get all right, but she's playing. She wouldn't still be there if she wasn't up for it, would she? She certainly wouldn't be saying anything to her father.'

His friend shrugged.

'I'd be careful if I were you, John. Word gets around.'

Rose heard none of this as she approached the bar where they were sitting.

'Rosy,' John said. He always called her Rosy after a few drinks. 'Had enough of the old dragon?'

Rose didn't bother leaping to her aunt's defence. John knew perfectly well that Rose agreed with him.

'I'm going down to East Beach. You stay here.'

'No, I'll come. I could do with a swim.'

'I'm hoping to meet up with Matthew and his fiancée.'

'Oh.' John's interest evaporated. 'I'll stay here then.'

★　★　★

Johanna and Timothy weren't alone in the gardens. Despite the grounds' disordered state, they were still a popular place to take the dog or to walk off a big lunch. The smaller paths had

154

disappeared in the wilderness of undergrowth, so most people stuck to the main ones, where regular foot traffic ensured a clear way. Timothy knew a disused track, just discernable if you were familiar with it. It ran behind a huge Norfolk pine and down towards the Moyne River. At a certain point, it flattened out to provide a place that couldn't be seen from either the park or the land on the other side.

He and Johanna sat down, or rather Johanna did, and Timothy lay back with his hands behind his head. His shirt rose up to expose his belly; but, despite the intimacy of that kiss, Johanna was too shy to place her hand on his skin. She did as he did, and lay back.

'We'll be all right, you know,' Timothy said.

'Maybe it'll all be over by the time you're 18.'

'I hope not.'

Johanna sat up.

'You don't have to prove how brave you are, Tim. Not to me, and not to anyone else either. There are plenty of blokes who haven't joined up, and no one thinks anything of it.'

Johanna didn't quite believe this. She understood why her father hadn't joined up. Shark fishing was a reserved occupation. Several other fishermen had signed on for the army. Tom Scotney thought those blokes were nongs, not heroes. They'd left their families in dire straits, and they'd expect to just waltz back into the industry when the war ended. Shark fishing was a protected industry for a bloody good reason, so those blokes were abandoning their duty, not heading off to do their duty. Johanna had heard her father crowing recently about the fact that the silly buggers were being sent home because there weren't enough fishermen left behind to fill the catch quotas. He'd been right all along. Someone like Matthew Todd, though? He should be in the army, Johanna thought. Timothy, on the other hand, was too young, and he ought to think about his mother. She already had one son overseas, and she probably worried herself silly that he'd end up like her husband.

'Does your mum want you to go?'

Timothy sat up.

'No.'

'I don't want you to go.'

Afterwards, she couldn't recall what prompted her to say what she said next. Perhaps it was the sudden call of a coot, or the splash of a black swan landing in the river.

'I want you to stay here to protect me.'

Timothy was silent for a moment.

'To protect you from what?'

'Men. Other men.' She began to cry, and Timothy was covered in confusion.

'Jo, what's the matter? Did I upset you?'

'Oh no. I'm sorry, I don't want to . . . I have to tell *someone*.'

Her sobs became so deep that she was unable to speak. She leaned into Timothy to reassure him that this had nothing to do with him. He let her cry because he didn't know what else to do.

'I thought I was coping with it, but it's too much, Tim. It's too much, and now I don't know what to do.'

She told Timothy that Matthew Todd had

touched her in intimate places. She also told him that John Abbot had made lewd suggestions to her, although he'd never touched her. Timothy didn't understand at first what Johanna was talking about. Matthew Todd was a respected man, and John Abbot was married. Surely Johanna had just misunderstood something that had been said to her, and maybe Matthew Todd had touched her accidentally. Johanna stared at Timothy, and her distress and embarrassment turned to anger.

'Do you think I'm making this up?'

Her voice was shrill with disbelief. The last thing she'd expected of Timothy was doubt. 'Do you think this is my *fault*?'

Timothy had never been so close to real fury before, and he fell back away from it.

'He pushed my hand against his penis!'

Timothy was now mortified. Johanna saying that word was shocking — so shocking that he couldn't grasp the full meaning of the sentence. They both stood up. Johanna was crying again. Timothy put his hand on her arm, but she slapped it away. She was incapable of speech. She walked quickly up the path's incline, and when she reached the main path she began running. She passed several people who were surprised to see Johanna Scotney in an hysterical state. They saw, too, Timothy Harrison, standing some distance away, his hands by his side, a stunned look on his face. Well, it was perfectly obvious what had happened, wasn't it? If word of this got back to Tom Scotney, Timothy Harrison could expect a thrashing.

'How far do you think he went?' Mrs Lucan said to her husband.

'Far enough to make her hysterical, so I'd say he went plenty far enough.'

'You can't trust the quiet ones.'

'I always thought there was something odd about the Harrisons. They've never had to struggle for a penny. It makes people feel entitled. Serves him bloody right if Tom Scotney does find out. I've a mind to make sure he does.'

Timothy barely noticed the Lucans, even though they were in his line of sight. He watched the retreating figure of Johanna. He'd done everything the wrong way, and he had no idea how to put it right.

★   ★   ★

Rose Abbot was some distance from the bridge when she saw Johanna run across it. She was obviously crying, but Rose was too far away to catch up with her and find out what was wrong. Johanna ran down Regent Street, and by the time Rose got there, she was nowhere to be seen. A male figure reached the bridge just as she did. He, too, looked upset, and Rose surmised that this must be Timothy Harrison.

'Timothy? You're Timothy Harrison?'

He was momentarily startled.

'Yes.'

'I just saw Johanna run past. What's happened?'

'I don't know who you are.'

'My name is Rose Abbot. Johanna works on our farm.'

158

Timothy looked stricken.

'She told me about your husband.' The words fell out of his mouth in a rush, and he pushed past Rose before she'd taken them in. She thought she was going to be ill. No, there'd been some misunderstanding. Timothy Harrison was just a boy. He'd got the wrong end of the stick. She'd sort this out later. She suppressed a sense of dread, and continued walking towards East Beach.

Rose wasn't a keen beach swimmer. It was John who enjoyed it. Rose didn't really understand the attraction, particularly on windy days, when the sand stung. There was no wind today, and there was a sufficient scattering of clouds to provide some relief from the sun. There weren't many people on the beach, and she quickly found Dorothy Shipman. She was sitting on her own. Matthew must have gone in for a swim.

'Hello,' she said.

Dorothy shielded her eyes, uncertain at first who the silhouetted figure looking over her was.

'Oh, Rose, it's you.'

She leapt up, wrapping a large towel around her already modestly clad body.

'May I join you?'

'Oh yes. How lovely.'

They both sat down.

She was pretty, Rose thought, even in bright sunlight. She could see why Dorothy had caught Matthew's eye, but how had she held it?

'We've never really had a decent conversation, have we?' Rose said.

'It seems a shame, doesn't it?'

'I hope Matthew has been giving you eggs and vegetables from our farm.'

'Oh yes. Thank you. I have asked him to tell you how grateful we are. I hope he's told you.'

'He's forgetful.'

'Oh, that's terrible. I'm so sorry. I'm embarrassed.'

Rose could tell that Dorothy was genuinely annoyed by Matthew's failure to observe the rules of etiquette.

'I'll have a word with him when he comes out of the water, if he ever does. He's been out there for ages.'

'No, no. Don't spoil your day. I know he can react badly to being dressed down, and he really wouldn't like being corrected in front of his sister.'

'Well, that's too bad for him. He needs to be trained.'

Rose raised her eyebrows at this prim declaration.

'I've found that if a man's not fully trained by the time he's 15, he goes beyond the reach of any regime designed to improve him.' Rose laughed as she said this, having given up trying to add civilising touches to John Abbot's limited repertoire of social graces. Dorothy looked surprised.

'Matthew doesn't mind being told when he's done some small thing wrong.'

Rose didn't believe this for a minute. If Matthew was on his best behaviour now, it was because it suited his purpose. Dorothy was in for

160

a nasty surprise. It wasn't Rose's place to warn her that her fiancé was capable of deceiving her without feeling guilt. *My God, the way he ogled Johanna Scotney.* Hard upon this thought, Timothy Harrison's words crept back. Ridiculous.

'Have you set a date for the wedding?'

'Not an exact date, but I'd like it to be in May. Summer weddings are uncomfortable, don't you think?'

'I suppose. I got married in February. It was hideously hot, now that you mention it. St Patrick's was sweltering.'

'Exactly.' Dorothy nodded sagely.

'I can't see Matthew. Can you?' Rose said.

Dorothy shielded her eyes again and looked at the sea.

'Is that him? No, it isn't.' There was a small hint of panic in her voice. 'I can't see him.'

'He's a strong swimmer.'

They both scanned the water.

'He's not there,' Dorothy said, her voice rising. 'He's not there! Oh! Is there a rip? Has he been caught in a rip?'

She stood up quickly, not caring now that her towel dropped to the ground. She ran to the water's edge and began calling, 'Matthew! Matthew!' Several small wading birds took flight.

Rose joined her.

'Oh!' Dorothy whimpered. 'Oh!' Her hands fluttered. To still them, she pushed her fingers into her hair.

'There!' Rose said. 'There he is, out behind that swell. He's perfectly okay.'

Dorothy burst into tears. As they walked back up the beach, Rose noticed the large, purple birthmark on the inside of her thigh. Matthew must have seen it, and Rose knew that he wouldn't like it. He found physical imperfections disgusting.

Matthew began swimming towards the shore. He stood up when he reached the shallows, paused when he saw that Rose was sitting next to Dorothy, and jogged across the sand to them, showering his sister with kicked-up grains. Dorothy was still crying.

'We thought you'd drowned,' she said. 'You were in so long, and then we couldn't see you.'

'Well, that's just absurd,' Matthew said. Rose noticed that he'd trimmed the hair on his chest and shaved it completely from under his arms. She found this vaguely distasteful and effeminate. She was certain that the birthmark would bother him. Why on earth was he marrying this girl? Was she pregnant? Unlikely. Dorothy Shipman didn't strike her as the sort to surrender her virginity before marriage.

'What are you doing here, Rosy?'

'Aunt Aggie said you'd be here swimming, and I thought it was a good opportunity to talk to Dorothy. We'd barely talked before this afternoon.'

'And what did you talk about?'

'I suppose you think we were talking about you,' Dorothy said, sufficiently recovered to be coquettish. 'You're not the only topic of conversation in the world, Matthew.'

Matthew looked at Rose.

'Well, you did come up, as it happens. I was telling Dorothy how wonderful you are, and how very lucky she is.'

From where Dorothy was sitting, she couldn't see the sour look that crossed Matthew's face. When he turned to Dorothy she was smiling broadly, so Rose probably hadn't said anything unpleasant about him.

'Dorothy was telling me that the wedding is in May.'

'Yes, and then we both flew into a panic about you drowning.'

'Both?'

'Yes, both,' Dorothy said, and Rose thought she detected a hint of disquiet.

★   ★   ★

Steven McNamara finished his shift at the Windsor at 5.00 pm. He'd be surprised if the bloke he'd met at breakfast actually showed up. McNamara hung around outside the hotel, smoking a cigarette. There was something about that bloke. He obviously had money. There was something crude about him, too, and he looked disconcertingly like a young Rudolph Hess, who Steven had seen in newsreels. He wasn't soft-looking. He'd have a hard belly, and maybe he enjoyed being roughed up. If he wanted to do the roughing up, that was fine. Maybe he'd misread the whole situation. Steven checked his watch. Ten past five. He wasn't going to show up.

'Sorry I'm late,' George Starling said. He'd been watching McNamara from inside the

163

Windsor, making up his mind. When he saw him draw on his cigarette in an elaborately feminine way, he decided he needed to put a stop to him.

McNamara turned at the sound of Starling's voice. *Oh yes*, he thought, *you'll do nicely*.

Starling moved past McNamara and kept walking. Steven knew that he'd been invited to follow and did so. This fellow was discreet, and didn't want their assignation noted by anyone associated with the hotel. Fair enough. He caught up with him a block or so along.

'I don't think I know your name,' Steven said.

'You don't. It's George, and that'll do. What's yours?'

'Steven McNamara.'

'The full title. That's formal. I'm new around here. Is there somewhere I can buy you a drink?'

'I know a place. You know the kind of place I'm talking about?'

'I hope we're talking about the same sort of joint — you know, a place where two blokes having a drink won't be bothered.'

Steven nodded and smiled.

'Follow me,' he said, and his turn was almost a pirouette. Starling wanted to knock him down on the spot, and stomp so hard on his face that no fairy would ever give him a second glance, except to note how ugly he was. He held fire and followed. Finding a nest of these people would be useful. He could burn it down, and all of them in it. He was developing a taste for burning.

McNamara led Starling down Little Bourke Street, and into an alley that smelled of garbage and urine. He pushed a door that opened onto a narrow staircase that looked as if it might collapse if stepped on.

'It's up here. It's not salubrious, but it's private.'

At the top of the stairs, McNamara knocked at a door. It was opened a fraction, and then fully. He gestured in a way that indicated he was vouching for Starling, and they were admitted into a small room. Starling didn't know what he'd been expecting, but it wasn't this. He'd imagined some large, bordello-like space, decorated with rich velvet and oversized cushions. This room, with two hurricane lamps rather than an electric light, would look crowded if ten people were in it. There was one table and a few chairs, and there wasn't even a bar — just a cabinet against one wall. Apart from the person who'd opened the door, and who now was arranging bottles in the cabinet, Starling and McNamara were the only people there. They sat at the table. The barman crossed to them, and even though the light was dim, Starling could see that he was wearing make-up.

'Your friend looks nice, sweet Stevie. Does he have a name?'

'The name's George,' Starling said. He smiled up at the barman, who took the smile at face value, and put his hand on Starling's shoulder. He squeezed it. Starling was careful not to flinch. He couldn't afford to drag this out for too long. It was early, and doubtless more punters would begin arriving soon. He'd already decided to kill Steven McNamara. He'd have to do the barman as well now. He didn't want a witness.

'What can I get you to drink?'

'You don't have any beer, I suppose?'

'No, love. The hidden miseries of war. We've got champagne, can you believe it? It's not cheap, but you don't look like a man who scrimps on anything.'

'Champagne all right with you, Steven?'

'That would be lovely.'

Steven relaxed completely. He felt safe here, safer than anywhere else in the world. He leaned back in the chair and put his hands in his pockets.

'What's your story, George?'

The barman brought a bottle of champagne to the table.

'We don't have a chiller, so it might froth when you open it. But that's festive, don't you think? Or would you rather I opened it?'

'I'll do it,' Starling said. He held the bottle and made to open it.

'You tell me your story first, Steven.'

'All right. Well, I'm 22 years old — I know, I look younger. Everyone says so — and I live with my mother-in — '

Starling swung the bottle by its neck, and hit the side of Steven McNamara's head with such force that the glass shattered, leaving Starling with the jagged shank. The barman had no time to register what had happened before Starling was on him, twisting the bottle's neck into his throat. He pushed so hard that it stuck there. Starling stepped back, well out of range of the spray of blood that gushed when the barman pulled the weapon away in horror. He didn't utter a sound as he first sat heavily, and then fell on his side. The astonishing volume of blood reassured Starling that he'd hit an artery. He checked Steven McNamara's body. There was a deep depression above his left eye, which was open and unseeing.

Starling took McNamara's identity card, and, very carefully avoiding the blood, took the barman's card as well. Starling checked his clothes. He was clean. He left, taking one more look at his handiwork, and quickly scanned the staircase. No one was coming up. He went back into the room, took each of the hurricane lamps, and threw them against the wall. A dribble of blue fire crawled down the wall, pooled on the floor, and looked as if it might take hold. Starling didn't stay around to make sure. If it didn't catch, it didn't matter — he'd made a good start to his evening. There was no one in the alley when he reached it, and he joined the throng of people in Little Bourke Street. He raised his hat to an elderly lady, and she smiled appreciatively. It was nice, she thought, that there were still some men with manners.

9

Martin Serong, whom Inspector Lambert considered the most compassionate and most accomplished of crime-scene photographers, had not yet finished his task when Lambert and Senior Sergeant Bob O'Dowd arrived. It was just after eight o'clock on Saturday evening, and Inspector Lambert had elected not to bring Sergeant Reilly or Constable Lord to the scene of this double murder. Each of them would benefit from a rest. He'd felt guilty about leaving Maude to make Tom Mackenzie's house in South Melbourne habitable, but Maude knew, and accepted without rancour, that victims of violence would call her husband away at all hours of the day and night. Sergeant O'Dowd's wife hadn't been so understanding, and had complained bitterly that she'd now have to entertain his parents on her own.

Nevertheless, when he and Lambert walked into the dingy upstairs room, laughably described as a club, thoughts of his small, domestic ruckus vanished. The intermittent glare of Serong's camera revealed two bodies and a great deal of blood. A single, electric bulb provided the only constant illumination. Three other detectives and the police doctor, who'd arrived ahead of Lambert and O'Dowd, were dusting and using torches to scour the room for evidence. They were experienced men, and Inspector Lambert knew that their practised eyes would settle on anything that seemed anomalous. O'Dowd placed his murder bag on the floor, and joined his colleagues. One of these, Detective Ron Dunnart, was Lambert's age. He came across to him.

'What do we know, Ron?' Lambert said quietly.

'The call was made to D24 anonymously. This salubrious establishment is apparently a private club — a private gentlemen's club where only gentlemen are welcome, which is why the informant didn't stick around. The bloke on the floor has had the business end of a broken champagne bottle rammed into his throat, and the bloke at the table has a crushed skull, the result of being hit with the same bottle when it was full. There's champagne all over the place. There are no signs of a struggle. This was done quickly and efficiently. I suspect both victims were taken by surprise. Our killer is a cool customer. The doc thinks they've been dead for no more than a couple of hours. The killer tried to burn the place down on his way out. Two hurricane lamps were thrown against the wall, but the flames went out.'

'So what do you think happened here?'

'I think one of these blokes — the one at the table, I'd say — brought someone here who didn't realise what kind of place it was until a hand went down his pants, and then he went berserk.'

'Berserk?'

'Wrong word. It's too controlled to be the result of someone going berserk. Still, I think he did this when he found out what sort of place it was.'

'Did you know the club was here?'

'No. I'll check with the CIB. Neither of the victims has any sort of identification on him. Maybe they got what was coming to them.'

'Do you really think that, Ron?'

Ron Dunnart shrugged.

'Well, Titus, some people don't like being felt up by perverts. I can't say I'd care for it myself.'

'And this is how you'd react?'

'I'd settle for a good punch.'

Martin Serong, who'd taken the last of his photographs, joined Ron Dunnart and Inspector Lambert.

'What do you think, Martin?'

'I'd say Ron's right about the killer having a cool head, but I don't think the place took him by surprise. He killed both these men within seconds of each other, which means both of them were relaxed at the time. If one of them had made an unexpected move on the killer, his shocked reaction, if he was going to have one, would have been impossible to control. That would have alerted one, or both, of his victims. The man at the table didn't know what hit him, and the man in the make-up would have had no more than a couple of seconds to comprehend what had happened.'

'Ron?'

'Sure. That makes sense. Maybe our killer hates queers, let himself be picked up, and then chose his moment.'

'I think that's what happened,' Serong said.

'Okay. Ron, I want you and O'Dowd to work this one. The CIB might know who the regulars here are, and I want you to be discreet. This isn't a witch hunt for homosexual men.'

He spoke briefly to the other detectives in the room, and before leaving he took Ron Dunnart aside.

'We've known each other a long time, Ron.'

Ron became immediately defensive. 'I'm not sure I like where this is going, Titus.'

'If I hear, Ron, that any member of my squad uses information about the men who use this place to blackmail them, I'll make bloody sure that that man gets a posting to Murray Bridge. Is that understood?'

'Loud and clear, sir.'

Titus ignored the sneering edge to the 'sir'.

'Good. Keep me fully informed. I'll leave you to it.'

Later, over a drink, Ron Dunnart and Bob O'Dowd agreed that the murder of a couple of queers needn't be a top priority. There were more pressing cases.

'We might learn something useful, though,' Dunnart said.

'Meaning?'

'You never know who you're going to find when you look under a rock, and you just never know how much they're willing to pay to stay under it.'

O'Dowd smiled. 'Interesting,' he said. 'Interesting.'

★　★　★

171

On Saturday morning, Peter Lillee drove Joe Sable into Russell Street. There, Joe spent the next three hours dealing with the consequences of having been the victim of arson. There were forms to fill in, statements to be clarified, insurance claims to prepare, and myriad bureaucratic impedimenta that seemed designed to punish him further. He knew he ought to make contact with the other residents, but he didn't feel up to accommodating their suspicion and blame. He looked briefly at the report that had been prepared on the dead neighbour, and noted the address of the next of kin. Would some form of condolence from him be appropriate, or even welcome?

He pushed the question to one side and walked up to the gymnasium on the fourth floor. It was only when he opened the doors and entered the impressive space — the ceiling here was two stories high — that he remembered he had no clothes to exercise in. As for many policemen — and the gymnasium was the exclusive preserve of men — the punching bags, rings, bars, and rowing machines offered Joe a release. He hadn't been able to exercise properly since he'd been stabbed, but just being in the gymnasium, among the echoes of grunts, slaps, and thwacks, and even breathing in the smell of sweat, lineament, metal, and leather, calmed him. In some ways this was odd, because he never felt part of the camaraderie and crude banter of the place. He didn't particularly like the men who exercised here. He understood, of course, that the culture of which he was a part was predicated on the ideal that one policeman would always support another. Society at large didn't much like them, except when it needed to call on them in an emergency, so the only people they could really depend on were other policemen. Only a policeman understood the peculiar stresses and demands of the job.

And yet Joe could see that the ideal, if not false, was more honoured in the breach than the observance. There were tensions at Russell Street between the Masons and the Catholics. Most people stayed well out of it, but it was a conflict that created divided loyalties, even among those who were neither Catholic nor Mason. The cause of the trouble between the two groups was a mystery to Joe. He thought them both secretive and ridiculous, and it was in the gymnasium that he'd occasionally overhear a derogatory remark made by someone about one or the other. The vitriol between several of the officers was so fierce that Joe was shocked by it. He'd never heard anyone of his acquaintance, either inside or outside the force, speak so savagely against Jews, although he'd become increasingly aware of simmering anti-Semitism in some sections of Melbourne society. Masons and Catholics — what was the difference between them anyway? Joe had spent most of his life thinking they were the same thing, but clearly he'd been wrong. The incomprehensible allegiances of each group were as closed to him as the arcane and excluding sects within Judaism.

There were several men in the gymnasium. Joe knew all of them by sight, but only a couple of them by name. One of these was a man attached to the arson squad, and although he wasn't assigned to the 'Rosh Pinah' fire, Joe assumed he might know something about the case.

Sergeant Prentiss was doing bicep curls with a dumbbell when Joe approached him.

'Sergeant Prentiss?'

Prentiss, who was short sighted, but who never wore his spectacles in the gym, squinted to identify the speaker.

'Sable.' He put the dumbbell down. 'I heard about your flat. Bastard of a thing to have happened. I heard you've got some lunatic after you. Is that true?'

'You're not doing your job properly if you haven't made a few enemies.' Joe said this automatically, without conviction.

'Too right,' Prentiss said.

'You haven't heard anything, I suppose.'

'I know the boys are working overtime on it, but it only happened yesterday, mate. They're doing their best.'

'Yes, of course,' Joe said quickly. The last thing he wanted was for Prentiss to report to his colleagues that Sable wasn't happy with the progress they were making. Homicide had already acquired a reputation for being up itself.

'I'm just checking. I think the Americans call it 'touching base'.'

'No worries. As soon as they've got anything, you'll be the first to know.'

There was nothing unpleasant in Prentiss's tone. It was just a statement of fact.

'Thank you,' Joe said. 'I appreciate it.'

Prentiss picked up his dumbbells.

'No worries,' he said again.

In the afternoon, Joe met Peter Lillee and Ros and Helen Lord at the Hoyts Plaza Theatre. They'd planned to see *The Moon and Sixpence*, but the session was full. Instead they found themselves at the Hoyts Regent watching Sonja Henie in *Marriage on Ice*. No one really wanted to see this, and Joe had agreed to go to the cinema anyway, simply because it seemed a better alternative than sitting in the Kew house on his own. Opinions on the film were divided. Helen and Peter thought it was dreadful, an insult to a person's intelligence. Joe and Ros quite liked it. It was inoffensive, Joe said.

'Which essentially means it was pointless,' Helen said, and wished she hadn't. So what if Joe liked the stupid movie? Maybe it was a brief distraction from his troubles. To make up for the sharpness of her comment, and in the hope that she might repair any damage she might have done — she didn't want to slip into fawning over Joe Sable, but she didn't want to antagonise him with contrariness either — she allowed that John Payne was good in his role and that his performance was probably worth the price of admission. The business on the ice was quite well done, too. Joe, who hadn't felt that Helen's difference of opinion about *Marriage on Ice* was of any consequence, was oblivious to the small torment she was putting herself through.

After the film, the quartet returned to Kew, and Joe went upstairs. He ran himself a bath, taking Peter Lillee at his word and filling it well above the Plimsoll line. His bath at home had been too small to stretch out in, and this one was generous. The hot water relaxed his body, but his mind was a circus of disconnected thoughts. He'd never before been the focus of another person's hatred, and it was both disconcerting and strangely exhilarating. He couldn't account for the exhilaration. He'd always thought he'd feel something like this when he knew for certain that the woman he loved loved him and him alone. Here, dozing fitfully in slowly cooling water, he found that George Starling's fierce, violent, and psychopathic loathing of him was thrilling. If he could go back into the Lamberts' backyard, he wouldn't now be afraid.

When Joe returned to the bedroom, he looked at his discarded clothes and decided they needed to be washed before he wore them again. He laid out a complete set of Peter Lillee's clothes and stared down at them for a minute before putting them on. It felt strange. Although these were casual in style, he'd never before worn anything of this quality. The cotton shirt must have been bought before the war, the fine material having been woven in England. Nothing like this could be produced in Australia. His first thought was how he could stop himself sweating in the clothes, or getting them dirty.

When he went downstairs, he found Helen alone in the library, reading. She looked up, and whistled. He was embarrassed.

'I feel a bit, I don't know, odd, wearing someone else's clothes.'

'If it's any consolation, you don't look odd.'

'Your uncle has expensive tastes in clothes.'

'Uncle Peter has expensive tastes in everything.'

'What does your uncle do for a living?'

'It's a mouthful. He's a banker, of sorts. He's on the Commonwealth Bank board. He advises the Capital Issues Advisory Committee on controlling private investment. The government wants to restrict investment to projects associated with the war effort. That's the limit of my knowledge about his job, and I'm not even sure I understand what I just said.'

'Very impressive. Where are they, Peter and Ros?'

'In the kitchen. Dinner on a Saturday night is always a decent one. Uncle Peter likes to help prepare it. It's become a sort of tradition with us. I stay out of the kitchen. I think they like that time together. They were pretty close when they were children.'

Joe sat opposite Helen, and for the first time felt truly comfortable in her presence. Perhaps it was the soothing influence of the long bath, and the softly diffused light in the library. There was still bright sunlight outside, but it was tamed by filtering trees and dusty windows. Helen had seen him at his most vulnerable, weakened by his unreliable heart, and wounded in a hospital bed, and he felt no awkwardness about this. Nevertheless, from their first acquaintance the previous December, there'd been a stubborn distance between them. He knew that Inspector Lambert thought she was a better detective than he was, and he couldn't shake how this galled him, even though he'd acknowledged to himself that it was true.

'I really appreciate . . . '

Helen stopped him.

'We could hardly say no to Inspector Lambert.'

Joe looked stricken, and Helen realised with dismay that the joke had fallen flat.

'I didn't mean that, Joe. It was supposed to be funny. We didn't have to have our arms twisted to have you billeted here. If Inspector Lambert had had some other idea, we'd have insisted that you come here. I mean, imagine ending up in the Reilly household.'

'You don't like him much, do you?'

'Is it obvious?'

'Oh yes, it's obvious.'

'Well, he's one of those unimaginative, dull-witted coppers. He'd be hopeless interviewing suspects.'

Conversation flowed easily between them when it was about work. They'd found this at the height of the last investigation.

'When you read the reports of the interviews in Warrnambool,' Helen said, 'you'll see what I mean.'

'What do you mean, so I know what I'm looking for?'

'Reilly was assigned to talk to a woman who was married to a German and who was once an enthusiastic National Socialist — although she's gone quiet now, of course, like most of them. He briefed us on the interview, and I didn't believe a word of it.'

'You think he made things up? Surely not.'

'No. I just mean there wasn't enough there. If he'd managed a proper interview, we'd have a much better sense of who the woman was. I've got no idea what she was like and whether or not it would be worth talking to her again.'

'He's done Detective Training. That should have taught him something.'

'And I haven't, is what you mean?'

'That's not what I mean.'

The conversation stopped. They avoided eye contact. Joe thought he'd probably said the wrong thing, but it was impossible to predict how Helen would react to the most harmless comment. She was touchy about her position in Homicide; he was aware of that. She'd spoken to him about it. Still, why did she always assume the worst when it came to things that he said? He drummed his fingers on the arm of his chair, and broke the silence.

'I actually meant that you'd think he'd be better at his job, given that he's done the proper training.'

'You do realise you've pretty much said exactly the same thing and that it's still insulting?'

Joe looked at her.

'*He's* done the *proper training*. You don't think that reveals anything about the way you see me? You've done the training, yes?'

'Yes, of course.'

'Of course. You've done Detective Training; every other nong in Homicide has done Detective Training. I, needless to say, haven't, because women can't do it. At some point in every day, someone helpfully reminds me that I'm unqualified to work with *proper* policemen, who've had *proper* training. From where I sit, the training hasn't done a lot of them much good. You can't train someone not to be stupid. Stupid is forever.'

'There are plenty of good men in the Homicide squad.'

Helen, who couldn't stop the diatribe once it had begun, hated how truculent she sounded. Or rather, she wished she could control it better in front of Joe.

'Yes,' she said. 'There are some good men in Homicide. Some. Don't ask me to name them.'

Another silence descended. This time Helen broke it, and for her this was almost an act of contrition.

'No one seems to know very much about George Starling. He went from fat to thin to invisible.'

'Even when you meet him he's invisible. He never said very much. There was something malevolent about him, though.'

'He's a kind of bogey man, isn't he?'

'No. He's just a nasty thug who thinks the world would be a better place if people like him were in charge, and if there were no Jews in it.'

'Is he stupid?'

'Let's hope he's at least slightly more stupid than we are.'

'Yes. Touché.'

'You have a pretty low opinion of police generally, don't you?'

'I've been around them my whole life. There

are good coppers. My father was a good copper, but up in Broome he worked with a couple of truly dreadful men. I'd listen at the door when Mum and Dad were talking late at night. There was one bloke who'd killed a black man, but there was no way he was going to admit it. The man died in the cells, and there was no proper investigation, until Dad started to agitate for one. Then he died, and nothing came of it.'

'How did he die?'

'There was nothing suspicious about it, nothing that anyone could point to, anyway. We were at Cable Beach — have you heard of Cable Beach?'

Joe shook his head.

'It's possibly the most beautiful beach in the world. We were there late one afternoon, along with a few other people. Dad went in for a swim, and he got into trouble. He was a strong swimmer, but when they carried him up the beach we could see that there were jellyfish tentacles sticking to him, and there were red welts on his legs and chest. He was dead when they pulled him out of the water. The coroner said that he'd had a bad reaction to the stings, and that he'd had a heart attack. I was about 14, and I didn't believe the coroner. A part of me still doesn't believe that dad's death was an accident. I don't know how it was managed. I was there, and I didn't see anyone approach him in the water. He went in, and he just seemed to die.'

'What does your mother think?'

'We don't talk about it. She's never got over it. What about you? Why are you a copper?'

'I don't think I would be if it weren't for the war. I'd be doing something useless like studying the International Gothic in art history. Manpower would take a dim view of that. I don't think I could convince them that studying the works of Gentile de Fabriano would contribute to an Allied victory.'

'That's a painter, I presume.'

'One of the greatest. I've never actually seen one of his paintings in the flesh, only in books.'

'So policing isn't your great passion?'

'It is now, I think. I've got lots to learn, and I know that Inspector Lambert sees me as only mildly competent.'

'I hope you're not fishing for compliments.'

'Just a few weeks ago you made it crystal clear that you don't think much of my skills, and sitting here, in another man's house and in another man's clothes, I can't argue with that. My heart means that I can't be relied on. I do know that, Helen.'

Helen stood up abruptly and walked to the window. She wanted to tell Joe that none of that mattered, and she was afraid that she'd blurt it out. That mustn't happen.

'You know, Joe, I don't think your heart makes you a poor policeman.'

'You think it's everything else.'

She laughed and returned to her seat.

'Are your parents alive?' She'd never asked him a personal question before. All their conversations had been about investigations. It seemed significant to her that she felt able to ask him such a question. To Joe, it was a natural and uncontroversial query.

'They're both dead.'

'I'm sorry.'

'It will sound cold, but I wasn't close to them — or, rather, they weren't close to me, and they certainly weren't close to each other. At some point in their marriage they stopped talking to each other. That is almost literally true. Hard to believe, I suppose.'

'But they spoke to you.'

'Less and less. I never doubted that they loved me, but at some point, when I was 12 or 13, I had to remember that, rather than experience it. It just became the way we lived.'

Helen found the ease with which he spoke of his family compelling. She was unused to this sort of intimacy, and she was both confounded and excited by it.

'Were your parents born here?'

'No. Their names were David and Judith, by the way. We were Jewish, but not observant.'

'Observant?'

'We didn't go to synagogue or live by any of the strictures about food and that sort of thing. They emigrated from England, and Dad's big boast was that he was English first and Jewish a very poor second. They were actually embarrassed by the Jews in Carlton, the refugee Jews from the *shtetls* in Europe. They thought they were peasants, and they raised me to think the same. Noble blood flowed through Sable veins, not *shtetl* blood. Jews spoke Yiddish and looked foreign. My parents wanted nothing to do with them. I didn't grow up feeling Jewish at all.'

'I didn't grow up feeling Presbyterian. That's apparently what we are.'

'Hitler isn't killing Presbyterians.'

The sudden fierceness in Joe's voice took them both by surprise.

'I'm sorry,' he said, and Helen noticed that his hands were shaking. He put them in his trouser pockets. Helen didn't know what to say. Her life suddenly seemed uncomplicated, and her concerns trivial. Joe Sable was a mess of contradictions and wounds of all stripes, and when Helen saw his shaking hands she knew without a shadow of a doubt that she loved him. The knowledge calmed her. She would wait now. The house in Kew was, after all, a house where people waited patiently.

★　★　★

It was well after 11.00 pm when Titus made it to Tom Mackenzie's house in South Melbourne. The place looked very different from when he'd seen it earlier in the day.

'It was all surface clutter,' Maude said. 'Tom and I tidied it away quite quickly.' She lowered her voice. 'It was amazing, Titus. As soon as we started, something seemed to happen to Tom. Maybe it was just that he was touching stuff that was his, but there were long periods during the day when he was like his old self. He got tired, but then he sat and he talked to me while I worked. He actually talked to me. He remembered last night, and he remembered Joe being there.'

'And Starling?'

184

'He wasn't sure. He said he finds it hard to separate his nightmares from real experience. But, Titus, he was able to talk about it in those terms, and with that level of clarity.'

'That's wonderful.'

'If we can string days like today together, I think he'll recover much faster than the doctors expect.'

Bed was the place where Titus brought his daily investigations to Maude. It had been like this since the early days of their marriage, and although Police Command might frown on it, Titus discussed everything with Maude. He spared her nothing. She'd demanded this of him, and his initial reluctance gave way to gratitude, and now the idea that she might be excluded was unthinkable. In fact, she had become so much a part of the way in which Titus did his job that he valued her opinion above all others. She examined crime-scene photographs, and read briefings and witness statements. No one in Homicide knew the full extent of her access, although most people suspected that she knew more than she ought to about investigations. If Command ever found out that photographs left Russell Street without authorisation, Titus would have been subject to serious reprimand and possibly even dismissal. However, for Titus it was worth the risk. Maude had the uncanny knack of seeing in photographs telling details that others missed, and she could ascertain from witness and suspect statements unexpected aspects of their characters.

It was deeply frustrating to Titus that almost

all material relevant to the investigation that had so damaged Maude's brother and Joe Sable had been taken away by Army Intelligence, and was now out of reach under the secrecy restrictions of the Crimes Act. He'd heard nothing from Intelligence since New Year's Day. If they had any continuing interest in George Starling, or any other Hitlerites, they weren't using Homicide to help them. That suited Titus. He hadn't liked the way they worked.

Maude was reading the briefings written in Warrnambool. She was fascinated by the difference between the Halloran brothers. She remembered Greg Halloran fondly, and she thought Helen Lord's description of her meeting with Stanley Halloran was evocative and brutally honest.

'She doesn't spare herself, does she? Most people would have left out that remark about her being ugly.'

'Why did she leave it in, do you think? Leaving it out wouldn't have mattered.'

'Yes, it would have. We need to know that Stanley Halloran would say such a thing because it lends credence to Helen Lord's recollection of everything else that he said. What he said to her is nasty; what he said about the Jews and Italians is doubly disturbing because we know his capacity for nastiness sits alongside his ideology.'

'What does he say? Remind me.'

' "This is what's fundamentally wrong with this country — Jews, Italians, Japs, blacks; no one likes them, but no one dislikes them enough. They don't want them in their clubs, or next door, but that's about as far as it goes." '

186

'Christ. The bloke Greg and I interviewed said that democracy was Jew thought. We all need to start worshipping Odin.'

'Yes. He was an oddball. He worried me, though. Anyone who believes that he knows the way to form a perfect society is suspect. It usually involves those in opposition being disposed of. Ideology and human nature aren't good bedfellows.'

'I wish I'd been able to remember the exact quotes he read to us from a book he had. Democracy leads to government by Jews. That was one gem.'

'I thought David Reilly's briefing notes were thin. I didn't get a good sense of this Maria Pluschow at all.'

'David's experience is wide but shallow.'

'You mean he belongs to the great D+.'

This was one of Maude's favourite shorthand tropes. There were smart people at one end of the social continuum, seriously stupid people at the other, and between them sat the great D+. These were the people who made everything work, but who weren't much given to analysing the world around them.

'I think Reilly's a bit better than a D+,' Titus said. 'He's not a bad detective, but he's constantly surprised that other people aren't like him and don't believe the things he believes.'

'Well, anyway, I don't trust his account of that interview. It's too smooth. She says everything he wants her to say without demur, and I don't believe for a minute that this Maria Pluschow would have been so charmingly compliant.'

'You're probably right. I think it's clear though

that none of these people have had anything to do with George Starling for years, and I don't think he'd approach any of them.'

'Besides, he's here in Melbourne.'

'I'm going to have to get in touch with Intelligence again.'

'Yes, you are. They might know people here, other than the ones who've been interned.'

'I really don't like those people. Sometimes, Maude, I think the number of people I can't stand far outweighs the number of people I can stand.'

Maude leaned across and kissed him.

'I'm so tired, Maudey. I don't have the energy to talk about the incident tonight. I wish we were in our bed. I don't like strange ceilings.'

Maude switched off the light and left her hand on Titus's chest until his breathing told her that he was deeply asleep. *We are a strange species,* she thought, as she drifted into sleep. *We kill each other.*

★   ★   ★

On Sunday morning, over tea and butterless toast, Titus saw for himself the change in his brother-in-law. His voice was firmer, his movements more assured, and there was something altogether more stable about him. Perhaps the shock of seeing Starling had had the unexpected effect of rebalancing rather than unbalancing him. Or perhaps Maude was right, and the effect of being in his own house was remedial. He reiterated that Starling's visit had merged inextricably into the landscape of his dreams, and he couldn't say with any confidence that it had actually happened.

'Joe was there. I know that was real. I didn't say anything to him. Why didn't I say anything to him?'

'You'd come straight from sleep, Tom,' Maude said. 'Maybe you were in a sort of fugue state — half-waking, half-sleeping. That can happen.'

'Like sleepwalking. I need to talk to Joe, Maude.'

Maude looked at Titus.

'The doctors thought you might need to talk to a professional — a psychiatrist — at some stage, Tom. Maude and I have found a good one, if you'd like to do that.'

Maude had never known Tom to express an opinion either way on the efficacy of psychiatry. She thought he would probably be suspicious of it, but he'd never been the type to express hostility without first looking into things. He surprised her, though, when he said, 'I'll have a go at that. I want to talk to Joe as well. There's so much that I can't remember.'

'Do you want to remember?' Maude asked.

'There are things that come at night. I can't get their measure. I want to know what horrors my mind is manufacturing and what it's remembering. Maybe if I knew the difference it would help. Maybe not, too. Is Joe a good man? I barely know him.'

'Yes, Tom,' Titus said. 'Joe is a good man.'

He decided not to tell Tom that George Starling was hunting Joe — that's how Titus thought of it — and that he'd burned down Joe's

189

flat and killed a man in the process.

'I keep seeing Joe in that room with me, at the end. He was there, wasn't he?'

'Yes, he was there.'

'Did they hurt him?'

'Yes they did, but not as much as they hurt you.'

Tom looked puzzled.

'Why not?'

'Only because we got there in time. The intention was to kill you both.'

Maude's hand covered her mouth. Titus's statement had seemed brutal to her. Tom wasn't shocked by it.

'Yes, I see,' he said quietly.

'I'll see if Joe can visit you here as soon as possible. Are you absolutely sure you're ready to talk about what happened to you both?'

'I'm not absolutely sure of anything anymore. I do want to talk to him, though.'

After breakfast Tom returned to the room where a camp bed had been made up for him. As Titus shaved, Maude sat on the edge of the bath and expressed her concerns about Tom and Joe talking together.

'I know Tom seems relatively fine, Titus, but he's been practically catatonic for two weeks. This sudden burst of clarity might be worrisome. What if it's just another, less alarming, symptom of shellshock, if that's what they still call it.'

'I know what I'm about to say will sound callous.'

'Pre-empting it doesn't necessarily excuse it.'

'I know, but I have to say this. Tom spent much longer in George Starling's company than

Joe did. He may have vital information that he gleaned that will lead us to Starling. If this period of clarity is a brief anomaly, I'm afraid I want Joe Sable to take advantage of it and see what Tom can remember.'

'Even if it means forcing Tom to confront things he's in no shape to confront?'

Titus put down his razor. He concentrated on his reflection rather than catch his wife's eye.

'Yes, even if it means that. I'm sorry.'

Maude stood up and left the bathroom without a word. Titus splashed cold water on his face. The chill of it against freshly scraped skin helped quell the sickening feeling in his stomach.

★ ★ ★

At Russell Street, Titus telephoned Victoria Barracks, but was unable to get through to any of the branches of Military Intelligence. The fact that he was an inspector in the Victoria Police didn't wash with the woman on the switchboard. She had her orders, and no one whose name wasn't on the list of authorised personnel in front of her was going to be put through to the Office for Native Policy in Mandated Territory. It didn't matter that Titus had been able to name that ludicrous cover title. The woman offered to take his name, and perhaps someone would call him back.

'Could you at least tell me if either Tom Chafer or Dick Goad is on the premises?'

This was met with silence, followed by the non sequitur, 'Is there anything else I can help you with?'

191

Titus hung up. He'd have to go down there and insist that he be admitted. Surely to God a murder inquiry meant something, even to those people.

An hour later, Titus had turned off St Kilda Road and climbed the front steps to Victoria Barracks. He was seething. He flashed his credentials to the air force man on the front desk and said in a voice that brooked no opposition that he needed to see either Tom Chafer or Dick Goad, who worked in the directorate designated the Office for Native Policy in Mandated Territory. The matter was urgent, and he'd appreciate being given full co-operation. Obstructing a police investigation was a serious offence. The air force officer was unfazed by Titus's anger. He was shouted at by someone almost every day. However, he picked up a telephone and asked to be put through to the requested department. There was a short wait. The officer put his hand over the mouthpiece.

'Who shall I say is calling?'

'Detective Inspector Titus Lambert of the Homicide Squad.'

The officer's eyebrows shot up. Someone began speaking at the other end of the telephone.

'Mr Chafer? There's a gentleman here who says he has urgent business with you — an Inspector Lambert from Homicide. Yes, I've seen his credentials. All right, I'll tell him.'

He replaced the phone in its cradle.

'He says he'll come down.'

Titus's anger had now subsided. It was a shame that it was Tom Chafer who was on duty.

Titus had found his manner objectionable. He predicted, correctly, that Chafer would keep him waiting. He crossed from where he'd been sitting to the officer on the desk.

'When Mr Chafer arrives, tell him I'm outside.'

'That's a bit irregular, sir.'

'Not for me. Flight Lieutenant, is it?'

'That's right.'

'I'll be on the other side of St Kilda Road, sitting on the bench directly opposite.'

'He won't be happy.'

'Mr Chafer's happiness is immaterial to me.'

It gave Titus unseemly pleasure to sit across from Victoria Barracks and watch Tom Chafer duck traffic as he crossed St Kilda Road. He was still unhealthily thin, his suit still looked too big for him, and he still wore a thin, blond moustache. His hair wasn't quite as closely cropped as it had been when he'd first entered Titus's office on Christmas Day. His prominent ears were red, either with indignation or the heat, when he sat down next to Titus. He was in his late twenties, but his self-importance extinguished any deference he ought to have shown.

'I don't appreciate being summoned.'

'I think when we first met I suggested you should make an effort not to be an arsehole. That suggestion still holds.'

Titus stood up and began walking towards the Shrine of Remembrance. Chafer was obliged to follow.

'What is it you want?'

'I want to know if you have any intelligence on George Starling. He's a dangerous, loose cannon, and he poses a serious risk to Sergeant Sable.'

'Oh?'

'He's issued threats, and is the main suspect in an arson attack on Sergeant Sable's flat.'

'All aspects of the case involving Ptolemy Jones, George Starling, and the others are now covered by the Crimes Act, and I'm not at liberty to discuss them with you.'

Chafer's pomposity pushed Titus's patience almost to breaking point.

'I'd rather discuss this matter with your partner, Mr Goad.'

'Dick Goad is not my partner, and he's been moved into another department. He'd be unable to help you.'

'This is intolerable. One of the people you were investigating has threatened the life of one of my officers.'

'We're not investigating George Starling — that much I can tell you. He has no affiliations that we can find with any known Hitler sympathisers. He is, as you say, a loose cannon. My job is to deal with matters of national security. Your job is to find common or garden murderers. George Starling is a common or garden thug. Intelligence has no further interest in him.'

'I need to know who his associates are, and who he'd be most likely to run to for shelter.'

'I've already told you — as far as we're concerned, he has no associates. His only associate was Ptolemy Jones, and Jones is dead. End of story.'

'You're an extremely unpleasant young man, Mr Chafer.'

'And you're wasting my time.'

Chafer stared at Titus blankly, and began walking back towards Victoria Barracks. To calm down, Titus walked around the Shrine.

★ ★ ★

George Starling stood under the shower for a wasteful ten minutes and thought about what he should do next. He knew no one in Melbourne now that Jones was dead. There'd been a couple of blokes who'd hung around Jones and talked politics, but he had no idea how to contact them. They came together to discuss National Socialism, and then they went away. He couldn't even recall any of their surnames.

Maybe he could buy a car. A new car was out of the question, of course — even if one were available, it would require too much scrutiny by the authorities for his liking. However, a secondhand car was a possibility. There'd be no need to go through the proper channels for that. A private car was a liability, though. There were no spare parts, no tyres to replace old or damaged ones, and the petrol ration allowed no more than 80 miles a month. That was barely enough to keep the battery alive. The motorcycle was useful, but it made him conspicuous, and if it broke down he'd have to abandon it. Once he'd dealt with Joe Sable he might return to Port Fairy. Maybe he'd invest in a couta boat, or a bigger one — one that could go further out. He'd hire fishermen. He didn't know if this was even possible, but as hot water relaxed his shoulders, he imagined himself swaggering along the wharf, checking the catch, calculating his cut. You'd never get him out on one of those bloody boats, though. He didn't want to work that hard. Peter Hurley would be surprised to see his old employee running things, and Peter Hurley might need to be persuaded to give him a cut of his black-market profits. Not much; just enough to guarantee his silence. Hurley'd buck at that. Well, George Starling had a fair idea about how to stop people bucking. These thoughts, fanciful though they might be, were pleasurable.

He towelled himself dry and assessed himself in the mirror. He'd done this yesterday, fully clothed. Now he was naked. There was no fat on his body. It was hard and well proportioned; darkly hairy, yes, but so what? It was a body that wouldn't let him down. It would respond to whatever demands he made of it. It was a body that could subdue people, injure them, kill them. He got dressed and went downstairs to the hotel barber for a shave. As he'd done the previous morning, he then entered the dining room for breakfast, and in a nod to his Port Fairy fantasy, he ordered fish — Sweet William, grilled and dressed with a burnt butter sauce and chives. The waiter who served him volunteered that this was meant to be his day off. The waiter who should be here hadn't bothered to show up.

After breakfast, Starling returned to his room. He flicked again through the folder of newspaper clippings he'd taken from Joe's flat. He'd become so used to reading about Allied victories in the papers that he'd accepted that Germany, and by extension National Socialism, would be defeated. But here in this folder was such a concentration of news about successful measures taken against the Jews that he began to think that readers of *The Age* and *The Argus* were being duped by propaganda. Perhaps the war wasn't being lost after all, and perhaps the healthy state of National Socialism could be seen in these reports of exterminations.

With Jones gone, his ideas lacked clarity and purpose. He needed to talk to someone about this, to show these clippings to people who would be keen to form a branch of the party. There were people he knew of in Warrnambool; they used to gather at the Starlings' farm. He couldn't remember any of their names, but he knew where one of them lived. It was in a house that was perched on a cliff above the Hopkins River. He was an old man, but Starling thought he might be worth a visit. He wouldn't tell him that he was John Starling's son, and as he bore no resemblance to the child this man might have noticed at the farm, he would pass himself off as someone else.

He felt in his pocket for the identity cards of the men he'd killed. He hadn't bothered to look at them yet, but now he took them out. He put Steven McNamara's aside — he was too young. The barman, though, was born in 1914, which made him 30. Starling was 28, but he could easily pass for an older man. Sturt Menadue — that was his name. Starling spoke the name out loud. Sturt Menadue. It was a good name.

197

Sturt Menadue sounded like the kind of man who'd wear decent clothes. Sturt Menadue, he said again. Mr Menadue would be leaving the Windsor Hotel that afternoon. He'd signed the register under his own name. That had been unavoidable. Starling wanted to put distance between himself and the place where Steven McNamara worked. The police would eventually discover who their John Doe was, and they'd come sniffing around the Windsor. He'd move to another place, and there he'd register as Sturt Menadue. He needed to buy a suitcase now that he had several changes of shirts, trousers, underwear, socks, and two pairs of shoes. He'd bought his clothes at different shops, using almost all the clothing coupons that remained in the books he'd taken from Sable's flat and his father's house.

Late on Sunday afternoon, an elegantly dressed man, wearing a soft, grey fedora and carrying an expensive suitcase, walked into the foyer of the Australia Hotel in Collins Street, and registered in the name of Sturt Menadue.

10

Rose Abbot sat in a pew at the back of St Patrick's church. She could see her Aunt Aggie with Matthew and Dorothy in the front pew. It would have been Matthew's decision to sit at the front. The Abbots were Port Fairy royalty, or so Matthew thought, and the front was their rightful place. Rose had arrived at Mass late, and she intended to leave early, after the necessary witnessing of transubstantiation. She didn't want Aggie to see her and smugly suppose that Rose had taken her advice about attending Mass. She'd come to Port Fairy two days in a row — a rare occurrence — because Timothy Harrison's words had eaten away at her overnight, and she needed to talk to Johanna Scotney. John had complained about the unnecessary use of fuel, but Rose had lied and said that if he wanted a cake for afternoon tea, she'd have to get flour, and that was all there was to it.

'You should've got it yesterday, and where'll you get it on a Sunday anyway?'

'Aunt Aggie — we've given her enough eggs to make a hundred cakes. She won't begrudge us a bit of flour.'

John snorted.

Father Brennan's sermon was short and uninspired. All his sermons were uninspired. Unfortunately, as John Abbot had said more than once, they weren't all short. Rose wasn't listening, in any case. He said something about the bushfires, and there was a reminder to keep Mrs Watson in the congregation's prayers. She was poorly, and was in hospital in Warrnambool, and wasn't expected to make a recovery, although miracles did happen, and she asked especially that people pray to St Ursula, who'd intervened on her behalf in the past.

Rose slipped out as soon as Communion had begun. She didn't know Johanna's address so she walked to the wharf, assuming that someone there would know it. The wharf was quiet. Three couta boats were tied up, and in one of them a man was coiling rope. Rose asked him if he knew Johanna Scotney.

'Ought to,' he said. 'She's my daughter.'

'Oh, Mr Scotney. I've heard so much about you from Johanna.'

'Oh yes, and how's that then?'

He smiled up at her. His weatherbeaten face would have been attractive, except that it showed the strains of a lifetime of fishing.

'I'm Rose Abbot. Johanna works on our farm during the week.'

Tom Scotney climbed up onto the wharf.

'Tom Scotney,' he said. 'Pleased to meet you, Mrs Abbot. Johanna seems to be enjoying the work.'

Rose was relieved. Tom Scotney was showing no evidence of having been told anything unpleasant about the Abbot farm.

'I was wanting to call on her at home, if that's all right — only I don't have the address.'

'Give me a tick to finish up here, and I'll walk

you there. Lunch'll be on if you're hungry.'

'Thank you, but I really need to get back. I just need to talk to Johanna for a minute.'

'You're not sacking her, are you?'

'Oh no, no. Nothing like that — just some small thing.'

'Good-oh.'

The Scotneys' house was a ten-minute walk from the wharf. It was run down, but respectable, and it needed money spent on it that the Scotneys didn't have; building materials were scarce anyway. Tom Scotney opened the front door and ushered Rose through to the small front room. Mrs Scotney, who'd heard two people come into the house, hurried to see who the unexpected visitor was. When she saw it was a woman, and before she'd been introduced, she made it clear to her husband, with an eloquent grimace, that he ought to have given her time to tidy up. Rose understood this at once, and immediately complimented Mrs Scotney on the room's furnishings.

'I'm Rose Abbot,' she added.

Mrs Scotney was uncertain how to proceed. What did you say to a Catholic woman who turned up to your house uninvited and unannounced?

'I suppose you want to talk to Johanna,' she said, as politely as she could manage. Rose, who wasn't fussed by other people's religious affiliations, couldn't guess at the cause of Mrs Scotney's discomfort. She put it down to having been caught off guard. She was saved from further awkwardness by Johanna, who stood at the door of the front room and said, 'Mrs Abbot.'

Rose could see her face, and she could see that it was ashen. Rose read in that face that Timothy Harrison's blurted accusation had substance to it. She asked Johanna if she might speak to her for just a moment, outside. Mr Scotney had gone through into the kitchen, and Mrs Scotney, who wasn't able to see her daughter's face, said rather stiffly that Mrs Abbot would be welcome to speak with Johanna in the comfort of the front room. She was a woman of considerable Christian charity, after all. She didn't go so far as to offer tea, reminded Johanna that lunch was almost on the table, and left the two of them alone.

Rose sat down. 'Has my husband behaved towards you in any way that has upset you?' she asked.

Johanna was unable to speak.

'I met the boy you're stepping out with, Timothy, yesterday. Well, I didn't actually meet him so much as run into him, and when I introduced myself, he said something. I can't remember the exact words, but he said something like, 'Johanna told me about your husband.' What did that mean?'

Rose realised that she sounded prim.

'Timothy had no right to say that, Mrs Abbot.'

'Because you told him something in confidence, or because he was making something up?'

'I don't want to lose my position. We need the money.'

'You won't lose your position, Johanna. You have my word. What has my husband done? Please.'

'Mr Abbot hasn't really done anything. I told

Timothy that. Mr Abbot says things sometimes — crude things — but he's never touched me, or anything like that.'

'So he's been vulgar and suggestive?'

'Yes. I know it's just words, but I told Timothy that I didn't like it. That's all.'

'I saw you running away yesterday, and you were very upset. So that's not quite all, is it?'

Johanna shook her head.

'What else did you tell Timothy?'

'I told him about Mr Todd.'

'Matthew?'

Johanna subdued her emotions by speaking matter-of-factly, as if she were reciting a shopping list.

'Mr Todd has been making lewd suggestions to me for several weeks. The things he says are disgusting and insulting. I think he thinks they're all right.'

'He would.' Rose's sour note encouraged Johanna.

'He grabbed me on Friday and touched me in private places, and he forced my hand against his trousers. He tried to kiss me, but Mr Abbot came out of the house, and he stopped. We heard the door slam. He said something awful about Mr Abbot, and he said that the next time he came to the farm I'd better be more co-operative or he'd make sure I lost my job. And he said that he could make sure that none of my dad's catch got to market. I told all that to Timothy, and he thought I must have done something to lead Mr Todd on. That's why I was so upset. How could he say that?'

'Because he's still a child, Johanna.'

'What Mr Abbot says to me is nothing, really. It's schoolboy stuff.'

'My brother, on the other hand, is another matter.'

'Do you think I lead him on?'

'No, Johanna, I don't, and I believe every word of what you said. The question now is, what do we do?'

'Should I report him to the police?'

'You should, but I know my brother, and I know that he'll make your life hell, and that it will be your reputation that gets destroyed, not his. He's worked hard to get where he is, and he'll do anything to protect himself. He'll ruin your family, and think nothing of it.'

'Can you stop him coming out to the farm?'

'I don't see how. What I can do is make absolutely sure that I'm with you at all times when he's there. I know that's not satisfactory and that just having him there is threatening, but I can protect you. Has he ever approached you in Port Fairy?'

'No, never.'

'That'd be risky for him. I think you'll be okay here. What about Timothy? He won't do anything silly, will he, when he thinks about what you've told him?'

Johanna was suddenly uncertain.

'I don't think so, but I don't know him well enough. Like you say, he's a child in lots of ways.'

'But he's a tall, strong child. I think we can sort this out with time. I'll talk to Matthew, which will be extremely unpleasant, and threaten him with telling Dorothy that her fiancé isn't the man she thinks he is. I think that has to come from me, Johanna. He can't attack my reputation without compromising the family name.'

As soon as she'd said this, she realised that Aunt Aggie might be an unwilling ally in curbing Matthew's baser instincts. He might listen to her. If he felt her disapproval, he might even feel some remorse. He was close to Aggie. Her opinion mattered, or so Rose thought.

'Please come out to the farm tomorrow, Johanna. We can't do without you. I can assure you that you'll hear no more silly remarks from John, and I think I can safely say that Matthew won't ever step out of line again.'

Johanna wasn't entirely reassured, but she was relieved not to have been dismissed, and so relieved that Mrs Abbot hadn't doubted her story that she agreed to turn up for work in the morning.

'My parents must never know,' she said. 'I don't know what Dad would do if he found out.'

Rose stood up, and the sound of her doing so covered Tom Scotney's retreat from where he'd been listening at the door.

Rose remained at the Scotneys' front gate for a moment. She thought that the interview with Johanna had gone as well as could be expected. The fact that John had been no more than vulgar had removed an enormous weight from her shoulders, and the news about Matthew hadn't really surprised her. If Johanna had told her that Matthew had actually raped her, she would have seen this as entirely consistent with his character. *My brother*, she thought, *is an awful man*. She didn't hate him, did she? She thought about this as she walked to Aunt Aggie's house. She hoped Matthew and Dorothy hadn't gone back there with her after Mass. She wanted to speak with her in private, and she decided that she wouldn't spare her feelings. Aggie wouldn't want to believe that Matthew was capable of sexual impropriety — and Rose would use the term in the hope that it shocked Aggie into listening to her attentively.

Aggie answered Rose's knock. She'd only just got back from Mass, and hadn't yet changed out of her good clothes.

'I didn't see you at Mass.'

'I was there, Aunt Aggie, down the back.'

'Was John with you?'

'No, he wasn't.'

Aggie made a small sound, and admitted Rose. She offered her a cup of tea, which Rose declined. She wanted to get this out of the way.

'Aunt Aggie, can we sit down? I want to talk to you about something very important, and it's very difficult for me to do it, so I'm going to go feet first. What I'm going to say will upset you.'

'Why would you want to upset me?'

'I don't want to do it, but something bad has happened, and I need your help.'

Aggie became less defensive.

'Has your husband been hitting you? I always thought it would come to this. He's a brute. No one in the family has the foggiest notion why you married him in the first place.'

206

'My husband is not a brute, and he would no more hit me than he'd hit you, or anybody else, for that matter. He certainly would never hit a woman.'

Aggie, unconvinced and unapologetic, said, 'Well, so you say. Go on.'

'The person whose behaviour has been disgusting is Matthew.'

Aggie put up both hands.

'No, no, no. I won't get involved in some trivial sibling dispute. Whatever Matthew has done, I'm sure he had good reason, and if he said something unkind to you, I'm sure he was well and truly provoked. You can be very provoking. To call it disgusting is hysterical and ridiculous.'

'Matthew interfered with Johanna Scotney.'

Aggie stared at Rose.

'I was at Mass this morning,' she said, 'with Matthew and his fiancée and his future father-in-law. I can't bear to repeat what you just said. It's too ugly, and it's quite simply an evil thing to say, and yet you come into my house and you say it.'

Aggie's face was contorted with an emotion that Rose took to be hatred. Hatred — her aunt hated her.

'It's the truth, and it has to be said.'

'The truth, is it?'

'Johanna Scotney has no reason to lie.'

'She's that girl who works for you. She's a Protestant slut who doubtless was surprised when Matthew turned away her advances, and this is her revenge.'

'That's absurd, Aunt Aggie.'

207

Aggie's voice was ominously calm.

'Did you think, did you really think, that you could come to me and ask me to help you ruin Matthew's reputation by accepting the truth of that wicked accusation?'

'I'm here because I want you to help me protect Matthew's reputation by getting him to see that he has to stop.'

Aggie laughed.

'You're a stupid woman, Rose. You're jealous of your own brother — of his looks, of his position in this town, and of his intelligence. I will not let you go any further with this nonsense. I have absolutely no intention of mentioning this conversation to Matthew, and I assure you, if I hear a whisper of this in the town, Johanna Scotney will pay dearly. I'd suggest you let her go. She's a trollop. Next she'll be accusing John of interfering with her.' She paused. 'She's a poisonous little bitch, and so are you.'

Rose's head snapped back in shock.

'I don't want you to come here any more. Your visits have never been pleasant. I'm ashamed of you. I'm ashamed that you're my niece. Your mother, of course, is a Presbyterian.'

'She's also Matthew's mother.'

'Matthew is all his father. You should leave now.'

'This isn't going to go away, Aunt Aggie, just because you don't want to talk about it. Matthew interfered with Johanna Scotney, and something must be done about it.' These words were said fiercely. Aggie's face flushed red.

'Leave my house.'

Afterwards, Rose was amazed by her aunt's control. Everything she'd said had been expressed without raising her voice. The effect was to make Rose see for the first time the extent to which Aggie was in Matthew's thrall. There was something disturbing about this. This was more than an aunt's affection for her nephew; it was more than family loyalty. There was an obsessive quality to it. All right then, Aggie was out of the picture. Not being welcome in her house was hardly a punishment. The only thing about it that Rose regretted was that it made their family one of those tawdry ones whose members engaged in feuds, or refused to speak to each other. There was nothing for it now but to confront Matthew. He'd be as unreasonable and hostile as Aunt Aggie, and Rose didn't feel up to approaching him that afternoon.

She walked back to the church, where she'd left the truck. To calm herself down, she drove around the streets of Port Fairy. It was a neat town, its uncomfortable, small cottages lending it an air of quiet, English respectability. People worked hard to earn a living here, and they weren't given to extravagance of any kind. The houses themselves seemed to impose a modesty of expression and expectation. Port Fairy was not a place for grand gestures, either civil or personal. There were, of course, undertows beneath the slightly tired, surface elegance. Someone like Johanna Scotney could be dragged under by cruel innuendo. She had to be protected. Rose pulled over and tried to think how this might best be accomplished.

Late on Sunday night, Aggie Todd sat up in bed, reading. She always did this before going to sleep, and her preferred author was Trollope. She'd read it before, but she'd taken up *The Eustace Diamonds* again. For a moment, she thought she heard an odd sound near the front of the house. She always locked her back door to keep Selwyn from wandering into the kitchen uninvited. She rarely bothered to lock the front door, despite Matthew encouraging her to do so. 'There are bad types in this town,' he used to warn. It would never occur to Selwyn to come around to the front. He was too stupid — Aggie was confident of that. She listened for a moment, heard nothing more, and returned to her book. On the edge of sleep she turned out the light and splayed the novel on the bedclothes beside her. She'd always been a good sleeper, and would often say that she'd sleep through a bombing raid, should the Japs ever make it to Port Fairy. She slept deeply, and she hardly ever slept in. She was usually up and dressed by 5.30 am, especially in summer.

Monday morning was no exception. She looked through the kitchen window to Selwyn's shed. The door was open, but Selwyn would still be in there, snoring and farting. Sometimes she locked him in at night. Mostly she didn't. She'd rather he urinated in the backyard or the toilet than in a bucket, which she'd have to empty and clean. She put wood on to get the stove going, and set about making a cup of tea. She'd also have one of the eggs Matthew had brought. She thought about the incident with Rose, and her indignation flared. How dare that silly, jealous woman make such outrageous accusations against her own brother? She was tempted to warn Matthew that his sister had turned against him, but decided it was best he not know. Why should a man of his calibre have to be put in the ignominious position of defending himself against the slander of some jumped-up little slattern like . . . what was the girl's name? . . . Johanna something-or-other? He shouldn't be exposed to the poisonous jealousies of others.

As the egg clattered around the side of the saucepan in which it was being boiled, Aggie thought she might write her vile niece a letter, telling her exactly what she thought of her, what she'd *always* thought of her. She had no intention of ever speaking to her again, and she didn't care if people noticed. They probably wouldn't notice anyway. They were too busy with their own lives, and how often was she seen talking to Rose, anyway? At Mass from time to time, but when the ladies visited for morning tea they never asked after Rose — only Matthew. On a couple of occasions, Matthew had visited during an apostle-spoon event, and how he had beguiled them!

'Such a good-looking young man,' Mrs Crockett had said, 'and such lovely manners. Dorothy Shipman is a lucky girl.'

Well, Lucy Crockett was right about Dorothy Shipman being a lucky girl. She wasn't nearly good enough for Matthew.

A few sips of tea quelled Aggie's fierce feelings about her niece, and she took the top off her egg and ate its just-right centre with one of her apostle spoons. It was the perfect size for scooping out the insides of an egg. The scrabbling of a bird's feet on the edge of the guttering made her recall that unusual sound she'd heard the night before. Perhaps Matthew had left something for her on the doorstep, and it had been far too late to disturb her. He was thoughtful like that. She left the kitchen, and as she walked down the corridor towards the front door and passed the front room, she saw a shape of someone sitting in the armchair. She gave a little cry of fright, but relaxed immediately when she realised that it was Matthew. He was sleeping. He'd never done this before. Perhaps he'd had a row with Dorothy and hadn't wanted to be on his own, so he'd come to her, let himself in, and fallen asleep in the chair. That must have been the sound she'd heard. It was so like him not to upset her, or disturb her. She smiled. He was so beautiful. Should she let him sleep? He looked uncomfortable. He'd have a terrible crick in his neck when he woke up. She decided to wake him, but before she did, she returned to the kitchen, made a fresh pot of tea, and put another egg on. At least she could give him something for breakfast. She went back to the front room and called his name softly.

'Matthew — time to wake up.'

She opened the curtains, and sunlight flooded the room. When she saw Matthew's face, she couldn't immediately make sense of why his skin was such a peculiar colour. His tongue protruded from his lips, and drool had dried on his chin. A nasty smell came off him, which, to her horror, she recognised as excrement. She shrank back to the door of the front room and tried unsuccessfully to make some sort of sound. She was dizzy, and sat heavily against the corridor wall. For several seconds, Aggie's world was one of echoes and nausea. She couldn't force meaning onto the scene in the room. She must have passed out, because she found herself lying on the floor, the linoleum cold against her cheek. Something had happened, but what was it? Had she had a stroke? She'd been dreaming something, and now she was on the floor. Was she paralysed? She moved her limbs. Everything was working. There was something or someone in the front room. She stood, weak and juddery. That dreadful smell seemed to have been released by the sunlight, and it reached her. It hadn't been a dream. Matthew Todd, the most important part of her life, the very best part of it, sat there, dead in the armchair. And Aggie knew who had killed him. Oh yes, she knew all right.

★ ★ ★

Aggie ought to have telephoned the police. However, a strange calm had come upon her, and with it an absolute certainty that she had to act on Matthew's behalf. Retribution was her duty. Matthew would demand nothing less, and he certainly deserved nothing less. There was a higher justice that needed to be attended to here,

213

higher than the clumsy, slow-moving justice of the courts. The smell now coming from the front room threatened to diminish Aggie's sense of Matthew's death calling her to noble acts, as did the hum that signalled the arrival of the first flies. She closed the door, being careful not to catch another glimpse of that awful blue-and-purple face, and telephoned the Abbot's farm. It was barely 6.00 am, but Rose and her husband would have risen long before to begin the first milking. Presumably the slanderous and wicked Johanna would also be there. There was a pause after the telephone was picked up, and Aggie surmised that John Abbot had answered it and passed it to Rose. Rose's simple 'Yes?' was full of surprise that anyone would ring at such an hour.

'It's your Aunt Aggie, Rose.'

Aggie's voice was unstrained.

'Aunt Aggie?'

'Yes. I've slept on what you told me yesterday, and I feel I was rather harsh and unfair to you.'

'I see.' Rose didn't see at all.

'I spoke to Matthew after you left, and I must say I was rather set back by the way he spoke to me. I mentioned that girl's name, and he was, well, he became quite vulgar about her. I don't know what's come over him, but I'm sure there's more to this than meets the eye. He'll be here in half an hour. We need to sort this out now, this morning. Can you come? It won't take you 15 minutes to get here, and we can discuss what it is we're going to say before Matthew gets here. And come through the back gate. Matthew might not come in if he knows you're here.'

Aggie spoke quickly, not giving Rose time to comprehend fully what she was saying.

'It's very early, Aunt Aggie. There's the milking . . . '

'Rose, if you don't come I'll have no choice but to take what you told me to the police.'

'So you believe Johanna Scotney?'

Aggie paused for effect.

'Yes, I'm afraid I do. I'll tell you why when you get here.'

'All right.'

Aggie collected her thoughts. She had only a vague idea what she was going to do. She had no choice; that much was clear. Matthew's desecrated body gave her no choice. As she waited for Rose to arrive, she was elated by the sensation that she'd always had this in her, this capacity to act decisively and righteously. She'd never been called on to do so before. Her life had been one of quiet service, but building inevitably to this great test. The burden that Selwyn had placed upon her, and which she'd borne with fortitude, made sense to her now. Her reward wouldn't be in Heaven — Father Brennan was wrong about that, but he was wrong about most things. Her reward would come to her in a few minutes.

There was one thing she needed to do. She went out into Selwyn's shed, holding her breath against the fug of body odour and stale air, and picked up his slate. He was sound asleep, and didn't hear her. Outside, she scratched on its surface, 'I done it because I hate them.' She held the slate away from her. That wouldn't do — the letters were too well formed, and the word 'because' was too sophisticated to be convincing. As far as the people of Port Fairy were concerned, Selwyn had no vocabulary at all, but Aggie knew she could claim that this wasn't the case, and that when he was at home he would often say a few simple things. People saw him scratching away on his filthy slate every day. How would they know whether or not he could form letters?

She cleaned the slate, and in laborious, infantile script, wrote, 'Me do bad. Them bad, but.' She was satisfied with that. She wiped around the edges of the slate, put it on the end of his bed, and took up the shovel that leaned near the back door. Matthew kept its blade sharp for her. Just for a moment she faltered, but the opening of the back gate galvanised her. Rose entered the yard, saw Aggie, and raised her hand in a small wave. Aggie strode towards her niece, holding the shovel in both hands. Rose thought nothing of this. Aggie was always digging in the garden.

'I came as quickly as I could . . . ' were the last words Rose Abbot spoke. The flat of the shovel caught her full in the face, and she'd barely hit the ground before Aggie drove the blade into the side of her head. Two movements — that was all it took. Aggie had no idea that she had such strength in her body. She began to move rapidly. She wiped her fingerprints from the handle of the shovel, and, using a towel to manoeuvre it, scooped blood into its bowl and splashed it about Selwyn's shed. She then placed the shovel on the floor beside his bed, used the towel to soak up blood from Rose's wounds, and smeared Selwyn's hands and face. He woke up, confused. But by the time he'd sat up, Aggie had locked the shed door and returned to the house.

She telephoned the police, and the exchange put her through to Constable Paddy Filan's house. He was half awake when Agnes Todd told him that her retarded brother, Selwyn, had gone berserk and murdered her nephew Matthew and her niece Rose. He was safely locked in the shed, but she didn't know his strength, and someone needed to come immediately. She hung up before Constable Filan could ask any questions. She hoped he would take this as the action of a woman on the edge of hysteria. She then walked out into James Street and waited.

11

As soon as Constable Paddy Filan entered Aggie Todd's house and saw the bodies of Matthew and Rose, he knew he was out of his depth. There were usually three policemen in Port Fairy, but Sergeant Macpherson was in hospital in Warrnambool with a kidney infection, and the junior constable, Jimmy Doggart, was laid up with a heavy summer cold, made more severe by his asthma. Filan was on his own. He was well liked in the town. His father had been the sergeant here back in the 1920s, so no one was surprised when Paddy Filan had followed in his footsteps. Filan never threw his weight around, and even the Protestants found him agreeable and helpful. He was used to dealing with drunks, and could hold his own in a fight, but he had never seen anything like the scene on Aggie Todd's property. Selwyn was banging on the locked door of the shed and making noises that sounded like distress. Having quickly checked the state of Rose Abbot's head, there was no way that Paddy was going to let Selwyn loose. He touched nothing, except Rose's wrist to make sure that she was dead. There was no need to confirm that Matthew was dead.

Filan telephoned Warrnambool for advice and assistance. He was told what procedures needed to be followed, and he then went out into James Street, where Aggie Todd was sitting on the grass. She seemed to be in a daze. She stared up at Filan as if she couldn't quite make out why he was there. Her look reminded him of the look he'd once seen on the face of a man who'd been pinned under a tractor — shock, disbelief, wonder. He felt a little like this himself. He knew Miss Todd. He used to see her at Mass, and he knew both Matthew and Rose to say hello to. He knew Selwyn, too, of course. He'd never been any trouble.

'I know this is very difficult, Miss Todd, but can you tell me anything about what happened here?'

Aggie made to form a word, but appeared unable to do so.

'Would you like a glass of water?'

Aggie nodded, and Paddy Filan returned to the house. As carefully as he was able to, touching nothing except the glass and the tap, he filled the glass and took it to Miss Todd. She swallowed the water slowly.

'Can you tell me anything?'

'Selwyn became violent. I've always been afraid that he might. He's so strong. I don't know what set him off. I couldn't stop him.'

'What did he do?'

'He strangled Matthew. I didn't see him do that, but I heard them struggling, and then he came out of the room, looking like a maniac, like some sort of wild animal, and he chased Rosie into the backyard and he . . . ' She paused, as if what she was about to say was almost too difficult to manage. 'I saw him take the shovel and hit her in the face with it, and then he, then he . . . '

'Yes, I understand. How did you get him into the shed?'

'I didn't. It was so strange. He just walked into the shed of his own accord. It's his bedroom, you see. I rushed out, terrified, and locked the door. It will be dreadfully hot in there.'

'There'll be policemen coming from Warrnambool in half an hour. They'll take him into custody. So, after you'd locked your brother, Selwyn — Selwyn is your brother?'

'Yes.'

'After you'd locked him in, what did you do?'

'I went into the front room to see if Matthew was all right.'

'You didn't check on Rose first?'

'Of course I did. She was right there, and I could see that she was ... I checked on Matthew, and I found him sitting there. At first I thought he might be alive, but when I went closer I could see that he wasn't.'

Constable Filan had been discreetly taking notes while Aggie was talking.

'Is there someone we can get to come and keep you company?'

'No, thank you. I don't think I could bear it. Matthew's fiancée will have to be told, and Rose's husband.'

'I've already telephoned Mr Abbot. He's coming into town as soon as he can.'

'He's not coming here!'

'No, Miss Todd, he's going to the police station. My wife will meet him there if he gets away from the farm early. I can't leave here until Inspector Halloran arrives from Warrnambool.'

'What about that awful Macpherson, or Doggart?'

'I'm afraid I'm all that there is for a few more days. Can you tell me anything else?'

'No.'

'Why were your niece and nephew here at such an early hour?'

Aggie thought quickly. There'd be more of this sort of question. She mustn't seem flustered.

'It's a private, family matter.'

'I'm sorry, Miss Todd, but privacy is the first thing to go in a murder investigation.'

'Murder?'

Paddy Filan was taken aback by Aggie's incredulity.

'Yes, Miss Todd, murder. That's what this is.'

Until the word had been spoken, Aggie hadn't considered that this was the crime *she* had committed. Rose had murdered Matthew. She'd simply dealt with Rose. They hanged people for murder in the state of Victoria. She felt faint, and began breathing rapidly. Paddy Filan diagnosed this as continuing shock. She recovered, her face beaded with sweat.

'They can't hang Selwyn, can they? He's retarded.'

'I don't know, Miss Todd. Can you tell me what the private family matter was? Would it help if Father Brennan was here?'

Aggie straightened her shoulders.

'Father Brennan? Certainly not. If you must know, we were discussing what was to be done about Selwyn. I'm getting too old to look after him. Living on a busy dairy farm is out of the question, and Matthew and Dorothy can't be expected to take him. They're getting married soon.'

'That's Dorothy Shipman, isn't it? I didn't know they were engaged.'

'Well, they are.' Aggie realised what she'd said, and choked. Paddy Filan fetched another glass of water.

'We were discussing putting him somewhere.'

'The lunatic asylum in Warrnambool?'

'Somewhere. Perhaps he overheard us, and that's what set him off.'

Aggie was pleased with this scenario.

'But why were they here so early?'

'My nephew and niece work long days, Constable. The very early morning was the only time that suited everyone.'

Among the notes he was taking, Filan made short observations about her demeanour. He'd noticed the sharpness in her reference to John Abbot, and he'd noticed, too, that she always mentioned her nephew ahead of her niece. 'Niece and nephew' was the usual order, and surely it was easier to say than 'nephew and niece', yet Miss Todd carefully put 'nephew' first. But maybe it meant nothing.

The banging on the inside of the shed had stopped. Paddy worried that Selwyn might have passed out in that hot box. He hurried through the house and into the backyard.

'Selwyn Todd?' he called.

Scuffling noises and then giggles assured him that Selwyn was fine. Filan had had no experience of a murder scene, let alone the scene of a double murder. He was, however, an observant man, and there was something about this that didn't fit Miss Todd's version of what had happened. She, of course, was above suspicion. She was a good, boring, Catholic spinster. The idea that she would have had the strength to strangle Matthew Todd or batter Rose Abbot was ludicrous. Her story of Selwyn going berserk made sense, especially if he'd overheard them planning to lock him up in an asylum. But would Selwyn Todd know what an asylum was? Was Miss Todd covering for someone? No. He put the thought out of his head.

When he returned to the front of the house, Inspector Greg Halloran was pulling up in a police sedan. Close behind him was a second car, this one fitted with a coal burner at the rear. Halloran and a uniformed man got out of one car, and a second uniformed man got out of the other. Aggie, alarmed by the spectacle of so many policemen — whose job it would now be to expose her, and see to it that she was hanged — retched dryly.

★ ★ ★

Constable Filan gave a thumbnail sketch of what they would find beyond the front door. In anticipation of the obvious first query, he said that the suspect was securely held in a shed down the back.

'His name is Selwyn, sir, and he's known around here as the village idiot, I'm afraid. Until now, he's been harmless.'

Inspector Halloran asked if the Port Fairy lock-up had anyone in it at the moment. Paddy Filan said no, and that it rarely had anyone in it for very long — the odd drunk-and-disorderly, but even they mostly staggered home without causing trouble.

'All right,' Halloran said. 'I want this Selwyn character out of harm's way, so that's the first job.'

The policemen entered the house, gave a cursory once-over of the body in the front room, and moved through to the backyard, where Rose Abbot's body lay exposed in full sunlight. Only Greg Halloran had seen anything like this before. The others experienced a mixture of horrified fascination and fear. The man who'd done this was inside that shed, and it was their job to contain him. Paddy Filan pulled back the bolt on the door and swung it open. They'd all been expecting someone to rush out at them. Instead they heard a barking laugh. Halloran called.

'Selwyn?'

There was no response.

'You need to come out now, Selwyn.'

Still nothing.

Halloran approached the shed, and slowly, in full expectation of having to avoid a blow, put his head around the door, and withdrew it instantly. This was an automatic response. The glimpse he'd caught of Selwyn Todd, sitting on the edge of his bed, naked in the heat, assured him that he was in no danger. He indicated to the others that they should stay back, and he stood in the shed's doorway, where Selwyn could see him. Selwyn's eyes hadn't adjusted to the light, and he squinted up at the strange man. It wasn't Matthew, so he needn't be afraid. He was only afraid of Matthew. Halloran saw that Selwyn had blood on him. He saw, too, the bloodied shovel leaning against the wall near the bedhead.

'It's hot in here, Selwyn. You should come out where it's cooler. You must be thirsty.'

Selwyn stood up, unselfconsciously. Halloran stepped back from the shed door, and Selwyn stepped into the sunlight. The sight of him made Constable Adams, one of the Warrnambool men, laugh. Selwyn laughed in response. Halloran shot the constable a look that silenced him.

'Hand me my murder bag,' Halloran said. He opened it and took out a swab.

'Can you show me your hands, Selwyn?' Halloran pointed to Selwyn's hands as he spoke.

Selwyn, who hadn't yet noticed Rose Abbot's body, looked down at his hands. Why were they sticky? He held them up. Was the man going to hose them for him? Halloran took a sample of the blood, put it in a bag, and sealed it.

'Would one of you go into the house and get a blanket or a sheet so that this man can be covered?'

'Shouldn't he just get dressed, sir?' Constable Adams was trying to make amends for his undisciplined laughter.

'No, he shouldn't. I don't want anything in that shed disturbed until we've gone over it properly. And I don't want Selwyn cleaned up until he's been thoroughly examined. But he can't stay here. Constable Filan, if you'd take Selwyn to your lock-up, I'd appreciate it. Constable Adams will go with you. Constable Manton will stay here with me. We'll come to you as soon as we can.'

Aggie watched as Selwyn, swathed in one of her best cotton sheets — she'd have to burn it if she ever got it back — was helped into a car and driven away. He'd been no trouble; a curious fact that wasn't lost on Constable Filan.

Inspector Halloran questioned Aggie briefly. She told him what she'd told Paddy Filan. Inside the house, Constable Manton was photographing the bodies. He'd been asked to do this because photography was a hobby of his, and Warrnambool didn't run to a professional police photographer. He was doing his best, although he wasn't confident that his shots were either in focus or properly exposed. When Halloran came back into the house, he found that Manton had finished and that he was taking notes in the front room.

'Constable Filan said that the local doc will be here as soon as he can, sir. A woman is inconveniently giving birth, even as we speak.'

'We're going to need help with this, Constable. I don't want the bodies moved until Homicide gets here from Melbourne, and I know that won't be until late this afternoon, at the earliest, assuming they can send people at all. We can cover the body of the woman once the doc has had a look, but I'm afraid I'd prefer that they stay where they are. Awful, I know.'

'This isn't as straightforward as it looks, is it, sir?'

'Does it look straightforward, Constable?'

'Well, Filan said that the old lady's story was that the retarded bloke went berserk and killed them. They're related, apparently.'

'Yes, that's the story. Does it look that simple to you?'

'No, sir, it does not.'

'It doesn't to me either. Gut instinct, Constable?'

'I don't think the person who killed the man in the front room is that same person who killed the woman in the backyard. I think the bloke's been dead for a longer period of time.'

'You'll make a bloody good detective, Constable Manton. Why do you think he's been dead longer?'

'The spittle and mucous around his mouth and chin are dry and crusted. The blood around the woman's head is still wet and sticky. Also, the lady . . . '

'Her name is Miss Agnes Todd.'

'Miss Todd said that Selwyn went crazy and that she heard him struggling with her nephew in the front room. There are no signs that there was a struggle. It's neat and tidy. The body looks like it's been placed there. It doesn't look like he died there.'

'So that nice old lady — and she's not that old — sitting out on the footpath is lying to us about what happened?'

'Yes, sir, I think she is. Constable Filan said as much as well.'

'Constable Filan is as sharp as you are. Any theories, off the top of your head?'

'No, sir. It does look as though Selwyn hit the woman.'

'It does look that way, doesn't it?'

Halloran asked if Manton had photographed the interior of the shed. He had. He then examined Matthew Todd's body. He pulled the shirt collar down to reveal raw ligature marks.

'He certainly wasn't strangled while he was sitting in this room. I'd say he was brought here, either from somewhere else in the house or from outside the house. There's a bit of sand in the tread of the shoes, which is hardly unusual in Port Fairy. There's no damage to the hands, and nothing under the fingernails. He didn't, or couldn't, put up a fight.'

'Which means the killer was strong.'

'And that rules out Miss Todd. I don't see how those skinny arms could draw a cord this tightly around his neck. Any sign of the cord?'

'No, sir — not in the room. We haven't had time to do a thorough search.'

'Let's look at the woman. Her name is Mrs Rose Abbot.'

In the backyard, the early cohorts of flies had arrived. Halloran waved them away.

'We need to get Mrs Abbot covered.'

Constable Manton went inside and returned with a tablecloth. Halloran looked down at Rose.

'This is a very different crime. Her face is unrecognisable. Are we even sure this is Rose Abbot?'

'According to Filan, Miss Todd says that she saw Selwyn attack her niece with the shovel.'

'And then he took it and drove the blade into

the side of her head? That seems very precise for the man who came out of that shed. He didn't react at all when he saw her on the ground. Did you notice that?'

'I got the impression that he didn't understand what it meant.'

'Could he kill her in a rage and then forget almost immediately that he'd done it?'

'I suppose that might depend on what sort of retarded he is.'

'Not very well put, Constable, but I see what you mean.'

'When I was photographing in the shed, I noticed that there was a slate with writing on it that you might want to look at, sir. I made sure I got close-ups of it.'

There was very little to see in the shed. The only furniture was the bed, and Selwyn's clothes were piled in a corner. The shovel was there — that would need to be dusted for fingerprints. And the slate that Manton had mentioned was on the end of the bed. It was an ordinary slate, the kind used in every primary school. Halloran cocked his head so that he could read what was on it: 'Me do bad. Them bad, but.'

'Who's 'them'? Rose and Matthew, or Rose and Miss Todd? Maybe he wanted to go after Miss Todd, too, but she locked him up first. What do you think, Constable? Is this a confession?'

'It certainly looks like one.'

'I can't get a handle on any of this. It looks like an open-and-shut case, at least as far as Rose Abbot's death is concerned. Miss Todd says she saw Selwyn attack Rose, and he's more or less confessed to it on his slate. And yet I don't believe it. There's not a single thing that rings true. I feel as if someone's throwing sand in my eyes, and I don't like it. This is a small town, and a murder in a small town is like a hand grenade going off. A lot of people can end up getting hurt. This needs to be solved quickly, before it starts to fester. I'll telephone Melbourne and insist on someone from Homicide coming down here. And so, Constable, the grim and tedious process begins.'

★   ★   ★

Inspector Lambert took Inspector Halloran's call at 8.00 am.

'A case that fitted your department's brief better than this one would be difficult to find, Titus.'

'We're pretty stretched here, Greg.'

'I understand that. Let me outline the case, and you'll see why my inexperienced men aren't equipped to deal with it on their own.'

'You don't have confidence in your people?'

Greg Halloran ought perhaps to have been offended. He wasn't. He thought the question a reasonable one.

'I've got one first-class man. You've met him — Constable Manton. The local bloke in Port Fairy is excellent, too, but none of them have had detective training, and they'd benefit from being guided through this. When I said I was rusty, Titus, I meant it.'

'I'm listening.'

Halloran ran through the details, sketchy though they were.

'Tell me about Port Fairy, Greg. I've never been there.'

'It's small, about 30 minutes out of Warrnambool along a terrible road. I suppose you'd say it was a picturesque place, although what that really means is that nothing's been done to it since about 1900. Farming and fishing keep it going. No one's been murdered here since God knows how long. It's quiet, orderly, with Western District certainties that will find these murders hard to accommodate. Murder in a small place like this can create all sorts of tensions. I've seen it in Warrnambool. Old wounds open up, even when they've got nothing to do with the crime. People settle scores with gossip or with malicious accusations. It can take a generation for a community this size to recover from murder, which is why I want this cleared up as quickly as possible.'

'I can't come down, Greg. There's too much going on here.'

'I wasn't expecting you to, Titus. I'll run the investigation. Just send me someone who knows what he's doing.'

'Would you be willing to work with Constable Helen Lord? She'll have someone with her, of course.'

'I need someone who's trained.'

'The person she'll be with is a trained detective. Helen Lord is better than trained, Greg. She's good.'

'My blokes aren't going to like deferring to her.'

'They won't have to. She'll be under strict instructions to follow your orders, and she's perfectly aware that her rank means she can't throw her weight around. Not that she would.'

'I don't know, Titus. I know she's good. I've met her.'

'Under normal circumstances a policewoman wouldn't be let near a homicide, but these aren't normal circumstances. Nothing has been normal since Darwin was bombed. It won't hurt your blokes to work with Helen Lord. I'm happy for you to decide how best to use her.'

'Has she ever seen a mutilated body, or smelt it?'

This question shook Titus's confidence in his decision to send Helen Lord to Port Fairy. He realised that she hadn't, in fact, been exposed to the brutal reality of a violated corpse. She'd examined photographs of particularly unpleasant murders in the case involving George Starling, and she hadn't flinched. On the contrary, she'd done what many seasoned officers still found difficult to do — she'd stared and stared at those photographs, extracting from them as much as she could. She hadn't looked away for the same reason that Maude hadn't ever looked away. She was on the side of the victim, and sometimes the victim spoke through an overlooked detail in a photograph.

'I don't expect you to expose Helen Lord to the bodies, but you don't need to protect her from the photographs. She'll be a tremendous help to you.'

'All right, Titus. Who'll be coming with her?'

'I haven't decided that yet.'

'It'll be faster if they come by train.'

'And how long will you need them?'

'With two extra people we can get through interviews quickly. This might turn out to be much simpler than it looks.'

'I want them back in three days, Greg.'

'Fair enough. By the time they get here I'll have a much clearer idea of what we're dealing with.'

Titus needed to make a decision on the spot. He ran his eye down the list of continuing investigations. There was no one he wanted to take off a case. Alternatively, he could borrow someone from the CIB, but he didn't like doing that. The Homicide department was still finding its feet, and it seemed important to Titus that it be seen to manage whatever case load it found itself carrying. Sergeant Reilly was an obvious choice, but Titus knew that there was tension between Reilly and Lord, and Greg Halloran wouldn't appreciate having to sort out any arguments that might erupt between them.

With mild trepidation, he decided that it might be time for Sergeant Sable to return properly to work. This would mean delaying a meeting with Tom Mackenzie, but that couldn't be helped. There were several advantages to sending Joe to Port Fairy with Constable Lord. He'd be well away from George Starling, who was still in Melbourne; Titus had no doubt about that. And work would offer Joe a distraction that he sorely needed.

Hoping that Helen and Joe wouldn't have yet

left for work, he telephoned the house in Kew. Ros Lord answered and said that they were almost out the door. She called them back and handed the telephone to Joe. Joe listened as Inspector Lambert issued his instructions. When he hung up, he gave the gist of it to Helen.

'Port Fairy,' she said. 'I've never been there. I know where it is. It's the other side of Warrnambool.'

'I've never been there either. The other side of Warrnambool — it might as well be Timbuktu.'

Ros Lord, who'd discreetly withdrawn after she'd handed Joe the phone, reappeared and asked if anything was wrong.

'Nothing's wrong, Mum. We have to pack a few things. We'll be away for a couple of days.'

'But where are you going, darling?'

'We're being sent to Port Fairy, Mrs Lord. There's been a murder.'

Helen would never have been so explicit with her mother, and she expected her to object to her daughter being involved in something as sordid as murder.

'I *do* work in Homicide, Mum.' She was defensive, even though Mrs Lord hadn't said a word.

'I know you do.' She paused, and then, to Helen's mortification, she said firmly, in front of Joe, 'I am proud of you, Helen, and I know that your father would have been proud, too.'

Helen blushed and was unable to appreciate the compliment calmly. She mumbled about needing to pack, and hurried upstairs. Joe found himself similarly mortified when Ros Lord put her hand on his arm and said, 'Don't worry, Joe, Helen will look after you.'

He had no idea how to respond, so he said, 'Thank you,' and wondered immediately why he should be grateful that Ros Lord saw him as some sort of damaged child. He went upstairs to pack.

★   ★   ★

A large sign at the entrance to Spencer Street Station read, 'Is your journey really necessary?' The fact that a priority permit had been organised quickly for Joe and Helen was proof enough that this journey was really necessary. The train to Warrnambool, and on to Port Fairy, was scheduled to leave at 9.30 am, and they made it in plenty of time. In any event, it didn't actually leave until 10.00 am and was unexpectedly crowded. Apparently, large numbers of people were making necessary journeys. Joe was glad that he'd escaped having to walk into Russell Street wearing a suit that was not his own, and the quality of which reinforced this fact. Neither Helen nor Joe had had time to assimilate the situation. A solid five hours on the train would rectify that. They'd gone straight from Kew to Spencer Street, so the only information they had was what Titus had told Joe. There'd been two murders, of a brother and sister, and a suspect was being held for questioning. The suspect, who was the deceaseds' uncle, was problematic, as he was severely mentally deficient. They were to be under the direction of Detective Inspector

Halloran, and they were to be accommodated at Douglas House in Gipps Street. This was close to the courthouse and the police station.

'Is this an expression of Inspector Lambert's confidence in us,' Joe asked, 'or are we all that's available?'

'I expect it's an expression of confidence in me, at any rate.'

Helen smiled to reassure Joe that she was kidding. She'd noticed that his sense of humour had been blunted recently, that he was apt to put the worst possible construction on things.

'Actually, Joe, we're not all that was available. Inspector Lambert could easily have sent someone else — someone from the CIB even, if Homicide was too over-stretched. And there's Sergeant Reilly, of course. I could be sitting opposite him right now and wondering if there was going to be a third corpse before we'd finished investigating the first two.'

'He really isn't that bad.'

'Let's not go down that rabbit hole again. All I'm saying is, I'm glad you're sitting where Reilly might have been sitting.'

'Why do I feel like we're a couple of lame ducks?'

Helen's mood began to darken.

'What's that supposed to mean?'

'I'm not being rude, Helen, but look at me. Do you think they're not going to wonder why someone who looks like he's been hit by a car has been sent to investigate a crime they probably think they're perfectly capable of investigating on their own?'

236

'You said, 'We're a couple of lame ducks.' I presume you mean that the fact that I'm a woman is my handicap.'

'You know you're going to be treated as an oddity by those country coppers. They're not going to make this easy for you.'

'You have a low opinion of other men, Joe. At least that's something we have in common.'

'I'm just being realistic.'

'I'm in a constant state of readiness to meet my opposition. I have no illusions, Joe. I'm not going to win their respect, no matter what I do. I'm a novelty, a sideshow freak. Maybe I'll be pleasantly surprised, although having met a couple of them already, I doubt it. Halloran is a good man, though. I like him. The thing is, I'm not interested in winning their respect. Wouldn't it be amazing if they were interested in winning mine? When you say that out loud, you can hear how ridiculous it sounds, how very outlandish.'

'I think, well, I know, that Inspector Lambert respects you.'

'Yes, I'm starting to believe that he does.'

'That's why he asked you to do this.'

'And that's why I'm doing it.' Helen was tempted to admit that Inspector Lambert's respect was of great importance to her. Her desire for it was new and strange, and a small, angry part of her still thought it might be a weakness.

'I shouldn't have included you in the lame-duck remark. I'm sorry.' Ros Lord's parting words came back to Joe as he said this.

'Pardon, what did you say?' Helen hadn't

heard what he'd said. His words had been lost in the clatter of the train.

'Nothing. It was nothing,' he said.

★ ★ ★

Doctor Marriott, a sturdy-looking man well into his sixties, found the task of examining the bodies of Matthew Todd and Rose Abbot very difficult. He knew both of them, and although he'd never much liked Matthew, to see him *in extremis* like that was disturbing, and Rose's wounds made him feel physically ill. He'd attended innumerable dead people, but the circumstances of these two deaths got to him. He didn't betray this to Inspector Halloran; instead, he hoped he gave the impression of dispassionate professionalism, which was the quality that Halloran displayed. Dr Marriott declared each of the victims dead, and said that although he couldn't give an exact time of death before an autopsy, he believed that Matthew Todd had been dead for several hours — perhaps as many as six or seven. This would put his time of death at before midnight. Rose Abbot, on the other hand, had been dead for fewer than two hours. He would perform an autopsy on each of the bodies as soon as they were released to him. It had been Halloran's intention to leave the bodies *in situ* until the Homicide people arrived. Now, knowing that one of these was Helen Lord, he decided to have the bodies removed to the small mortuary. He'd done a thorough examination of the scene, and photographs had been taken, as well as fingerprints. He'd take Titus's advice and allow Constable Lord full access to the photographs.

By 10.00 am the neighbours had discovered what had happened. They'd watched, fascinated, as the bodies, outlined under sheets, had been carried out to a waiting van. By 11.00 am each of the immediate neighbours had been interviewed. No one had seen or heard anything unusual, either the previous night or that morning. Selwyn had made a bit of noise, but he generally did, and it had been no different from the noises he usually made.

Aggie consented eventually to go into Mrs Cuthbert's house, next door to hers. Mrs Cuthbert was deaf, so Aggie wasn't subjected to a stream of questions. She accepted a cup of tea and sat quietly, waiting for the inspector to turn his attention to her. She was nervous about this. He didn't look like the kind of person who would be fooled easily. She'd stick to her story, and if she did that, she couldn't see how it could be proved that she was lying. Selwyn had Rose's blood all over him, and there was his confession on the slate. That had been clever. What was it she'd written, exactly? She pictured it in her mind's eye, and when she did, something about it leapt out at her, and her stomach lurched. It was such a small thing. Surely they wouldn't notice.

At 11.30 am, having been briefed by his men on what the neighbours had said, Inspector Halloran sat down to interview Aggie Todd. Constable Manton took notes, and Mrs

Cuthbert went next door to the Hendersons so as not to intrude.

Aggie told Halloran the same story she'd told Paddy Filan, with no refinements, no additions, no suddenly remembered details.

'You say you heard, rather than saw, the disturbance between Selwyn and your nephew in the front room?'

'Yes.'

'So it sounded to you as if they were fighting, knocking things over, making a racket.'

'I don't know about knocking things over, but they were certainly fighting. Matthew wouldn't have given up without a struggle, Inspector.'

'How do you account for the state of the room?'

'What do you mean?'

'The room was remarkably tidy for a place where a fight had taken place.'

This hadn't occurred to Aggie. It was too late to spin the police a tale that it was Rose who'd killed Matthew, and that she must have taken him by surprise from behind.

'I imagine the room was a bit of a mess, but Selwyn's been well trained to tidy up after himself. He would automatically have put things back where they belonged. It's one of his few redeeming features.'

'So he strangled your nephew and then thought he might be reprimanded for making a mess.'

'Selwyn doesn't *think* anything, Inspector. He acts according to a routine he's become used to.'

'You mentioned to Constable Filan yesterday

that you think Selwyn must have overheard you discussing putting him away somewhere.'

'That sounds dreadful, 'Putting him away somewhere', but I suppose that's what it amounts to. We have to be practical. I can't look after Selwyn forever, and I don't think it matters to him where he is, so long as he has a routine.'

'It would seem, though, that it matters to him very much — enough to kill two people, in fact.'

Aggie began to feel that her story was unravelling. She wasn't going to panic. She could outwit this policeman.

'Yes. I sometimes underestimate Selwyn's understanding of things. You would, too, if you lived with him day in and day out.'

'Does he speak?'

'He speaks when he's at home — when he feels safe, I suppose. I wouldn't call what he says a conversation. He says single words. That would surprise people who only see him sitting there, giggling, in Sackville Street.'

'Did he say anything this morning?'

Aggie considered the minor embellishment of having remembered Selwyn saying something incriminating, but decided against it. It would strike a false note. If he'd said anything, she'd have told Constable Filan already.

'No, he said nothing. Even when he was hitting Rose, he was quite silent. I think that made it even more frightening.'

'Can Selwyn write, Miss Todd?'

'I wouldn't call it writing. He makes letters on that slate of his, and he knows a few words I've taught him. I can't bear to touch that slate. He

241

cleans it with his saliva.'

Inspector Halloran didn't tell Aggie that no fingerprints had been found anywhere on the slate, which was consistent with it having been wiped clean by someone — and that someone was unlikely to have been Selwyn.

'Apart from Selwyn, Miss Todd, do you know anyone who would want to harm either your niece or your nephew?'

'What do you mean? I heard Selwyn attack Matthew, and I saw him attack Rose. Whatever can you mean by that question?'

Halloran allowed the silence to grow between them. It gave Aggie a moment to think.

'Are you suggesting, Inspector, that someone might have encouraged Selwyn to kill Matthew and Rose?'

Halloran had to admit that Aggie Todd was sharp. Aggie was buoyed by this inspired suggestion.

'Matthew was well respected in Port Fairy, although there might have been disgruntled fishermen who resented his success.'

'Why would they resent him?'

'I don't know much about it, but I know there's a fish Co-operative that represents fishermen, and they don't like competition outside the Co-op. Matthew was a forwarding agent, and he represented individual fishermen who chose not to join the Co-op. He got them good prices, better usually than they would have got through the Co-op.'

'Did Matthew ever tell you that he'd been threatened by anyone?'

Aggie thought for a moment. It wouldn't hurt

to throw up some smoke.

'He didn't take any of it seriously, and he certainly wasn't afraid, but he did mention once or twice that a man named Scotter, was it? Or Scotney? Yes, Scotney — that this Scotney person had had words with him.'

'What sort of words?'

'I don't know the details. Matthew just mentioned in passing that Scotney had used abusive language and that he threatened him in some way.'

'And your niece?'

'Oh, Rose. No, I can't imagine that anyone would hold a grudge against Rose. She wasn't entirely happy in her marriage. Her husband is something of an oaf, and I know that he'd raised his hand to her on occasion. She confided that much in me.'

'You think he'd want to have his wife killed?'

Aggie expressed shock.

'Oh, no. But who knows what goes on within a marriage, Inspector?'

Halloran had to hand it to Aggie Todd. Her stories were almost plausible.

'Perhaps, Inspector, whoever influenced Selwyn, the intention was to frighten or punish either my nephew, or my niece, and Selwyn misunderstood and killed them both. Or perhaps he was meant to teach one of them a lesson and he went too far.'

'Why would Selwyn write what amounts to a confession?'

Aggie looked suitably aghast.

'A confession?'

'On his slate.'

'There was nothing on that slate when Selwyn went to bed last night. I saw it, and it was blank. What did he write?'

Halloran checked his notes.

'Me do bad. Them bad, but.'

'I wouldn't have thought Selwyn was capable of writing anything quite so coherent. I'm frankly astonished.'

'Do you think someone else might have written it?'

'I don't see how. The slate was blank last night. He must have written it after I'd locked him in the shed. As I said, I don't have a full understanding of Selwyn's abilities. I don't think anybody does.'

'Are there any questions you have for us, Miss Todd?'

'Has my brother in Melbourne been told about his children?'

'Yes, he has. He and his wife are coming by train tomorrow.'

'It was his wife who insisted that Selwyn stay with me. She's a selfish woman, but she doesn't deserve this. She's partly responsible, of course. If Selwyn had stayed in Melbourne, this would never have happened.'

Halloran signalled to Constable Manton that he could put his notebook away.

'Thank you, Miss Todd. I'm afraid you won't be able to go into the house for a while. Homicide detectives are coming from Melbourne, and they'll need access to the property.'

'I couldn't sleep there tonight anyway, Inspector. Mrs Cuthbert has a spare room, and ladies from the church will descend any minute with casseroles.'

Halloran caught Manton's eye. Afterwards, in the street, he asked the constable for a reaction to Aggie Todd's testimony.

'Grief can show itself in all sorts of ways, sir, and so can shock.'

'Give me four words or less.'

'Well-ordered self-righteousness.'

'You're wasted in Warrnambool, Constable — you really are.'

★　★　★

The Australia Hotel wasn't as salubrious as the Windsor, although by George Starling's standards it was still pretty flash. His clothes, especially perhaps the hat — he'd never owned anything as beautiful as that fedora — ensured that the staff at the Australia treated him with immediate deference. His room had a radio in it, and he spent much of Sunday afternoon listening to what was on offer. A piano recital and orchestral music were on 3LO, National Farm Topics on 3AR, and nothing of interest on any of the other stations. He switched it off, but not before he'd heard an advertisement on 3XY for the natorium at the City Baths: 'Roman rings, hot showers, private hot baths, filtered water, and mixed bathing every night at 8.00 pm, Sundays excepted.'

Starling was interested enough to decide that he'd pay the baths a visit the following evening. He'd seen them from the outside often enough, but he'd never been in. The exercise on the rings would do him good, and mixed bathing seemed tantalisingly erotic to him. Unless the kind of women who swam there were stout matrons with psoriasis; the promise of filtered water would be compromised if it had to battle the flaky leavings of skin diseases. He'd be sure to check the other bathers before he slipped into the pool. He was fastidious when it came to contact with strangers. The more he thought about it, the more he thought he might stick with the private bath. He'd go into the public pool area and consider carefully before immersing himself in the soup of sweat, mucous, and ooze from ugly men and ugly women. He'd look at them. He'd enjoy that. There was pleasure to be had from feeling a rush of disgust for other people.

On Sunday evening, Starling ate at the Australia Hotel's dining room. There were tables of women — shop girls probably, he thought, or women with some sort of war job — who could afford to eat here because of the fixed price. Their laughter annoyed him. He was sitting alone, and he became aware that he'd become the object of attention for three women nearby. They were trying to catch his eye. He wasn't flattered. They wanted him to buy them a drink, he was sure of it, and he found it objectionable. They probably thought they were being daringly flirtatious, in a manner learned from the movies. Starling met their eyes finally, and the expression on his face wiped the smiles off theirs. They turned away, and made no further effort to engage with him.

He wasn't hungry, and was uninterested in the waiter's apology for the absence of potatoes and tomatoes. He ordered a soup, ate it quickly, and left. He wanted to say something to the silly women, to put them in their place, but he passed their table without even glancing at them. He'd have an early night. The following morning he wanted to walk up to Russell Street and see who came and went from police headquarters. The only policeman he knew by sight was Joe Sable. He might get lucky though and recognise one of the cunts who'd been there the night Ptolemy Jones was killed.

Starling didn't bother with breakfast on Monday morning. He was pleased that the Australia Hotel had a barbershop for guests, where he had indulged himself with a close shave. He'd become attached to this small luxury, so much so that he hadn't yet bothered to buy himself a razor. As he walked east along Collins Street towards Russell Street, he marvelled that the people he passed would have shrunk from him if they could see themselves as he saw them. They had every reason to fear a man like him, and they didn't know it. They led lazy, pointless lives, the sole aim of which was to protect their laziness and their pointlessness. Joe Sable's folder of clippings proved that, elsewhere, people like him, George Starling, were engaged in a fierce and noble struggle against the Jew. He could do his bit by removing undesirables whenever he came across them. The thought put a spring in his step.

When Starling reached police headquarters, he

leaned against the wall of the Magistrate's Court opposite. He was surprised at the number of women who went in and out of the building. He was too far away to see any faces properly, so he crossed the street and loitered near the corner of Russell and La Trobe Streets. He walked back and forth in front of the main door a few times. He bumped into one man, who apologised and passed into the building.

★   ★   ★

David Reilly was preoccupied, which was why he'd almost knocked that pedestrian off his feet. Fortunately, the man had been polite about it. It was reassuring when people were decent and didn't lose their tempers. He was preoccupied because, when he'd come into work that morning, he'd discovered that Helen Lord and Joe Sable had been dispatched to Port Fairy to investigate a double murder. He was senior to both of them. He didn't allow himself to linger over the thought that he'd been overlooked in favour of a woman, although that was how he saw what had happened. There were a couple of other cases that he was working on, that was true, yet he couldn't help but interpret this as an expression of Inspector Lambert's lack of confidence in him. He didn't have any illusions about his skills as a detective. He was a good, steady worker, and a reliable one. He was certainly no shirker, and he wasn't on the take. He knew coppers who were, and he despised them for it. He was ordinary, but no more ordinary than Lord and Sable, surely. His feelings about each of them were rapidly curdling, and if there was one weakness he was willing to admit to, it was that he held a grudge. He had a brother he hadn't spoken to for ten years, and he wasn't one of those people who forgot the *casus belli*. He remembered it, all right.

He'd thought about what he was going to say to Inspector Lambert all morning. He'd gone for a walk, found a telephone booth, and called his wife to ask her opinion. She was in no doubt that Helen Lord was at the bottom of this, and what a disgrace it was that a woman like that should be given more opportunities than he was being given. She repeated her belief that Helen Lord was a poor sort of woman anyway — wanting, as she did, to work in Homicide. You wouldn't catch Barbara Reilly poking around dead bodies. She had better things to do.

'You're too good for them, David. You should get out of Homicide. I don't like you coming home after looking at dead people and then looking at me.'

Barbara Reilly's opinion about Homicide wasn't a surprise. She'd often expressed her misgivings about the job's effect on David's health. He'd telephoned her, really, to reassure himself that her opposition to his grim work remained undiminished. This gave him the courage he needed to ask Inspector Lambert if he might see him on a matter of some importance. Titus, who'd been reading notes on the progress of the case involving the two men at the private club, invited Sergeant Reilly to sit down. The notes were worse than useless; no progress had been made. He closed the folder and looked up at Reilly.

'I have some concerns, sir,' Reilly said.

'Is this about your case load, Sergeant?'

'No, sir. My case load is perfectly manageable. It's no heavier than anyone else's.'

Reilly suddenly began to feel that he ran the risk of sounding petulant. Trying to keep this note out of his voice, he said, 'Sergeant Sable isn't yet fully recovered from his injuries, sir, and yet you chose to send him to Port Fairy, and to keep me here. I was wondering why.'

'My reasons for choosing the people I do for particular jobs are nothing to do with you, Sergeant.'

'In this instance, sir, I don't think that's absolutely true.'

Another man might have flown off the handle at what could be construed as both impertinence and insubordination. Inspector Lambert wasn't so insecure as to feel undermined by a member of his staff questioning his judgement. He was surprised by David Reilly's frankness, and surmised that something serious must have driven him to it.

'Do you think I should have sent you instead of Sergeant Sable?'

'No, sir. I think you should have sent me instead of Constable Lord.'

'Ah. If it's any consolation, there are a large number of people in this building who find Constable Lord's presence in this department inexplicable and regrettable. Fortunately, they have no say in the matter. Her position isn't permanent and poses no threat to anyone else's job, so the objections can only spring from an ignorant belief that a woman must be constitutionally unequal to the task of investigating a crime. I don't happen to share that belief, and I'm well aware that that puts me in a minority. I don't value her more than I value you, Sergeant, if that is what you were thinking. I hope it wasn't. I wouldn't like to think that a man of your experience could be quite so childish.'

David Reilly lost his nerve. Inspector Lambert hadn't raised his voice. The accusation of childishness embarrassed Reilly — partly because it was true, and partly because, like everyone else close to Lambert, Reilly wanted his approbation. Lambert moved on brutally.

'But if you're unhappy in Homicide, for whatever reason, you're no good to me. Your heart wouldn't be in your work. I can organise a transfer to the Company Fraud Squad. It's still in its early days, so you wouldn't be stepping into established routines and loyalties.'

Reilly had entered Lambert's office with the idea that he would ask for a transfer to this very squad. However, the fact that the suggestion came from Lambert shocked him. Titus saw the shock register on Reilly's face.

'I'd be reluctant to lose you, Sergeant, but if that's what you'd prefer, I'll grease the wheels for you. Aren't you curious to know why I wanted you moved into this section of Homicide?'

'I thought it was a question of office space. It's

pretty crowded down the corridor, and there was a spare desk in the area.'

Titus sighed, and Reilly was convinced that the inspector was now officially certain that he was a dolt.

'You've been a policeman for a long time, Sergeant. Apart from whatever other qualities you may have, you do have one that I admire and that I think I can use to the advantage of this department. You're honest. That's not a quality I take for granted. We both know men who abuse their authority. I know that you don't have any time for bent coppers. You don't like associating with them, and you'd never be tempted to go along with them.'

'Thank you, sir. I appreciate that vote of confidence.'

'It comes with a sting. There's something I want you to do, if you're willing to stay in the department.'

Reilly's reasons for leaving Homicide were now unclear to him.

'I'd like to remain in Homicide, sir.'

'Good. While Constable Lord and Sergeant Sable are away, I want you to diplomatically oversee the investigation being done by Dunnart and O'Dowd. They won't like you poking your nose in, and they'll know I've sent you, and they'll know why; at least Dunnart will. That's fine. I want Ron Dunnart to know that someone's looking over his shoulder on this one.'

'This is the murder of those two queers?'

'It's the murder of two men, Sergeant.'

'Of course, sir. I didn't mean . . . '

'Ron Dunnart is of the view that a dead homosexual is the best sort of homosexual. We still don't even know the names of the victims, and they've been dead for a day and a half. One of the men was quite young, probably no more than 20. It's likely that he lived at home, and he may well have been reported as missing. I want a rocket put under Dunnart and O'Dowd.'

'May I speak frankly, sir?'

'Please.'

'Ron Dunnart is the kind of man who'd use information in a case like this for his own advantage.'

'You mean blackmail. Yes, I've already warned him. When you announce that you've been instructed to join the case, it will be like an exclamation mark after that warning. Ron Dunnart has friends, so this isn't going to do your popularity any good. You can see why I couldn't ask Constable Lord or Sergeant Sable to do this, can't you?'

'Yes, sir.'

David Reilly was flattered, even if he doubted the sincerity of that final, unnecessary, implied compliment to his experience and authority. Titus handed Reilly the notes.

'Read these meagre offerings and then pop down the corridor and break the good news to detective Ron Dunnart that he's getting an extra man to lighten his load. He'll be thrilled.'

David Reilly, who'd begun this interview with the glum certainty that it would go badly, smiled.

'Not half as thrilled as I'll be, sir.'

★   ★   ★

253

George Starling had impressed himself with his successful imitation of gentlemanly restraint when that bloke, who must have been a detective, almost knocked him down. He wandered up and down for a few minutes more, and decided that the exercise was pointless. He was at a loose end. He could go to the pictures. He liked the pictures. He liked Gene Tierney, Joan Crawford, and Gary Cooper. He didn't like Leslie Howard, Charles Boyer, Errol Flynn, or Mickey Rooney — he wouldn't bother going to a picture if one of them was in it. He didn't have a preference for a particular type of picture. He watched westerns, musicals, gangster movies, and even women's pictures with equal pleasure. He headed back into the centre of town to see what was on.

A movie had to be spectacularly awful for George Starling not to get lost in it. Movies had been a refuge from his dismal upbringing, and their capacity to free him temporarily from the demands and insults of daily life remained into adulthood. Bad films made him angry because they breached the promise he'd come to expect, and so it was that he felt agitated when he left halfway through *Behind the Rising Sun*. It was just after midday. If he returned to the alley that Steven McNamara had taken him down, there were sure to be detectives still hanging about. He wanted to see who they were, and he also wanted to see whether or not he'd managed to burn the place down. There was even an outside chance that Joe Sable would be there. Starling hoped that the death of two fairies might be the sort of case that Sable would be assigned to. If the club had burnt down, of course, the identification of the bodies would have been stalled. Still, with nothing better to do, and feeling jittery from the bad movie, he found the alley off Little Bourke Street, and passed it two or three times, pausing to look into its shadows. There was no evidence of fire damage. A uniformed policeman stood at the door, his white helmet standing out in the gloom. So the bodies must have been been found. That was good. It pleased him to think that detectives were wasting their time trying to find the killer. There was absolutely nothing to connect him to the crime. A random murder was the perfect murder. Police liked the comforting reassurance of statistics which showed that victims almost always knew their killer. They'd work on that assumption in this case, and that would waste hours, days, of their time. There wasn't any activity in the alley. Perhaps the detectives were upstairs.

★　★　★

Ron Dunnart and David Reilly had arrived at the crime scene at 11.30 am. Dunnart, as Inspector Lambert had predicted, had known precisely what Reilly's appointment to the case signified. All right, then — he'd tread carefully, show due deference to Reilly's face, and keep him in the dark as much as possible. He took Reilly to the private club, but waited until they got there to discuss the progress of the investigation. He pre-empted the criticism of the briefing notes he'd given Lambert.

'I'm trying to keep Inspector Lambert informed as we go, but so far there's not a lot to go on. He must think we're dragging our heels. We're not.'

'You still don't know the identities of the bodies.'

'No. No one has been reported missing, and whoever the person was who found them hasn't come forward.'

'For obvious reasons.'

'And what reasons might they be?'

Reilly wanted to say that the fear of being blackmailed was probably the reason. He refrained diplomatically.

'He'd have to explain what he was doing at the club, and that might be awkward. I'm surprised that no one has missed either of the victims.'

'Maybe they had a habit of not turning up at home regularly.'

Dunnart was right about this. Steven McNamara's mother was used to him disappearing for days at a time. He would always turn up, explaining that he'd been staying at a friend's place. The barman, Sturt Menadue, lived alone. His friends wouldn't notice that no one in his circle had heard from him. He liked to keep his friends separate from one another — a habit that allowed Dunnart to say truthfully that finding out the name of either of the men was proving surprisingly difficult.

'They had no identification papers on them, and not so much as a set of initials on any of their clothing.'

'Who's the landlord of this place?'

'We do know that. We haven't been sitting on our arses.'

'Nobody said that you had.'

'He's a bloke by the name of Jimmy O'Farrell. He's in his eighties, and he lives in South Australia. He owns a few properties in Melbourne, and they're managed by his son, Brendan O'Farrell. We haven't yet spoken to O'Farrell the younger; but when we do, I suspect we'll have the name of at least one of the dead men. Unless, of course, the older of the corpses is Brendan O'Farrell himself.'

'Do you have his address?'

'O'Dowd should be there now. He lives in St Kilda.'

'None of this was in the notes you gave Inspector Lambert.'

Dunnart, whose patience was wearing thin, allowed a hint of annoyance to creep into his voice.

'That's because the information only came in late this morning. Christ. It only happened on Saturday night, and Sunday isn't the best day for tracking things down. The bloody Titles Office is closed on Sunday, or did Lambert expect us to break in and go through their records?'

'Keep your hair on, Ron. No one's criticising the way you're handling the investigation.'

This was such a blatant lie that Dunnart's estimation of Reilly's abilities plummeted. If Reilly was the best that Lambert had to offer by way of a watchdog, Dunnart had nothing to worry about.

Outside, in the alley, Dunnart asked the

policeman on the door if anybody had approached it. A couple of men had taken a few steps into the alley and then turned back into Little Bourke Street on seeing the uniform. Dunnart and Reilly headed back to Russell Street.

★   ★   ★

George Starling recognised one of the men who came out of the alley: he was the bloke who'd almost knocked him down at Russell Street. Starling tore himself away from examining the contents of a shoe-shop window, and followed the two detectives up Little Bourke Street. He moved quickly, kept his head down, and obscured his face with the brim of his hat. It was unlikely that either of the men would turn around, but it was a sensible precaution just in case one of them did. He managed to get close enough to hear that one of them, the one who'd bumped into him, was named Reilly. It gave Starling a real lift to know that the man they were looking for was a few feet behind them. In an act of brazen pleasure, Starling quickened his pace, passed the two detectives, and walked ahead of them. *What first-class fools they are*, he thought. Reilly — he'd remember that name. Maybe he'd find a way to introduce himself to Detective Reilly. Maybe Reilly could be per- suaded to tell him where the Jew boy Sable was hiding. As soon as this thought occurred to Starling, he saw its merits.

12

Helen Lord and Joe Sable arrived in Port Fairy at 4.00 pm. They deposited their belongings at Douglas House, and were taken by Constable Manton to the police station. Manton had met Helen Lord before, and was unsurprised by her presence. The situation at the small police station was a little different, however. Inspector Halloran wasn't there when introductions were made, and Constable Adams, who hadn't met Helen when she'd been in Warrnambool, was confused by her being there. Was she some sort of secretary to the Homicide bloke? Helen clarified matters for him by requesting a full briefing, followed by an interview with the prisoner. The use of the word 'prisoner' shocked Paddy Filan. Selwyn was being held in a cell because there was nowhere else to put him. He supposed that that did indeed make him a prisoner. Adams, meanwhile, thought that they should wait for instructions from Inspector Halloran before discussing the case with a female.

'Constable Lord and I require a briefing immediately, Constable. Which of you was first on the scene?'

The authority in Joe's voice overcame any doubts that had been aroused by his youth and by the fading bruises on his face.

'I was called to the house early this morning.' Paddy said.

Halfway through the briefing, Inspector Halloran arrived and signalled that it should continue. When Constable Filan had finished, Halloran welcomed Helen and Joe, careful to make no distinction between them, and identifying them both as representatives of Homicide. He outlined his reading of the case, and expressed his doubts about Aggie Todd's version of events, while acknowledging that he had no idea who she might be protecting.

'Aggie Todd isn't a suspect herself, sir?' Helen asked.

A little snort escaped from Constable Adams, who was amazed that this female blow-in could even contemplate the bizarre possibility that that staid, dried-up old spinster would be capable of murder. The snort drew a look of unalloyed fury from Inspector Halloran. He expected better from his men.

'Miss Todd is absolutely a suspect, Constable Lord. We would be foolish to limit her role to being an accomplice. We need to consider, however unlikely it might seem, that she might have been directly involved.'

He turned to Constable Adams.

'Old ladies don't kill people — is that what you're thinking, Constable?'

In an effort to regain lost ground, Constable Adams said, with more confidence than he was feeling, 'Well, poison maybe, sir, but these were such violent deaths, and Miss Todd seemed frail to me.'

Helen, who'd resented that snort, nevertheless came to his rescue.

'I haven't met Miss Todd. If she's a frail old lady, I can certainly see why you might want to eliminate her as having physically committed these murders.'

Inspector Halloran wasn't so forgiving.

'Miss Todd is not a frail old lady. Constable Adams here thinks that anyone over 40 is elderly. He sees a woman over 60 and assumes she's frail. Miss Todd is fit, strong, and calculating. She provided us with a self-serving list of plausible suspects, and I found her cool indifference to the fate of her brother frankly repugnant. She's a force to be reckoned with. Your question was a perfectly reasonable one, Constable Lord.'

While he was speaking, he opened a briefcase and took out an envelope.

'A commercial photographer here in town developed these for us in a hurry.'

He tipped the photographs, still smelling strongly of chemicals, onto the table. Helen reached for them, knowing that this would horrify Constable Adams. She spread them in front of her and Joe. There were eight photographs in all.

'There are more, of course,' Halloran said. 'I thought we needed to get at least some of them done as quickly as we could.'

Nothing was said as the photographs were examined.

'Where are the bodies now?' Joe asked.

'They've been taken to the morgue, which is attached to the hospital.'

Helen knew not to ask to see the bodies; it

would put Halloran in the position of having to refuse her. The photographs were adequate, although they lacked the incisive, penetrating assurance of Martin Serong's photographs.

'Could we speak to Mr Selwyn Todd before we see the Todd house?' Helen asked.

'Sure, but you'll have to excuse the smell,' Constable Filan said. 'The cell's hot, and Selwyn was already a bit on the nose when we brought him in. We cleaned him up a bit, which he didn't take kindly to.'

'He had blood on his hands, is that right?' Joe asked.

'Yes,' Halloran said. 'We're assuming that it's Rose Abbot's blood.'

'Has he said anything at all, Constable, since this morning?'

It had taken a while, but Joe was now comfortable addressing men his own age, or older, by their rank.

'Not a word, sir.'

He wasn't yet comfortable with being called 'sir'.

Paddy Filan suggested that the interview take place in the station's backyard. There was a table there.

'You don't consider him a flight risk?' Joe asked.

'It's been a long time since Selwyn did anything in a hurry. The thing about running away is that it involves running. When you meet Selwyn, you'll see that the Stawell Gift isn't on his list of things to do.'

'And you don't consider him dangerous?'

'He'll be handcuffed.'

'You didn't answer my question. Do you consider him dangerous?'

'Given that he's suspected of having murdered two people, I'd have to allow the possibility. If you'd asked me yesterday if Selwyn Todd posed a danger to anyone, I'd have said no, and I'd have said it with absolute confidence. There are marks on his body that might explain why he snapped, if he did. The doc examined him, and said that he had welts on his back and on his buttocks consistent with being beaten.'

'I noticed those when he came out of that shed of his,' Halloran said.

★   ★   ★

Helen and Joe sat at a picnic table in the yard of the station, with their notebooks open. Inspector Halloran and Constable Manton stood nearby. Constable Filan brought Selwyn Todd out of his cell. He was dressed in baggy trousers and a shirt that was too small for him, which was all that Filan had been able to find at short notice. Selwyn's hands were manacled, and he kept pulling at them as if he couldn't quite understand why his arms could move so far and no further. Filan spoke soothingly to him.

'There are some people here who want to ask you a few questions, Selwyn. All right?'

Selwyn giggled and tried again to pull his hands apart. Paddy Filan led him to the table and sat him down opposite Helen and Joe.

'Hello, Selwyn. My name is Helen.'

Selwyn giggled so that his jowls wobbled, and saliva made his protuberant lower lip glisten.

'My name is Joe, Selwyn.'

Joe raised his hand to wipe sweat from his face. The movement made Selwyn flinch, and he automatically put his manacled hands up to protect his face. His giggling stopped, and he became wary.

'It's all right, Selwyn. No one's going to hit you,' Joe said. 'Are there people who hit you?'

Selwyn gave no indication that he understood the question. When no blow came, he relaxed and made small, incoherent sounds.

'Do you remember what happened this morning, Selwyn?' Helen asked. 'Did anybody make you very angry?'

Selwyn looked about him, focussing not on the people in the yard, but on a tree, the sky, and a bird that landed on the fence. The bird ruffled its feathers, and Selwyn giggled. Both his legs began to jiggle uncontrollably, and he seemed distressed. Paddy Filan guessed that he needed to go to the toilet.

'Toilet, Selwyn?'

Selwyn still said nothing. He simply jiggled more vigorously. Paddy helped him up and showed him the backyard dunny. The handcuffs now caused Selwyn to panic.

'He can't work out what to do,' Paddy said.

'Free his hands,' Halloran said, 'before the poor man soils himself.'

As soon as the cuffs were removed, Selwyn hurried to the toilet. He didn't bother closing the door, and the odour of carbolic and sawdust drifted into the yard as Selwyn emptied his bladder into the can. When he'd finished he turned around, unsure what he should do next.

'I think you can take Selwyn back inside, Constable,' Inspector Halloran said. 'And don't bother with handcuffs.'

With Selwyn gone, Halloran asked Helen and Joe for their impressions.

'Does he speak?' Helen asked.

'His sister reckons he speaks when he's at home, because he feels safe there.'

'Did you see how he flinched when I made a sudden movement?' Joe said. 'I'd say he's used to pretty harsh treatment, and that home isn't a safe place at all.'

'His sister is adamant that he's more intelligent than he appears.'

'His sister is lying,' Helen said. 'I'm not saying he mightn't be capable of sudden, explosive violence. Is there any history of him losing his temper, or hurting animals? Anything at all?'

Paddy Filan had returned to the yard, and said that nobody in Port Fairy had ever reported seeing Selwyn do anything out of the ordinary. They were scared of him, but not because they thought he might hurt them. It was because he was so . . . Paddy struggled for the right word. 'I suppose he's just so . . . other. That's the only way I can describe it. He's other.'

'Miss Todd believes that he might have been following the instructions of someone who wanted to teach Matthew a lesson,' Helen said.

'Do you think Selwyn Todd, now that you've met him, is capable of retaining an instruction, let alone carrying it out?' Inspector Halloran asked.

'No, sir. I don't.'

'Sergeant Sable?'

'No, sir. He couldn't work out how to open his flies with handcuffs on. Managing a hit on his niece and nephew seems impossible.'

'I'll take you to the house and introduce you to Miss Agnes Todd.'

★ ★ ★

The first thing that struck both Helen and Joe at Aggie Todd's house was the lack of disturbance. There was a faint odour of Matthew Todd's body, and they could see dried blood on the lawn in the backyard.

'The report said that there were no fingerprints on the handle of the shovel,' Helen said.

'That's right.'

'So whoever wiped it down understood about fingerprints. Aggie Todd claims that she actually saw Selwyn swing the shovel.'

'She does.'

'Is she suggesting he wiped it down afterwards?'

'That's a question you can ask her yourself. She's had a good few hours to think about what happened here. I'll be interested to hear how she answers your questions.'

Helen and Joe examined the inside of Selwyn's shed, and Joe expressed his disbelief that a person could be banished there when the house had a spare bedroom.

'I got the impression that Miss Todd didn't consider Selwyn house-trained.'

'You can't accuse her of starving him at least,' Joe said, 'although I don't imagine she ever sat down with him at the dining-room table.'

The sheet on Selwyn's bed was stained with blood, and the slate was where the photograph indicated it would be.

'No prints on the slate, either,' Halloran said.

Helen peered down at the slate and frowned.

'It's so obvious, isn't it?' she said.

'Yes. If Selwyn was the last person to handle that slate, his prints would be all over it.'

'Well, that too,' she said.

'There's something else?'

'I'd like to talk to Aggie Todd.'

Neither Helen nor Joe was expecting a frail old lady after the sharp riposte that Inspector Halloran had given to Constable Adams. Nevertheless, it was difficult to read the emotions in Aggie's face, which was composed, but tense.

As for Aggie, she was astonished to find herself being questioned by a woman. Initially, even though Helen led off, Aggie directed her answer to Joe. They asked her the same questions Halloran had asked, and Constable Filan took notes.

'You've been very patient, Miss Todd,' Helen said. 'This must be very difficult for you.'

'I don't know what I'm going to say to Matthew and Rose's parents tomorrow. I really don't. It's just beginning to hit me now. The town will be devastated by Matthew's death.'

'And your niece's death, too?' Joe said.

'Yes, of course. Both their deaths will upset people terribly.'

'There are one or two things I'd like to clarify with you, if I may, Miss Todd?'

Aggie Todd nodded. Inwardly she was wary of this plain young woman who spoke to her as if she, Aggie Todd, were her equal. She was used to a certain level of respect in the town.

'You're very clear that Selwyn was in the front room subduing Matthew, and when he'd finished, he came out and attacked Rose.'

'I've already explained to the inspector that Selwyn would have made the room tidy if anything had been knocked over. That's why it was so neat.'

'Yes, I see. I just want to be absolutely clear about this. You heard Matthew and Selwyn scuffling, is that right?'

'Yes.'

'Matthew didn't call out?'

Aggie couldn't remember if she'd told the inspector whether Matthew had made any sound. Should she change her story, and tell them what she believed to be the truth about Matthew's death — that Rose had murdered him? She could still stand by her version of Rose's death. Why hadn't she thought of this earlier? She'd sleep on it, and construct a convincing reason for lying about Selwyn and Matthew fighting. They'd understand an aunt's reluctance to accuse her own niece. For now, she'd stick to the version she'd given Inspector Halloran.

268

'I can't think. I'm sorry — it was all so fast and hideous. I don't think Matthew cried out. No, I'm sure he didn't. There was just the noise of them fighting. Selwyn is strong.'

'And when the fighting stopped, Selwyn came out of the front room . . .'

'He came out, walked right past me, and attacked poor Rose. He bashed her with that shovel as if she was no more than a fence post or something.'

Helen left a gap for Joe to jump in.

'Miss Todd,' he said. 'At the time you say Selwyn was noisily fighting Matthew, Matthew had been dead for at least four hours — maybe more.'

Aggie's mouth dropped open, and the colour drained from her face. Helen didn't give her an opportunity to speak.

'I want to talk to you about Selwyn's confession.'

It hadn't occurred to Aggie that the police would know the time of Matthew's death, and in her panic she hadn't heard Helen's question.

'Miss Todd?'

Inspector Halloran was curious as to why neither Helen nor Joe was capitalising on the time-of-death discrepancy. With admiration, he realised what the strategy was: strip Aggie Todd of all her lies, and deny her the opportunity to deal with them one at a time.

'Miss Todd?' Helen repeated. 'Selwyn's confession?'

Almost with relief, Aggie remembered the confession.

'Yes, that's right. I was very surprised when

Inspector Halloran told me about it.'

'Were you also surprised that there were no fingerprints on it?'

'No. Selwyn was always spitting on it and cleaning it with his shirt.'

'I've interviewed your brother, Miss Todd. I find the idea that the man I spoke to might be capable of writing anything at all, let alone a confession, absurd.'

The word 'absurd' startled Aggie. It signalled a change in Helen Lord's tone. Aggie reacted to it with indignation.

'You know next to nothing about my brother. You've spoken to him once. I imagine he was unco-operative. Of course he was. He'd just killed my niece.'

'And your nephew,' Joe said.

Aggie rallied. 'Well, according to you, he was struggling with a corpse in my front room, and perhaps he was. I can't explain why you believe Matthew was already dead, but . . . '

'There's something about the confession that struck me most particularly,' Helen said firmly.

'Oh?'

'You said Selwyn could scratch out a few letters and the odd word that you'd taught him.'

'I said that because it's true.'

'*Me do bad. Them bad, but.* Each of those words is among the words you taught him?'

'I suppose they must have been.'

'An odd selection to teach someone.'

'Selwyn has been writing on that slate for 20 years, and I've been teaching him words for 20 years. I don't think it's in the least bit odd.'

'How large do you think his written vocabulary might be?'

'I have no idea. What is the point of these questions?'

'Is that the first sentence you've known him to write?'

Aggie was getting flustered.

'Why are you asking me this?'

'Is that the first sentence you've known him to write?' Helen's repetition was calm and measured.

'I'd hardly call it a sentence, but yes, I've never known him to string words together. As I say, no one's ever been sure about the true nature of Selwyn's intelligence.'

'I don't believe that for a minute, Miss Todd.'

Aggie reacted as if she'd been slapped.

'How dare you talk to me like that, young lady.'

'You wrote that confession, Miss Todd. I know you wrote it, because you weren't able to forget rules that had been drummed into you, that have been drummed into all of us. There are two sentences in the confession. Each of them begins with a capital letter, and each of them ends with a full stop. The biggest mistake you made, though, was that comma. *Them bad, but.* Do you really want us to believe that Selwyn had a good grasp of punctuation?'

Aggie put her face in her hands. She needed to buy time. What, after all, did these people actually know? All right. Matthew had died a few hours before Rose. They knew that. She could still claim that she was protecting Rose's name.

She was certain they'd have no way of proving that Selwyn hadn't killed Rose, perhaps in a rage after discovering that his beloved Matthew was dead. She'd insist that Matthew and Selwyn were close. She took her hands away from her face, breathed in deeply, and said, 'Yes, I wrote that confession.'

There was silence in the room.

'It was wrong of me, and it must seem callous to you that I'd do such a thing to my own brother.'

No one offered her any prompts.

'I've probably committed a crime of some sort. I don't care. What I'm about to tell you is the absolute truth. It's difficult for me to say these things, because our family has a position in Port Fairy, and has had that position for several generations. This will destroy our family. I found Matthew's body in the front room just when I told you I did. At first I thought he must have been asleep. I didn't know what he was doing in my house at that hour. I tried to wake him, and when I realised that he was dead, I was terrified. I could see that he'd been strangled. Without thinking, I rushed to the backyard to see if Selwyn was all right. Rose was there, just standing, looking at the house vacantly. 'I killed him, Aunt Aggie,' she said. It was as if she was in a trance. 'I killed Matthew. I've always hated him.' It all happened so quickly after that. Selwyn must have heard her, because he rushed out of his shed and hit her with the shovel. Selwyn adored Matthew. Then he just went back into his shed as if he'd done nothing. I know it was wrong of me, very wrong, but I wanted to protect the family as much as I could. How would Rose's parents bear knowing that their daughter had murdered their son? I wrote Selwyn's confession because I thought it would help you. He killed Rose, after all, so why not have him confess to both murders, and that way Rose's name wouldn't be sullied? I can't tell you how Rose killed Matthew, or how she managed to get his body into the front room. She must have had help — her husband, I suppose. That's the truth. It's shocking and devastating and destructive, but it's the truth. I can't tell you how ashamed I am of what I've done. Everything is ruined. Our lives have been ruined.'

'That's quite a story, Miss Todd,' Halloran said.

'I thought I was doing the best thing. It's a Greek tragedy, Inspector.'

★   ★   ★

No one noticed the photographer in the front garden of the house opposite Mrs Cuthbert's house. He fired off half-a-dozen quick shots and hurried back to the offices of the *Port Fairy Gazette*. News of the events in James Street had spread quickly through the town. Some people locked their doors, with stories of what had happened varying from Selwyn Todd having gone on a rampage to a Japanese assassin having come ashore from a submarine in the night.

'Constable Adams will take the first shift watching the house,' Inspector Halloran said. 'I want Miss Todd to stay put.'

The four police officers were walking back to the station.

'What a bizarre and extraordinary story,' Helen said.

'Well done catching her out on the punctuation, Constable. That wouldn't have occurred to me.'

'It wouldn't have occurred to me, either,' Joe said.

'You have to hand it her, she's fast on her feet,' Halloran said. 'Was there a single thing about her story that was convincing, do you think?'

'She was making it up as she went along,' Joe said. 'You could drive a truck through the holes in it.'

'Let's break this down into simple parts,' Halloran said. 'We're certain Matthew Todd was killed sometime just before or after midnight, and that he wasn't killed at Aggie Todd's house. There was sand residue under his shoes, and there was no trace of it in Aggie's front room. In other words, he didn't walk into that room.'

'So whoever killed him carried him there,' Joe said.

'Yes. Todd was a fit young man. It would have taken someone of equal or greater strength to strangle him. There's no bruising on his body, no damage to his hands, and nothing under his fingernails. He was taken by surprise, from behind, and dispatched quickly. I'd say that Aggie Todd is not a suspect in the murder of her nephew. I'd say that pretty much eliminates Rose Abbot as well, despite Miss Todd's view to the contrary.'

'Unless she had an accomplice,' said Joe.

'And Miss Todd kindly offered us one, didn't she? Rose's husband, John Abbot.'

'He hasn't come into town?' Helen asked.

'Rose drove the truck into town this morning, so he wasn't able to come in. Constable Manton is with him. Abbot runs a dairy farm, and the herd has to be milked. It's tough on Abbot. Manton telephoned earlier to say that he was shattered. He's our next port of call.'

'So,' said Helen, 'we're assuming that Matthew Todd was killed by a person or persons unknown. What about Rose Abbot? Is there any possibility that Selwyn Todd is responsible for her death? If he isn't, it means that Aggie Todd is lying about having seen him do it. Why would she do that?'

'Because she did it herself?' Joe asked.

'I reprimanded Constable Adams for dismissing her as a suspect,' Halloran said, 'yet I can't see her wielding that shovel. And why? Why would she hit her own niece in the face with a shovel?'

At the police station, Constable Filan's wife, Anne, had left a bowl of stew and vegetables for Selwyn. Constable Adams, who'd been given instructions to occasionally open the slot in the cell door and talk to Selwyn, had grown bored with the exercise. Selwyn never replied, so he left him alone — which was why he missed Selwyn's signs that he needed the toilet. A pan had been left in the cell, but Selwyn had never used a pan. He grew distressed, and began to make a noise. By the time Constable Adams responded, the smell that assaulted his nose when he opened the slot told him that Selwyn had soiled himself.

When Inspector Halloran and the others entered the police station, they were met with the pleasant odours of mutton stew, which was sitting, covered with a cloth, on the front desk.

'Constable Adams!'

Adams came in from the cell.

'Why hasn't that been taken out to the cells?'

'I'm sorry, sir. Mrs Filan just delivered it. I was going to take it out, but the prisoner has had an accident.'

'What kind of accident? You were supposed to be checking on him.'

'I mean, he's shat himself.' He paused and added, 'Sir.'

Halloran was livid.

'He'd have signalled that he needed the toilet. Where were you?'

'I was in here, sir. I didn't hear him.'

'This is completely unacceptable.'

For the second time that day, Helen felt sorry for Constable Adams. It was humiliating to be dressed down in front of other officers.

'You'll have to clean him up.'

Adams recoiled.

'How?' he said weakly.

'I'll help,' said Paddy Filan. 'There's a hose in the yard. It'll be the simplest solution. He'll need another change of clothes.'

'Perhaps Constable Adams can donate his uniform,' Halloran snapped.

★ ★ ★

Selwyn knew that he was in trouble. When two men came into the room, he began to whimper.

'It's all right, Selwyn,' Paddy said. 'We're going outside again, into the yard.'

Constable Adams was holding his breath as he and Paddy put a hand under Selwyn's arms and lifted him to his feet. Selwyn didn't resist; he knew what would happen if he didn't do what he was told. Outside, Paddy indicated that he wanted Selwyn to undress, while Fletcher Adams attached the hose to a tap. When Selwyn saw the hose, he began to shake, but he took his clothes off and stood with his eyes squeezed shut. His body was quivering. Paddy turned him gently around, and again saw the welts on Selwyn's body.

'Okay, Fletch, turn the hose on. Gently, gently.'

'Christ, I hate this fucking job. Halloran fucking hates me, the pay is lousy, and here I am, hosing the shit off some fat fucking retard.'

Filan took the hose from Adams.

'I'll do it. You go back inside.'

This seemed to Paddy to be the best way of avoiding punching Fletcher Adams in the balls.

'That suits me,' Adams said. 'I can't wait to get back to Warrnambool.'

Halloran hadn't had time to give Adams his instructions to watch Mrs Cuthbert's house. Adams found a note to that effect beside the stew. He was to go to the house immediately, and someone would relieve him at midnight.

'Fuck,' he said. Before he left, he lifted the cloth off the stew and, using his fingers, picked out chunks of the meat. It was good, so he helped himself to some more. Selwyn's meal was reduced to mainly potatoes and gravy and carrots, with a couple of small pieces of meat.

⋆   ⋆   ⋆

'Mr Abbot, my name is Detective Inspector Greg Halloran, and this is Sergeant Joe Sable and Constable Helen Lord, from Homicide in Melbourne.'

John Abbot was sitting in the kitchen. His eyes were red, and he looked more than usually dishevelled.

'We're very sorry about your wife. We need to ask you some questions, if you feel up to it.'

Abbot nodded. The back door opened, and Johanna Scotney came into the kitchen. Her eyes, too, were red and puffy from crying.

'Johanna works here,' Abbot said dully. 'I've told her she can go home.'

'You can't do the milking on your own, Mr Abbot. I'll wait outside.'

'No,' Abbot said. 'I'd like you to stay.'

Johanna was reluctant. Helen Lord said that it would be fine, that anything she could add might be valuable.

'Some of these questions might be upsetting, Mr Abbot,' Joe said. 'We need as much information as we can get in order to find out who took your wife's life.'

'If I find out,' Abbot said, 'I'll kill the cunt.'

'What time this morning did Rose leave to go to her aunt's house in Port Fairy?'

'Stupidly early. The old battle axe telephoned at some ungodly hour, five o'clock or five-thirty, and told Rose that she had to hightail it over there.'

'Miss Todd telephoned Rose?'

'Yes. I picked up the phone and handed it on to Rosie as fast as I could. I didn't want to talk to that bitch of a woman at that hour of the day.'

'Do you know of anyone who might want to hurt Rose?'

'What? No, of course not. It was that bloody simpleton they keep at the bottom of the garden, wasn't it? People have been ringing here all day saying it was him.'

'We don't know for sure who killed your wife, Mr Abbot. I'm sorry I have to ask you this, but did you leave the farm at any time last night?'

Abbot stood up.

'What kind of question is that?'

'The kind that will help us eliminate you from our inquiries, Mr Abbot.'

'Are you insinuating that I murdered my wife?'

Joe remained calm.

'Rose wasn't the only person murdered last night, Mr Abbot. Matthew Todd died several hours before Rose, so we need to know where you were and when you were there. Please, sit down.'

Abbot sat.

'So, did you leave the farm at any time last night?'

'No, I didn't. We went to bed at the usual time — early. We have to get up to do the milking. Rosie can vouch for that. She was here with me all night.'

He realised what he'd said, and pulled hard at his ear in frustration. 'Except that she can't, can she?'

'Do you know of anyone who might want to harm Matthew Todd?'

Helen noticed a slight widening of Johanna Scotney's eyes, and the clenching of her fists.

'I didn't have any time for Matthew Todd,' Abbot said. 'He was a prick. He'd come out here and swan about like he owned the place. Oh, and that aunt hated me. I wasn't good enough to marry a Todd. As it happens, Rosie thought I was plenty good enough.'

'What was Rose's relationship with her brother?'

'So what are you saying now — that Rose killed Matthew?'

'Mr Abbot, please. No one is accusing anyone of anything. All we're trying to do is assemble as many pieces of the jigsaw as we can. Please don't look for insinuations in the questions. If you could answer them as honestly as you can, that would be helpful.'

Abbot was sufficiently mollified to give his view of Rose's relationship with both Matthew and Aggie Todd.

'She was so much better than they were. They looked down on her, and it didn't bother her one bit. She . . . '

A great wave of emotion crashed over John Abbot. He lowered his head and began to shudder as sobs took hold of him. Johanna Scotney rose and discreetly went into another room. Helen followed her. She found Johanna in the lounge room, which was large and well furnished. It didn't look as if it got much use.

'I didn't think Mr Abbot would like me to see him like that.'

'May I ask you some questions?'

'Me?'

'Do you mind?'

'No, of course not — only I don't see how I can help.'

'Sometimes people who aren't involved see things that other people miss.'

Helen hoped that this might put Johanna at her ease. Those fists remained clenched. Why?

'Do you like working here, Johanna?'

'Very much. Mr and Mrs Abbot have always treated me well.'

'Did they treat each other well?'

'Yes, they did. I never saw them argue, not once. I think they loved each other. I know Mr Abbot would never do anything to harm Mrs Abbot.'

'Were you here when Matthew Todd visited?'

Johanna's response took Helen by surprise. She turned her back on Helen, and when she spoke, her voice had a tremor in it.

'He used to come here a bit.' No more words would come.

'Johanna?'

Johanna's body gathered itself tightly and then uncoiled as a dreadful cry escaped and echoed through the house. The men in the kitchen looked up. Joe made to move towards the lounge room. Halloran shook his head.

'Stay,' he said.

Johanna turned to face Helen Lord. The

muscles in her face were jumping. Helen waited.

'Matthew Todd tried to rape me!' She stood rigidly, her arms by her side, her fingernails biting into the palms of her hands.

'He tried to rape me.' Her voice was quieter now. Helen's instincts overrode her position, and she took Johanna in her arms. She felt Johanna surrender to the comfort of the embrace; the tension ebbed out of her body until she was limp with exhaustion. Helen eased her into a large armchair, its antimacassar incongruously still in place.

'He tried to rape me,' she whispered one more time. 'I told Timothy, and he didn't believe me.'

⋆   ⋆   ⋆

Tom Scotney admitted without obfuscation that he'd overheard his daughter telling Rose Abbot that Matthew Todd had assaulted her. Johanna and Helen Lord were sitting in the Scotney's lounge room, with Johanna's parents. It had taken less convincing than Helen had expected to get Johanna to reveal Matthew's crime to her parents. The only reason she hadn't done so already, she told Helen, was that she was afraid of what her father would do. It was when she sobbingly tried to explain this to her parents that Tom Scotney had admitted that he'd been listening at the door.

'I'll tell you this,' he said. 'If someone else hadn't got to that little bastard first, I'd have done for him myself. I'm only sorry someone beat me to it.'

Mrs Scotney sought reassurance for the second time that Matthew's assault hadn't actually ended in rape. It was as if, thought Helen, she could cope with a certain level of violation, but anything beyond it might change the way she thought of her daughter.

'Were you at home last night, Mr Scotney?'

Tom laughed.

'Having just said I'd happily kill Todd, I suppose I need an alibi, don't I?'

'I suppose you do.'

'I was here until 4.30 am. There are two people who can prove that — my wife and my daughter.'

'Why 4.30?'

'That's when I left to take the boat out fishing. Sharks don't catch themselves. I was later than usual because . . . '

Mrs Scotney blushed a deep scarlet.

'Well, let's just say I was later than usual. Johanna made me a cup of tea before she headed out to Abbot's farm. We get up early in this house.'

'And you didn't leave the house between midnight and 4.30 am?'

'No, I did not. I was in bed, which the wife will confirm, and I was probably snoring, which Johanna can confirm.'

'Dad was definitely here,' Johanna said.

'I'm glad I've got an alibi, but you know what? I see it as a missed opportunity.'

Helen saw no point in questioning the Scotneys any further. Either Tom Scotney had a solid alibi, or his wife and daughter were both lying. Johanna walked outside with her. Helen realised that she was hungry, having eaten nothing since lunch on the train. It was 8.00 pm.

'Is there anywhere I could get something to eat?'

'There's a fish-and-chip shop in Sackville Street. That should still be open. I'll walk you there.'

The light was beginning to fade, and the smell of the sea was strong in the town.

'That detective, the one with the bruises, he's talking to Timothy, isn't he?'

'Sergeant Sable will be doing that now, yes.'

'Timothy couldn't have killed Matthew Todd. He's a boy.'

'You said he'll be 18 soon.'

'Yes, but he's very young. He wouldn't. He couldn't.'

'Did Rose Abbot ever talk to you about her brother?'

'Mrs Abbot used to listen to me prattling on about Timothy. She was good like that. She didn't talk about her own family much. I know she didn't get on with Mr Todd. When he came to the farm she was never very friendly to him. She didn't like him being there, and she didn't like the way he spoke to her.'

'How did he speak to her?'

'Like he couldn't understand why she'd married Mr Abbot. He really didn't like Mr Abbot. I'm surprised they never came to blows. They were rude to each other.'

'What about Rose and her Aunt Aggie?'

'Oh, Rose definitely didn't get on with old

Miss Todd. Matthew was Miss Todd's favourite. Mrs Abbot did tell me that. She said that whenever she visited her, Miss Todd used to talk about Matthew as if he was the best thing on two legs. Once she said that she thought Miss Todd was in love with Matthew. Not that she loved him, as an aunt would, but that she was in love with him. I thought that was creepy.'

The fish-and-chip shop was on the point of closing. Helen said she'd make it worth their while to stay open, and ordered what she hoped would be enough to feed whoever was still at the police station when she got there.

'What's good?' she asked Johanna.

'Sweet William. It's got no bones, and Dad might've caught it this morning.'

★   ★   ★

The Harrison house was, by Port Fairy standards, rather grand. It was in Philip Street at the western end of the town. Joe drove there in Inspector Halloran's car. There were no lights visible — the result of blackouts still being up. Perhaps the Harrisons were paranoid about an attack from the sea. It was dusk, so finding his way to the front door wasn't a problem, even though there was a long driveway from the street to the house. Joe was glad of the half-light; it would soften the bruises on his face.

The door was opened by a woman in her late fifties. She was thin, elegantly dressed, and with expensively styled hair, which would have been auburn had it not faded to grey.

'Mrs Harrison?'

'Yes.'

'I'm Sergeant Joe Sable, from Melbourne. Is Timothy at home?'

'Are you from the army?'

'No, Mrs Harrison. I'm a police officer from Homicide.'

Mrs Harrison's hand flew to her mouth.

'This is about those dreadful murders, isn't it?'

'May I come in?'

The house smelled of the evening meal being cooked. It was a rich, pleasant odour of something roasting. It didn't smell of austerity.

'I suppose you want to speak to Timothy because he's been stepping out with Johanna. She worked for the dead woman, Rose Abbot, didn't she?'

'Is Timothy home, Mrs Harrison?'

'Yes, yes. He's in his room. Please come through to the living room. My husband is in there. He's an invalid.'

The living room confirmed, if it needed confirming, that there was money in the Harrison family. There was a piano, with silver-framed photographs sitting on top of it, and above the fireplace a portrait in oils of two young boys. It was competently done, a thoroughly professional job, and Joe could see that the signature was William Dargie's. It would have been an expensive commission.

'This is my husband, Albert.'

A good-looking man, his hair thinning, but his face retaining the unlined skin of a much younger man, sat in a plush armchair. He'd been reading a Josephine Tey novel.

'Mr Harrison, I'm Detective Joe Sable.'

Mr Harrison nodded.

'I'm afraid speech is quite difficult for Albert, Sergeant. He was gassed in the last war, and it did a great deal of damage.'

'I'm sorry,' Joe said.

Mr Harrison smiled, stood up, and whispered. 'I heard you say you wanted to speak to Timothy. I'll tell him you're here.'

Joe had expected Albert Harrison's incapacity to have affected his mind, but he should have seen as soon as he laid eyes on him that this wasn't so. His face had none of the slack, imbecile quality of Selwyn Todd's. It was a taut, intelligent face. This might be a quiet house, but it didn't feel to Joe like an empty one. Albert Harrison, unlike Joe's own father, wasn't the embodiment of a paradoxically absent presence.

Timothy Harrison entered the living room, and his mother made the introductions.

'Would you like me to stay, darling, while the detective speaks to you?'

'No,' Timothy said, his voice betraying his nerves. This was probably the first time he'd ever been interviewed by a policeman, so Joe understood that nervousness was a reasonable response. Joe's initial impression of Timothy was that he was tall enough and strong enough to have killed Matthew Todd. There was something not yet fully formed about him.

'You've heard, I presume, Timothy, that Mrs Rose Abbot and Mr Matthew Todd have been murdered.'

'Yes, of course. News like that gets around pretty quickly in Port Fairy.'

'Could you tell me where you were last night between midnight and 5.00 am?'

'What?'

The question seemed to stun Timothy.

'It's a routine enquiry, Timothy.'

'But why would you ask *me* that?'

'You have a friendship with Johanna Scotney, do you not?'

'Johanna is my girl.'

Good grief, Joe thought. *He's seen too many Andy Hardy pictures.* There was no time to watch him grow up slowly, so Joe spoke to him roughly and directly.

'Miss Scotney has told us that she confided in you that Matthew Todd had tried to rape her.'

'She told you that?'

'Do you mean that she'd confided in you, or that she'd been assaulted?'

'She told me those things yesterday, in the gardens.'

'She also said that you didn't believe her.'

Timothy Harrison looked as though he was about to cry.

'But I did believe her. I didn't know what to do.'

'You were the only person she'd confided in. Are you sure you didn't know what to do?'

'What do you mean?'

'Matthew Todd had made obscene advances to your girl. Maybe you thought about that, and maybe you thought someone ought to do something about it.'

Timothy shook his head rapidly.

'So, Timothy, where were you between midnight and 5.00 am yesterday?'

'I was here, asleep.'

'Would anyone know if you slipped out?'

'Timothy didn't slip out, Sergeant.'

Joe hadn't noticed the quiet entrance of Albert Harrison into the room. He was standing just inside the door. In a hoarse, painful whisper, he said, 'Timothy had a nightmare around 2.30. I'm a poor sleeper. I heard him cry out, and I went to him. He's had nightmares since he was a child. I sometimes think that they must be contagious, that he caught them from me. I sat with him until he went back to sleep. My wife will corroborate that.'

'I didn't know I had a nightmare last night.'

'You're lucky, Tim. You don't recall your nightmares.'

'That was at 2.30. What about between midnight and that time?'

'As I say, Sergeant, I'm a poor sleeper. I was awake until well after 1.30, and I would have heard Timothy if he'd left the house. The floorboards in this house are better than a burglar alarm.'

Mrs Harrison, who must have been hovering near the door, came into the living room. She knelt by the chair that Timothy had sat in.

'Oh Tim. Poor Johanna. You must bring her here. She must feel like the world is a terrible place.'

Timothy was trying to keep his tears in check. He failed. Joe let himself out of the house and made his way back to the station. The Harrisons were, he thought, decent people who didn't give a tinker's curse that their son was stepping out with a fisherman's daughter. It was a house where nightmares lay in wait each night for sleepers, but where they were endured and patiently soothed.

★ ★ ★

The smell of fish and chips and malt vinegar assailed Joe's nostrils when he returned to the police station. The newspaper in which they'd been wrapped had only just been torn open. Inspector Halloran, Constables Manton and Filan, and Helen were busy eating their share. A small parcel had been set aside for Constable Adams, which Constable Manton would take him as soon as he'd finished eating.

'There's plenty,' said Helen. 'Dig in.'

They ate in silence, each of them going over the information that had been gathered so far. When everyone had stopped eating, Inspector Halloran said, 'Let's line all our ducks up in a row and see if any of them quack. Sergeant Sable, before we do that, what did you think of Timothy Harrison?'

Joe outlined his interview and his impression of the Harrison family.

'All right,' Halloran said. There was a chalkboard on the wall, and he began to write a list of names on it.

'We have two bodies: Rose Abbot and her brother Matthew Todd.'

He underlined Matthew's name.

'Let's start with him. If his Aunt Aggie is correct, he was a popular and respected member of the Port Fairy community, with one or two enemies, whose names have been supplied by Agnes Todd. We know, however, that our Mr Todd was accused by Johanna Scotney of attempted rape. This alone gives us three credible suspects for his murder: Johanna's father, Tom Scotney, who overheard her telling Rose Abbot that Todd had attacked her; Timothy Harrison, the boy-friend in whom Johanna had confided; and Johanna herself. We'll throw John Abbot in there on the basis that he loathed Matthew Todd. All of these people have solid alibis.'

He underlined Rose Abbot's name.

'We have no suspects in the murder of Rose Abbot. Instead, we have a man who can't tie his own shoelaces, whose sister, Agnes Todd, saw him hit Mrs Abbot with a shovel. Or so she says. Wouldn't it be nice if her death were as straightforward as that? My problem is that I don't believe a word of what Agnes Todd has told us. She wrote a false confession, and it can only have been she who wiped fingerprints from the shovel handle and from the slate. Having interviewed her myself, and having watched Constable Lord slice and dice her version of events, I've changed my mind, and I'm now firmly of the view that it is entirely possible that Agnes Todd wielded the shovel that killed her niece, and that she is willing to sacrifice her brother, Selwyn, to cover her tracks. Why would she do such a terrible thing? I have no idea. And

I have no idea, short of getting her to confess, how we pin this on her. I don't give any credence to her notion that Selwyn was acting on someone's instructions. She helpfully offered up John Abbot to us, but she neglected to mention that it was she who telephoned Rose and summoned her. I've checked with the exchange, and that call was definitely made.

'Now, what muddies these waters into a turbid mess is the murder of Matthew Todd. He was killed much earlier, and elsewhere. I've been to his house; there are no signs of disturbance. The door is unlocked, but no one locks doors in Port Fairy. It would have been simple for someone to enter his house — he might even have invited that person in — and overpower him. It must have been someone strong. Dr Marriott says that the ligature dug deep into his throat, and that strong arms would be necessary to achieve this. That person, either alone, or with help, carried the body to his aunt's house, and propped it grotesquely in her front room. Why? The obvious answer is to both incriminate Agnes Todd and force her to make the discovery of her beloved nephew's corpse. I'd say Matthew Todd's killer hated Aggie Todd almost as much as he hated Matthew Todd. Who among our suspects fits that bill?'

'The only one who comes close,' said Joe, 'is John Abbot. His alibi for the hours between midnight and 4.00 am was his wife, and his wife is dead. We can say with absolute certainty that he had nothing to do with the death of his wife. We can't say that about the death of Matthew

Todd. We know he couldn't stand either Matthew or Miss Todd.'

'Does a person kill someone because he doesn't get on with him socially?' Constable Filan asked. 'The streets of Port Fairy would be knee deep in Catholic and Protestant dead if that was the case.'

'There are people we haven't yet spoken to,' Helen said. 'Matthew's fiancée, Dorothy . . . ?'

'Shipman.'

'Dorothy Shipman. I understand she's been informed of Matthew's death.'

'Of course. Father Brennan has been with the Shipmans all day.'

'He's the Shipmans' priest?'

'He's our parish priest, yes,' Filan said.

'I saw in the notes,' Helen said, 'that Miss Todd suggested that there might be some tension between the fishermen who turned their catch over to the Co-operative and those who used Matthew Todd as their forwarding agent. Is that worth pursuing?'

'Anything is worth pursuing at this stage,' Halloran said. 'This looks too personal to be about money, though.'

'Is it outlandish,' Joe said, 'to suggest that Rose Abbot might have killed her brother, and that Agnes Todd then killed her in revenge?'

'The times don't fit,' Halloran said.

'Unless she and John Abbot came into town and killed Todd. He'd have let them into his house. She could have distracted him. John Abbot could have slipped the ligature around his neck, taken the corpse around the corner to Miss

Todd's place, and driven back to the farm. Miss Todd finds the body in the morning, works out what's happened, and calls her niece.'

'How would she work out what's happened?'

'Maybe John Abbot had issued threats recently. I don't know.'

'Why would Rose, who knew her brother's body was in the front room, agree to drive to her aunt's house?'

'And that,' said Joe, 'is where my scenario falls over.'

They all looked at the blackboard, now with lines, arrows, and under-scorings that made the names on it resemble a physics equation.

'What do we do, sir,' Helen asked, 'if we can't break Agnes Todd's claim about Selwyn?'

'He'll be charged with murder, found incompetent to plea, and locked away in Brierly Mental Hospital.'

'That isn't justice, sir,' Paddy Filan said. 'That just isn't right.'

★   ★   ★

Aggie Todd sat in a chair beside the bed in the spare room of Mrs Cuthbert's house. She didn't want to lie down, and she wanted no light. '*That it should come to this,*' she thought. Could she remember the bit that preceded that fragment from *Hamlet*? Something about the Everlasting having fixed his canon 'gainst self-slaughter, and then, '*Oh God, God, How weary, stale, flat and unprofitable seem to me all the uses of this world.*' God? Where was God in all this? Her

294

soul was now condemned to eternal damnation. Eternal damnation. She remembered a story a nun had told them in an attempt to get them to understand the idea of eternity. Imagine, she'd said, the world as a ball of the hardest material in the universe. Once every thousand years, a sparrow flies by and brushes the edge of the world with its wing. When the sparrow has worn the world down to the size of a pea, eternity hasn't even begun.

Did she really believe all that? Could a dullard like Father Brennan really turn water into wine, and bread into the body of Christ? She couldn't confess and gain absolution for what she'd done to Rose. Would God really blame her for punishing the person who'd murdered Matthew, who was worth ten Roses? What kind of God was that? A vengeful one. Yet if God was vengeful, surely he'd understand righteous vengefulness in others? No. Aggie was too smart to bother with this sort of sophistry. If there was a Hell, she was already in it. One mortal sin was the same as two. Thus, with absolute clarity of purpose, Agnes Todd made the decision to take her own life.

Mrs Cuthbert, deaf as a post, didn't hear her leave by the back door. She went out through the back gate and opened the gate into her own property. She turned the light on in the kitchen, found what she was looking for in the cupboard under the sink, poured a glass of water into a saucepan on the stove, and stirred the embers in the firebox into flames. She took a bottle of brandy from a shelf and opened it.

Fletcher Adams was impatient to be relieved of his surveillance. He was bored numb. The fish and chips had been welcome, and he had to admit that he was glad to have copped the first shift and not the second. At least he'd be in his own bed soon. Filan was expected to get a few hours' sleep and to take over at midnight, which was fast approaching.

Adams crossed the road, and walked up and down in front of the Cuthbert house. On his second pass he noticed that a light had come on in Aggie Todd's house next door. He slammed his leather bobby's helmet on his head and ran around the corner and down the lane that ran behind the houses in James Street. The gate to the Todd house was open. Aggie Todd was in the kitchen, with her back to the window. The silly woman was supposed to stay away from the house. Adams strode to the back door, cross that she should oblige him to intervene so close to the change of shift. He opened the unlocked door and gave Aggie Todd such a fright that she yelped.

'What are you doing here?' he said tersely. 'This place is off limits. That has been explained to you.'

Aggie recovered quickly.

'I couldn't sleep, so I thought I'd just pop over and make myself a cup of warm water and brandy. Mrs Cuthbert doesn't have any brandy. She's a teetotaller.'

'The water's boiling.'

Adams' irritation abated rapidly. What was the harm in an old lady wanting a glass of warm water and brandy?

'Would you like a brandy?'

Adams thought for a moment.

'Why not?'

Aggie had replaced the item she'd taken from under the sink, and her mug was already out on the table beside the brandy bottle. She retrieved a glass from the cupboard.

'You can pour your own brandy,' she said, and handed him the glass and the bottle. She then poured hot water into her mug. Adams treated himself to a generous slug of brandy, and returned the bottle to Aggie. She splashed an equally generous amount into her mug. Adams raised his glass to his lips and sipped. It was good. The brandy caught pleasantly at the back of his throat. Aggie was watching him over the rim of her mug, the steam from which she was breathing in deeply.

'You're very young,' she said. 'They say policemen get younger as we get older. How old are you?'

'I'm 24.'

'Are you married?'

'Yes.'

He took another sip while, to his surprise, Aggie took large gulps from her mug. It must have burned her mouth, surely. She finished her drink and put the mug on the table, or tried to. It fell to the floor. She staggered, her eyes grew wide with fear, and her breathing became ugly pants. She fell, rather than sat, into a chair, where her body convulsed violently. Fletcher Adams was paralysed with horror. She gurgled and coughed, and her face became a jumping, quivering dance of muscles as great spasms of agony ripped through her. One final, terrifying rasp escaped her, and she was still.

Adams was open-mouthed, stunned into immobility. Aggie Todd's bladder emptied, and Adams knew that she was dead. *My God, was there something in the brandy?* He felt weak and nauseated. Had she poisoned them both? He picked up the brandy bottle, smelled it, and held it to the light. It was clean. She hadn't poisoned him. The mug that Aggie had drunk from hadn't broken when it hit the floor, and Adams was now sufficiently calm to use his handkerchief to pick it up. At the bottom of the mug were granulated white dregs. He smelled it and quickly put it down, well away from him. He was pretty sure it was cyanide. Where would Miss Todd get cyanide? Adams opened cupboards and drawers. He found nothing until he opened the cupboard under the sink. Very carefully, making sure he didn't smudge any prints, he withdrew a canister of wasp powder. He'd used this stuff in his own garden, and he knew how dangerous it was. The active ingredient in the wasp pesticide was cyanide, and Adams thought that Aggie Todd must have drunk enough of the stuff to kill a horse.

'Jesus Christ!'

Constable Filan stepped into the kitchen. He'd arrived to relieve Adams, found that he wasn't about, and seen the light in the Todd house.

'She's just fucking killed herself, right in front of me!'

'What are you holding?'

'Wasp dust. Cyanide. I couldn't stop her. It all happened so fast.'

'This looks bad, Fletcher. This looks very, very bad.'

★   ★   ★

Doctor Marriott had declared Agnes Todd dead, and taken blood samples. He'd arrived within half an hour of Agnes' death to find Sergeant Joe Sable, Constable Helen Lord, Constable Paddy Filan, and Constable Fletcher Adams gathered in the kitchen. Paddy Filan had photographed the scene. Marriott had hurried because Filan had told him that cyanide was suspected. Because cyanide dissipated quickly in the body, it was important to get a blood sample within the first hour to get an accurate sense of how much had been ingested. Inspector Halloran wouldn't yet have arrived back in Warrnambool; as the car wasn't fitted with wireless radio, he'd hear about Aggie's death from a message left with his wife. Joe had asked that he telephone the Todd house rather than turn around and drive back to Port Fairy.

Fletcher Adams was relieved that he wouldn't have to speak to Halloran until the morning. He answered all of Joe's and Helen's questions without ducking and weaving. He made no attempt to disguise the fact that he'd been offered a glass of brandy and that he'd accepted the offer. He knew that he faced probable dismissal, but he'd already decided to save

Inspector Halloran the trouble by resigning. Policing was a world he wanted nothing more to do with. Standing here, in a dimly lit kitchen, looking at the tortured face of an elderly dead woman wasn't his idea of a satisfying career choice.

The telephone rang, and Joe spoke with Inspector Halloran. He was incandescent with fury. There was, however, no point in his coming back to Port Fairy now. He needed to get some sleep. There were no suspicious circumstances. Constable Adams had witnessed Aggie Todd's suicide, which had the advantage of removing any ambiguities about her death. Discussions about its implications could wait until the morning.

With Agnes Todd's body having been sent to the morgue to join her niece and nephew, the police retired to their respective beds. Fletcher Adams, who was driving the coal-burning vehicle, couldn't help thinking that, with his luck, the unreliable bloody car would choose this night, of all nights, to break down. He was right. Halfway between Port Fairy and Warrnambool, the engine sputtered and died. He grimly accepted that this had been inevitable, pushed the dead lump to the side of the road, got back into the driver's seat, and tried to sleep. No doubt, Inspector Halloran would blame him for this, too.

13

Late on Monday afternoon, Sergeant David Reilly knocked on Inspector Lambert's door. He had information that was both disturbing and of great value.

'We may be getting closer to George Starling, sir.'

Lambert leaned back in his chair.

'How so?'

'Ron Dunnart has been busy. He's on his best behaviour, and, I have to say, he's more than competent as an investigator.'

'I've never doubted his skills, Sergeant — only his ethics.'

'We have the identities of the two bodies in the private club.'

'Excellent.'

'The building is owned by an elderly man named Jimmy O'Farrell. He lives in South Australia. All his properties, and he has a few, are managed for him by his son, Brendan. According to O'Dowd, who went to St Kilda and interviewed this Brendan O'Farrell, he's a bit of a standover man. He was very uncooperative until it was pointed out to him that being an accessory to a murder that happened in what a court might decide was a male brothel wouldn't be good for whatever reputation he had. He claims he had no idea that the room he rented out was being used for anything illegal. The man who paid the rent is a Sturt Menadue. O'Farrell was most reluctant, but O'Dowd was very persuasive and got him to go down to the morgue and identify the body. It's Menadue, all right. Menadue's home address is a flat in Prahran. It's been searched, and that didn't turn up much. There was an address book.'

Reilly produced the book. It was small and brown, bound in leather, with thin brass edging to protect the corners. Inspector Lambert flicked through it.

'There aren't many names here. They may just be friends, rather than regulars at the club.'

Two pages fell loose, from near the front of the book. The connecting pages, on either side of the stitched divide, were missing. Titus put the pages back and handed the book to Reilly. He didn't need to say anything. Both men suspected what this meant.

'And the young man?'

'We know who he is, too. He's a waiter at the Windsor Hotel, but he didn't show up for work this morning. He'd never been late or absent before, so the hotel telephoned his mother, whom he lives with. She wasn't concerned about his not coming home over the weekend; but when he failed to turn up for work, she contacted the police. She identified his body a couple of hours ago. His name is Steven McNamara.

'Now, this is where it gets interesting. Ron Dunnart had a look at the hotel's register, and a George Starling had booked in late on Friday, stayed Saturday night, and booked out on Sunday. The description given by the *maître d'*, and by waiters who recalled him, didn't sound like our George Starling. They described a well-dressed man who took great care with his appearance. He was always closely shaved, and his hair was trimmed and Brilliantined. They thought his manners were a bit rough. He was, however, obviously a wealthy man. He paid in cash. I took the sketch of Starling down to the Windsor, and the *maître d'* was almost positive that that was the man. The waiters in the dining room were less sure. Steven McNamara was this George Starling's breakfast waiter on Saturday morning.'

'What about the room Starling stayed in?'

'It's been cleaned, and an American officer and his wife are staying there. We had a quick look, but it was pointless.'

'And Starling didn't give any indication where he was headed.'

'No. Do you think it's him, sir?'

'He'd have to produce identification in order to register. It seems extraordinarily risky for him to do that, but he must have thought that the Windsor Hotel would be the last place we'd go looking for him — and he was right. It's an unusual name, George Starling. Where did he get the money?'

'He was at his father's house. There, maybe?'

'Yes, maybe. I think it's him.'

'Even if it isn't our George Starling, this man had contact with Steven McNamara on the morning of his death. Ron wants to find him. His sudden departure from the Windsor is suspicious.'

'What's Dunnart's strategy?'

'He thinks this man might move to another hotel. He's got people checking the register of every flash hotel in town. They're looking for either George Starling or Sturt Menadue, who had no papers on him. He wouldn't use McNamara's papers. The date of birth would give him away.'

'This is very good. Will you let Ron Dunnart know that you've brought me up to speed?'

'Yes, sir. Any word from Port Fairy?'

Titus looked at his watch.

'They'll only just have arrived. I'll keep you informed.'

★ ★ ★

Not long after George Starling had learned David Reilly's last name, he experienced a moment of intense anxiety. It had nothing to do with Reilly. It was about his money. He'd left it in his suitcase, in his room at the Australia Hotel. If he'd been a member of the hotel's staff, he'd have made sure that he checked people's rooms for valuables, and helped himself. He therefore assumed that someone would be stuffing his pockets with his, Starling's, cash. He ran most of the way back to the hotel, which drew stares from the people he rushed past and bumped into. No one had been in his room. The money was safe. He'd given himself a needless fright, and, as the suitcase wasn't heavy, he decided that he'd carry it with him wherever he went. If it became too much of an inconvenience, he'd put it in a locker at Flinders Street

Railway Station. He certainly wasn't going to hand it over for safekeeping at the hotel. He didn't trust them. The concierge asked if everything was satisfactory, or was Mr Menadue checking out?

'Everything's fine,' Starling said. 'I'm not checking out.' He offered no explanation as to why he was carrying his suitcase. It was none of their business.

The suitcase quickly became a nuisance, though. Starling hired a locker at the railway station, and because he'd never been inside it, he ducked into the Glaciarium nearby to watch people ice-skating. Music blared through loud speakers. 'Weekend in Havana', 'Don't Sit Under the Apple Tree', and 'Praise the Lord and Pass the Ammunition' sent people gliding around the rink, or squealing as they stumbled and fell. How ridiculous and frivolous they were. He left before his temper got the better of him. With nothing better to do, he retrieved his suitcase and walked to the City Baths at the top end of Swanston Street. A session on the Roman rings would do him good, and he couldn't be bothered waiting until 8.00 pm for the mixed-bathing session. He'd tire out his muscles, maybe swim, and have a hot bath. That would put him in a good frame of mind to extract information from the detective named Reilly.

Starling loved everything about the City Baths. The gymnasium wasn't crowded, and it smelled of sweat and lineament. The pool at this hour had only three men in it — two American soldiers, by their accents, and a flabby office worker. He had a lane to himself, and he swam ten laps. He was self-conscious about the clumsiness of his stroke, having learned it from observation and not instruction, so he was very pleased not to be looked at. He showered, and spent ten minutes in a deep, hot bath. It had been a long time since he'd felt something that came this close to contentment.

He changed into the second suit he'd bought. It was a dark, charcoal-grey number that had cost more than Peter Hurley paid him in a week. At 5.00 pm he was standing opposite police headquarters in Russell Street. With unusual patience, he waited for half an hour, and was rewarded when David Reilly stepped down into Russell Street. He wasn't alone: there were two other detectives with him. One of them was the man Starling had seen at the private club. The other was familiar, too. He'd seen him in the yard of his father's house in Mepunga. They were moving quickly. Starling followed them to Collins Street, and then realised where they were headed. Outside the Australia Hotel, three uniformed men were waiting for them. The man he'd seen in Mepunga gave them instructions, and they all went inside. Starling crossed to the southern side of Collins Street, put his suitcase down, and waited.

After a few minutes, two of the detectives emerged. The man named Reilly sat on a bench near the tram stop to the right of the hotel's entrance. The other man leaned against a shop window on the other side of the entrance. Starling knew that they were waiting for him. They'd identified the bodies, and they'd made a connection between him and Steven McNamara. They must have seen his name in the Windsor Hotel's register. One of them was smart, and had figured out that he might use Sturt Menadue's identity papers to register at another hotel. Well, he'd saved himself some money. He hadn't paid for his room in advance. He had his suitcase; he hadn't left anything in the room, except his fingerprints. They were welcome to those — much good it would do them. They would have checked all the hotels in town for George Starling and Sturt Menadue, so he'd have to postpone his meeting with the Reilly bloke. That was fine. He'd do that tomorrow. For now, he'd take a tram up to Carlton, where his motorcycle was parked near the cemetery, its spare fuel hidden nearby. There were plenty of hotels in the northern suburbs where no one would think of asking for identification papers, and where rooms were cheap. It'd be a bit of a comedown. Still, it pleased him to know that he was one step ahead of the coppers. Finding Sable was, however, more urgent now. He would take Reilly in the morning, and he had a whole night to think about how.

★　★　★

'Do you think the air will ever stop smelling of smoke?' Maude asked.

Maude Lambert and her brother, Tom Mackenzie, were sitting in his small back garden. It was late, well after ten, and Titus hadn't yet arrived from work.

307

'It's not an unpleasant smell, is it?' Tom said.

It was a simple-enough reply, but everything he said made Maude's heart sing. He was recovering at an astonishing rate, or he seemed to be. His physical injuries troubled him badly, but his mental state had improved so dramatically that it was as if someone had turned a switch in his head from 'off' to 'on'.

'I suppose it is quite nice,' Maude said. 'Aromatic. It represents such loss, though, doesn't it?'

'Titus works long hours. Is it always like this?'

'Not always. Unfortunately, people don't kill each other only during business hours.'

'I didn't imagine George Starling, Maudie. He *was* there.'

'The reason we're here at your house, Tom, is because Titus knows that you weren't just having a waking nightmare.'

'So he doesn't think I'm crazy.'

'No one thinks that.'

'I sometimes think it.'

By the time Titus made it to Tom's house, Tom had gone to bed. Maude had tried to keep a meal of cold lamb and salad palatable by putting it in the icebox. Titus, indifferent as always to the quality of the food he ate, cleared his plate. He was reluctant to join Maude in bed because he'd heard nothing from Port Fairy. He knew there would have been good reasons for this, and when the telephone call finally came through at 1.00 am, it took all his powers of concentration to overcome his exhausted mind and follow the complicated sequence of events.

The suicide of Agnes Todd was particularly frustrating, and the consequences for Selwyn Todd troubled him. He'd speak to Greg Halloran in the morning and get his advice on whether or not he should come down to Port Fairy. He woke Maude when he got into bed. She'd have been furious if he hadn't done so. She saw immediately that a great injustice seemed inevitable, and saw too that finding a solution to the murder of Matthew Todd might resist all the skills that the police had to offer. Short of a confession, the investigation looked depressingly as if it had been snookered. Having talked it through, at least Titus was able to sleep.

'I'm glad anyway,' he said, before dropping off, 'that Joe is out of harm's way in Port Fairy. George Starling is still in Melbourne. We know that for certain.'

* * *

The Lord Lutteral Hotel in Coburg, a suburb about three miles to the north of Melbourne's city centre, wasn't a dive. It wasn't grand either. At least Starling didn't have to share a room; and the linen, although it smelled damp, looked clean. The proprietor was surprised that a man as expensively dressed as Starling would request a room there. He told his wife later that the suitcase probably meant that he'd been thrown out of the house by his wife, that this sort of thing was none of his business, and that asking about it was a recipe for being shirt-fronted. He'd managed to avoid being worked over by his patrons by not asking them too many questions. If they wanted to talk, they'd do it at the bar after a few drinks.

On Tuesday morning, Starling rose early. He hadn't yet bought a razor, and he didn't much care for the beard-shadowed face that met him in the bathroom mirror. He went downstairs to pay the bill, and had to wake the hotel owner to do so. The man came to the bar in pyjama bottoms and no top — a sight that Starling found unappealing.

'Is there a barber around here?'

'There's a Greek bloke up the road. He opens at eight.'

'How far is it up the road?'

'About a ten-minute walk.'

Starling paid and left. By the time he got to the barber it would be eight o'clock, so Starling decided to walk instead of wasting petrol. He was the first customer. The barber was a bad advertisement for his own business: he could have done with a shave himself. As Starling waited for him to strop the razor and prepare the shaving cream, he flicked through that week's copy of *Truth*. It was a rag, but it was good for the stories that *The Age* and *The Argus* wouldn't touch. Divorce, rape, murder, and adultery were its bread and butter. *Truth* knew its patriotic duty, and reported war news on its front page. Beyond that, it was business as usual. Starling sat bolt upright in the chair, just as the barber was about to apply the cream. On page three, a headline screamed: 'Port Fairy Murders Rock Town. Village Idiot Main Suspect. Police

Tight-lipped.' There was a photograph of two detectives and a woman coming out of a house. They weren't identified, but they didn't need to be. George Starling would have recognised Joe Sable anywhere, and he'd seen that woman in Mepunga.

'You ready?' the barber asked.

'Quick as you can,' Starling said.

Thirty-five minutes later, Starling was on his motorcycle and on his way to Port Fairy.

★   ★   ★

The Belfast café in Bank Street served eggs from its owners' chooks, chokoes from the garden, and scones instead of toast. It was an unexpectedly satisfying breakfast. Also unexpected was the photograph in that morning's *Port Fairy Gazette*. It was similar to the one that had been flown to Melbourne the previous evening in time to make it into *Truth*. The headline in the *Gazette* was less lurid, more sensitive perhaps to local sensitivities: 'Todd Family Tragedy'. The story, cobbled together from neighbours' comments, speculation, and gossip, offered nothing of interest to Joe or Helen. No one from the press had approached them.

'Someone must have collared Paddy Filan or Inspector Halloran. They must have given them nothing,' Joe said.

'The parents are coming today. I can't imagine how they'll cope with this.'

The waitress, who was no more than 16, refilled the teapot.

311

'That's you in the paper, isn't it?' she said, and looked awestruck, as if a movie star had dropped into the Belfast café.

'What's your name?' Helen asked.

'Elizabeth, but Betty's what I'm called.'

'Did you know the Todd family, Betty?'

'Too grand to talk to me. I seen them at church and that. Rose was all right. I didn't like the way her husband gawked at me but. She was good. She come in here once or twice, for a malted milk. That Matthew wouldn't be seen dead in here. Pardon me. He was stuck up, walking around with his nose in the air. Thought he was it and a bit.'

'Did you know Miss Todd?'

'Saw her at church, too. Never spoke to her. There's the subo brother too. Selwyn. The paper reckons he went troppo and done it. Is that right? Is he locked up?'

Helen ignored the question.

'What about Matthew's fiancée, Dorothy? Do you know her?'

'She's all right. She works in the draper's. She's a bit stuck up, but not like the Todds. Don't know what she sees in Matthew.'

'Was he a bit of a gawker?'

Betty sniffed.

'They're all gawkers.'

'Thanks Betty, you've been most helpful.'

Betty took the hint.

'Happy to help, I'm sure,' she said and went back behind the counter. Another customer came in. Betty said something to her, and she turned to stare at Joe and Helen.

'The town's had 24 hours to talk about Rose and Matthew,' Joe said. 'Imagine the shock when they find out about Miss Todd.'

'Things like this can tear a small town apart. We need to find out who killed Matthew Todd before the rumour mill starts condemning innocent people.'

'Do you want to talk to Dorothy Shipman, or should we both do it?'

'I'll do it.'

'I'll talk to the priest, and see what he can tell me about the Todds. There must be someone lurking in this town who hated Matthew Todd enough to kill him.'

'And who doesn't have a bloody alibi.'

★   ★   ★

Helen and Joe checked in at the police station before beginning their interviews. Inspector Halloran and Constable Manton had arrived, but Constable Adams had been left behind in Warrnambool. Aggie Todd's death and its implications were discussed briefly. Manton was to visit the wharf and talk to the fishermen, if they weren't all out in the Southern Ocean. Aggie Todd had mentioned, probably mischievously, that there were men in the Co-op who didn't like Matthew Todd. Joe would join Manton after speaking to the priest. Inspector Halloran said that Inspector Lambert had asked whether he ought to come to Port Fairy, just as an extra pair of hands.

'I don't think he needs to come,' Helen said.

'We're scheduled to leave on Thursday as it is.'

Feeling that she sounded miffed, she added, 'What do you think, sir?'

'I agree with you, Constable.' He smiled. 'I've already told him that he'd be in the way. Are you happy with that, Sergeant?'

'Yes, sir.'

'Any thoughts before we go our separate ways?'

'Mr and Mrs Todd, sir,' Joe said.

'They'll be here at lunchtime. I'll talk to them. I'm not looking forward to it. Anything else?'

'This case, sir,' Helen said. 'It seems so contained. It should solve itself, yet the closer we look at it, the more elusive it gets. There's so much physical evidence, but it's so confounding that we're forced to work from assumptions. And what if every one of those assumptions is wrong?'

'What are our assumptions, Constable?'

'We're assuming that the person who killed Rose Abbot isn't the same person who killed Matthew Todd.'

'Because of Agnes Todd's evidence,' Halloran said.

'We're assuming that she was lying, in which case we're assuming she killed Rose.'

'We do know that Matthew died hours earlier than Rose, and that he died somewhere else. That's not an assumption.'

'But assumptions flow from it. We're still assuming it implies a different perpetrator. We're assuming that all the alibis are solid.'

'We're not assuming that at all. However, I

agree with you that none of our assumptions are safe. My own assumption is that we're all proceeding on that basis.'

'Yes, sir.'

'Thank you for reminding us of that, and I mean it. It's a timely reminder.'

⋆　⋆　⋆

Shipman's Drapery was closed.

'They're at home, love,' a woman said. She'd seen Helen peering through the window. 'There's been a tragedy in the family.'

'Yes. Can you tell me their home address?'

'Are you a friend of the family? I haven't seen you in town before.'

'Yes. I'm a friend from out of town.' This seemed easier than declaring that she was that freakish object, a policewoman.

The Shipman house was busy with people. Women were bringing pots of food, and men were standing outside, smoking. The door was open, so Helen walked into the house uninvited. Tragedy brought strangers along, so no one challenged her. For all anyone knew, she was a cousin of Dorothy's.

Dorothy was in the living room. She was seated, and people were moving around her. She, however, was perfectly still. She wasn't crying. Her face looked gaunt, as if tears already shed had drained it. Helen had never seen anyone so ruined by grief. She felt nervous about talking to her, but reminded herself that Dorothy Shipman might well have had a reason to kill Matthew

Todd. Had she discovered that her fiancé had tried to rape Johanna Scotney? The emotionally eviscerated woman who sat before her seemed an unlikely suspect, but questions needed to be asked. Helen knelt down in front of Dorothy and took a limp hand in hers.

'Miss Shipman, I'm a policewoman from Melbourne. My name is Constable Helen Lord, and I know this is a very difficult time, but I wonder if I could speak to you in private.'

Dorothy looked at Helen in stupefied wonder.

'A policewoman?'

'Yes. I'm here to help investigate the tragic death of your fiancé, and of his sister. Is there somewhere we could talk?'

Dorothy nodded. She wasn't quite the comatose person she appeared to be. She stood up, waved away anxious, fluttering hands that reached out to support her, and led Helen into the privacy of her bedroom. She sat on the bed, and Helen sat at her vanity.

'Please understand, Miss Shipman, that the questions I must ask are not intended to upset you.'

'Of course, I understand. You'll want to know if I had any reason to murder my fiancé, and you'll want to know where I was on Sunday night.'

'Thank you for making this easier for me.'

'I'm a practical person, Constable. It seems funny to be calling a woman 'Constable'. I had no reason to kill Matthew. I loved him. I loved him completely. I wasn't blind to his faults. I knew that I could fix those after we were married. Oh, they were small things.'

'Did you see Matthew on Sunday?'

'I saw Matthew every day. On Sunday, we went to Mass with Miss Todd, Matthew's aunt.' She stopped suddenly. 'Oh, poor Miss Todd. She doted on Matthew. This must be so terrible for her. I haven't even spoken to her yet. She must feel so terribly alone. She must come here. She must come here now.'

Helen couldn't withhold the truth about Aggie Todd from Dorothy, although she knew the blow would land with terrible force.

'Miss Shipman, I'm very sorry, but Miss Todd is dead.' She almost said 'has passed away'. This seemed ludicrously passive when applied to a suicide.

Dorothy's mouth opened in a silent gawp, and she fell back on the bed in a faint. Helen hurried to find her father, and he returned with her to the bedroom. They found Dorothy, white as a sheet, sweat running down her face, trying to stand. They sat her back down. Helen closed the bedroom door.

'Miss Shipman has had a shock.'

'What do you mean?' Mr Shipman asked.

Helen showed Mr Shipman her credentials.

'I'm afraid Miss Agnes Todd took her own life last night.'

'That's not possible,' Mr Shipman said firmly. 'Agnes Todd wouldn't endanger her immortal soul by taking her own life.'

'No, no, no,' Dorothy said. She began to tear at her hair. 'No! No! No!' Her screams brought people running to the bedroom. Dorothy, in the

317

grip of wild hysteria, began to thrash and beat at her face. Two women restrained her. They looked appalled, and admonished her not to carry on so. Dorothy began to convulse alarmingly.

'Put her on her side,' another woman said, 'on the floor. We don't want her biting her tongue.'

Mr Shipman was rigid with horror at the sight of his daughter, her dress dragged up over her thighs, her mouth flecked with saliva, and her limbs jolting grotesquely. The woman who issued the instruction to put Dorothy on her side took Mr Shipman by the arm and ushered him out of the room. This was no place for a man.

'Someone call Doctor Marriott,' she said.

Helen followed Mr Shipman, who was helped to the living room. The news of Aggie Todd's suicide passed from person to person, and Helen saw several people hurry away from the Shipman house, carrying the news to the town. A large brandy was brought to Mr Shipman.

'Mr Shipman,' Helen said firmly. 'Did either you or your daughter leave the house at any time between midnight and 4.00 am on Sunday night?'

It seemed such an extraordinary question in the middle of all the tumult that several people were taken aback.

'Of course not,' he said. 'Sunday night is always the same.'

Helen had no idea what that might mean, beyond its referring to an unchanging routine. She had no doubt, though, that the Shipmans were so overwhelmed by Matthew's and now Aggie's death that neither of them was implicated in this crime.

As Helen walked back to the police station, she berated herself for mishandling the interview. In her hurry to get out of that storm of emotions, had she made a convenient assumption? She had. Of course she had. She'd discovered nothing, and she'd come away without a firm alibi for either Dorothy or her father. She'd have to speak to them again, and she'd forewarned them that they both needed an alibi. *Please God*, she thought, *don't let it be one of the Shipmans.*

★ ★ ★

Father Brennan's housekeeper brought a pot of tea into the front room of the presbytery, where Father Brennan sat opposite Joe. The presbytery smelled of last night's chops and cabbage. Joe had never spoken to a Catholic priest before, and he thought it peculiar that this man, when asked how he should be addressed, said, 'Father.' Joe tried it.

'Father, Matthew Todd and Rose Abbot and their aunt, Agnes Todd, were members of your church?'

'Matthew and Rose were, and Agnes is, Sergeant.'

Joe was unable to repeat the word 'Father'.

'I'm sorry to tell you that Miss Agnes Todd died late last night, and I'm afraid all the indications are that she took her own life.'

Father Brennan crossed himself, closed his eyes, and said, 'May God have mercy on her soul. She can't have been in a sane state of mind.

319

Are you sure the poor woman took her own life?'

'Yes, we're sure.'

'God will see that the deaths of Matthew and Rose, Matthew especially, were too much to bear. He will be merciful. We'll pray the Rosary for their immortal souls. Are you a Catholic man, Sergeant?'

'I'm Jewish.'

'Ah. Our Lord was a Jew.'

'You said Miss Todd would have been especially distressed by Matthew's death. Why is that?'

'Agnes and Matthew were very close. I think she saw him as the son she never had. Rose and she were less so. I don't know why.'

'Did Miss Todd confide in you in any way?'

'Confession is a kind of confidence, I suppose.'

'Did she tell you anything in Confession that might be of assistance in this investigation?'

'Ah, now, Jews don't have the blessed sacrament of Confession, do they? The seal of the Confessional can never be broken, Sergeant.'

'This is a murder investigation.'

'My understanding was that poor, simple Selwyn lost his mind completely, and did these things in a rage.'

'Our investigations are ongoing.' Still he couldn't bring himself to say 'Father'.

'Was Matthew Todd a well-liked man in Port Fairy?'

'I think he was. I can only speak for my congregation.'

'Did the fishermen like him?'

'He did well by the men who employed him.'

'What about the Co-operative?'

'There was some tension there. Men don't like to think that other men are doing better than they are. It wasn't a big thing. No one came to blows.'

'Was there anyone in particular who made a noise about Matthew?'

'Now, I wouldn't like to name a man, but Teddy Turnbull used to mouth off in the pub about Matthew. I heard him do it myself.'

'And where might I find him.'

'New Guinea.'

Over the next half-hour, Joe formed the opinion that Father Brennan wasn't very bright. For a man who heard the private anxieties of his parishioners in Confession, he had little to offer by way of insight into their characters. He knew how much each person put on the plate, and who was married to whom, and who was prone to gout. He seemed not to know how any of them thought, or how they felt about themselves or one another. 'He was a grand man' and 'She was a good wife' were as complicated as he got. They all believed, and therefore felt, the same things. Doctrine calmed the chaos of people's thoughts. Father Brennan knew his doctrine, and he could apply it to any situation.

'We'll get through this terrible time,' he said to Joe. 'We'll pray hard for Selwyn and for the souls of the departed. Our greatest strength is prayer.'

Joe left the presbytery feeling slightly depressed. He'd hoped to find in the priest a man of quiet wisdom. Father Brennan wasn't a theologian. He was dull, mediocre, and pious — because, Joe suspected, that was easier than being brilliant.

At four o'clock, the five investigators reconvened at the police station. Inspector Halloran had met Andrew and Phillipa Todd. They were like sleepwalkers, he said. Mrs Todd had summoned a spark of anger when Halloran had asked if they'd like to see Selwyn.

'Are you serious?' she'd said. 'That ape killed our children.' She wasn't prepared to listen when Halloran tried to explain that this had not, in fact, been proven to be true.

'It's true, all right,' she'd hissed, and Halloran had seen no advantage in pressing her to understand the complexities of the case. They'd insisted on seeing all three bodies. Mr Todd had been stoic. Halloran could see the muscles in his jaw clenching and unclenching as he struggled not to break down. Mrs Todd collapsed when she saw her daughter's battered face. With Halloran's help, Mr Todd carried her to the car. She woke, and seemed dazed, and then she cried so violently that she was sick.

'They're staying at Matthew's house. The priest was going to call on them this afternoon.'

Will they find comfort there? Joe wondered. Brennan would pray. Perhaps that would be all that they'd expect. It seemed meagre to Joe.

Helen's retelling of what had happened at the Shipmans was as accurate as she could make it. Halloran said that grief and shock were forms of temporary insanity, and that getting information in those circumstances was difficult. The level of upheaval in that house was suggestive, as Helen had said, of emotions inconsistent with the planning and execution of a murder.

Joe tried to be polite about Father Brennan. Paddy Filan was a Catholic, after all. He was relieved when Paddy agreed that Brennan was the kind of priest who would never be given an important parish.

'You can't imagine him, can you,' Filan said, 'sitting down with Doctor Mannix to discuss some thorny issue?'

Brennan had mentioned the conflict between the Co-operative and the fishermen who used Matthew as their forwarding agent. Unfortunately, the only man he could name was currently in New Guinea. Joe, Manton, and Filan had spent the afternoon talking to men on the wharf. Several fishermen were out in the Southern Ocean, but there were some who'd taken the opportunity to earn a bit of cash by helping with the dredging of the river mouth. This had to be done regularly to prevent it silting up, blocking access to the sea. Matthew Todd wasn't the popular figure those closest to him insisted he was. He was seen on the wharf as a man who used his family name to big-note himself. The general consensus was that he looked down his snooty nose on the fishermen, even those he represented, and that he'd never done a decent day's work in his life. No strong leads came out of the interviews with the wharf workers. The fishermen out at sea would be followed up later, but feelings about Matthew didn't run hot. He was disliked, resented even. There wasn't much passion in the dislike or the resentment.

'The general feeling seemed to be,' Constable Manton said, 'that you'd cross the street to avoid him, but you wouldn't cross the street to kill him.'

'The town seems quiet, Constable Filan,' Halloran said. 'Two murders in a small community would usually generate fear and paranoia.'

'People think the murderer is already in custody, sir. They think this was a family matter. If they thought there was a killer at large, we'd have the town councillors breathing down our necks. This hasn't frightened people. It's given them plenty to talk about.'

'I believe Selwyn Todd is being transferred to Warrnambool tomorrow,' Halloran said. 'Agnes Todd's witness statement means we can't risk releasing him into the community. There's nobody who'd take him, anyway.'

'Where will they put him?' Joe asked.

'The Brierly Mental Hospital in Warrnambool. There are no other options.'

The group was silent.

'Will the funerals be held here, sir?'

'Mr and Mrs Todd want the funeral of their children to be held here in St Patrick's. They're hoping Monsignor Andrews from Warrnambool will conduct the service. The bodies should be released on Thursday.'

'What about Agnes Todd?'

Constable Filan answered.

'I don't think Miss Todd can be given a requiem Mass. She was a suicide, and suicides are generally denied a church burial. The Todds are influential, though, so perhaps they'll work something out with Father Brennan.'

'I don't think Phillipa Todd will be working too hard to do Agnes Todd any favours, even after death,' Halloran said. 'For now, I want us to sit down and review every scrap of information we have. Somewhere among all those convenient alibis there has to be a weakness. We have three bodies, and we're only certain about one of them — and we're only certain about that because one of us wasn't doing his job properly.'

No one challenged Inspector Halloran's assessment of Constable Adams. Each of them, though, wondered if he or she would have been able to prevent Agnes Todd from taking her own life.

★ ★ ★

George Starling didn't want to roar into town and draw attention to himself, so he parked his motorcycle in scrub above the rock pools known as Pea Soup. Leaving his suitcase with the bike, having first put the money in his pockets, he set out. It would take him 20 minutes to walk into Port Fairy. He turned into James Street and headed north. If he'd continued along the road he was on, he would have ended up in Gipps Street, which would have obliged him to pass the courthouse and the nearby police station. He wasn't ready to do this. He saw up ahead that there were people gathered in groups of twos and threes. Their attention was focussed on a house on the opposite side of the street. Starling pulled his hat low so that it obscured his eyes, and walked casually towards them. When he reached them, a woman who'd watched his approach said, 'Are you one of the detectives?'

It took Starling a moment to register that his suit must have led her to assume that he might be a person of some importance.

'No,' he said politely. 'Has something happened here?'

'Lord,' she said. 'You must have just arrived from the moon. Has something happened? I'll say it has. That house opposite? Three people dead in it. It gives you the creeps just looking at it.'

'Are the police inside?'

'Nah. It's all locked up. The detectives are at the station. That's what Mrs Henny says. She says she saw them all go into the station half-an-hour ago. Who'd have thought that such a thing could happen here? Like I say, it gives you the creeps.'

Starling was about to move off when she added, 'One of the detectives is a woman. Can you imagine that? I know they're collecting tickets on the trams now, but a lady detective! I mean, it doesn't fill you with confidence, does it?'

Starling smiled, but there was no warmth in it. He continued on his way. The town felt different to him now that he had money in his pocket. He didn't think anyone would recognise him. He'd kept out of everyone's way in the two weeks that he'd been there. He'd spoken to shopkeepers and to his landlord, but he'd never lingered for a chat. He was fairly sure that if they remembered

326

him at all, it wouldn't be with any clarity. He'd been scruffy, his clothes dirty, and his exchanges terse. If pushed, they might describe a workman with nothing remarkable about him. He thought he'd test this by having a drink at the Caledonian Hotel. How long would it take that fat barman, Stafford Giles, to recognise this visitor as the man who sometimes sat in the window, away from any possibility of conversation? He'd ask for a whisky. If he'd done this just a few days ago, Stafford Giles would have pointed out that whisky was expensive, and he'd have asked to see his money up front. Starling was willing to wager that he wouldn't do this to the gentleman in the grey fedora.

The Caledonian was busy. When Starling entered, a few men looked at him — not because they were curious about him, but because they were expecting someone they knew. The well-dressed stranger was of no further interest to them. At the bar, Stafford Giles poured him a whisky without hesitation. Starling kept his head bent forward so that Giles saw the brim of his hat, and not his full face. He took his whisky to an empty seat near the window. It was only a few days before that he'd been sitting in the same spot, with vague plans. His plans since then had become sharply focussed. Joe Sable would die tonight, he thought. No mucking about. The problem was, he was with a group of coppers. Starling needed to get him alone. There was that policewoman — he'd take her, and use her as bait to force Sable to come to him, alone. That, he thought, was definitely a plan. He drank another whisky, and watched Bank Street. The light would soon be fading. It was time to find Joe Sable, and the woman.

★　★　★

Helen had been honest about the failure of her interview with Dorothy Shipman, and despite the general consensus that there probably wasn't much more to learn from her, she wanted to speak with her again. The hysteria in the house had felt real, but that didn't mean that it *had* been real. It was 7.30 pm. Inspector Halloran had declared that any further questioning of Selwyn Todd was pointless. Selwyn didn't answer questions, and not because he wouldn't answer them — he couldn't answer them. His inability to defend himself would condemn him to Brierly Mental Hospital, where he would doubtless be isolated as criminally insane, unless doctors with expertise that was relevant to his condition were prepared to insist that he couldn't possibly have killed Rose Abbot.

Constable Filan's wife, Annette, offered to cook dinner for all the police. Halloran and Manton didn't want to impose, understanding that this would deplete the Filan household's larder. Nevertheless, she insisted that they shouldn't have to pay for their dinner in town. She had to cook for the prisoner, and as she and Paddy ate the same food, adding extra to the pot was no impost. One of the advantages of living in a small coastal town was that supplies that were difficult to secure in Melbourne were available here. Annette Filan made a fish soup and a rabbit stew that included potatoes and tomatoes. Aggie Todd would have been surprised that such food was to be lavished on Selwyn. Annette Filan's position had always been that even if it didn't matter to a prisoner what he ate, it mattered to her. There was something in the integrity of this young policeman's wife that reminded Helen of her mother.

They ate their meal in the police station, and afterwards Joe asked if Helen wanted him to go with her to the Shipman house. She declined — two detectives might be too alarming for them. The men agreed that a beer at the Star of the West Hotel would be a fine idea, before Halloran and Manton returned to Warrnambool for the night. The pub would have closed at six o'clock, but Paddy knew the proprietor, and he'd slip them in through the back. All five officers left the police station together and walked up Wishart Street. The lengthening shadows of dusk diminishing into night meant that the figure who followed them moved easily, fluidly, secure in the knowledge that he was unnoticed. The police turned into Cox Street. Starling's heart rate increased. Princes Street, the street where he rented a mean and filthy room, ran off Cox Street, just ahead. The police passed Princes Street. Starling stood at the corner of Princes Street and considered his options. Where were the coppers headed? He couldn't take on all five of them. Then the cards fell his way. A little way along Cox Street, the group stopped. A few words were said, and the four men moved off. The woman remained alone, looking at a house. She put her hand on the gate, and withdrew it. She seemed to be gathering her thoughts. The men turned out of sight, into Sackville Street. There was no one else about. The woman stepped back from the house and put her hands on her hips. Starling had moved to be directly behind her.

'Hey,' he said.

Helen turned, and in the last of the light she recognised George Starling. *How very ordinary you look*, she thought, before Starling struck her.

★　★　★

Starling stood over Helen Lord's still body, and was pleased with himself. One blow to the side of the head had been enough to knock her down. He gave her a vicious little kick to the stomach to make sure she wasn't feigning unconsciousness, then leaned down and picked her up and put her over his shoulder. She was slight, and he carried her with ease. His room was only yards away.

★　★　★

Eddie Rooney wasn't sure what he'd just seen. A few moments earlier, he'd watched from his front step as a group of people, one of whom he'd recognised in the dim light as Paddy Filan, stopped, spoke a few words to the woman who was with them, and then walked away. The woman approached the Shipman house opposite. Visitors had been going in and out of the house all day. Sheila, Eddie's wife, had been across to offer her condolences, and to drop off a casserole, and she'd told Eddie that Dorothy Shipman was a mess. 'All over Matthew Todd,' Sheila had said. 'I suppose it's nice that somebody loved him, although I can't see why anyone would myself.'

As Eddie watched the woman, a form seemed to materialise out of the half-darkness and obscure his view of her. It was a man. Eddie could see that he was wearing a suit and a hat. The man raised his hand, and almost immediately, after shuffling his feet in an odd way, he bent down and picked up the woman, who seemed to have fallen to the ground. The figure moved off with the woman over his shoulder.

'Sheila!' Eddie called through the open doorway of the house behind him. 'What do you make of this?'

★   ★   ★

For days, Starling hadn't been inside the house where he was renting a room. The front door was unlocked — it always was — and there were no lights on. The landlord wasn't home. He rarely was. He spent most nights with Shirley Rogers, a woman in her late forties who lived two streets away. Starling had seen her, but not met her. He didn't like to think of the ugly coupling of his unprepossessing landlord and the big-breasted, florid Shirley Rogers.

He dropped Helen Lord onto his mattress. The smell of sweat and stale fish rose from it, and it was so acrid that it took Starling a moment to realise that this was how he must have smelt. He turned on the overhead light. It was weak, which ought to have disguised the meanness of the room. Somehow, though, it exacerbated it. Starling looked down at Helen Lord. She moaned and opened her eyes. The expression on her face was of puzzlement. He saw her nose twitch as the stink from the mattress registered. She made a small movement, but was too groggy to sit up. Starling took off his hat and sat on the bed beside her. He held her chin between his fingers and moved her head from side to side. She was wearing a jacket, which he unbuttoned. In an inside pocket, he found a thin wallet, which he withdrew. There were papers in the wallet.

'Helen Lord. *Constable* Helen Lord. Well, fuck me. You really are a copper.' He patted her face, and slapped it hard, once. Helen's eyes opened wide, and she stared at the face that looked down at her.

'You're properly awake now, are you?'

He moved one hand under her skirt and let it rest on the inside of her thigh.

'We're going to get your friend, Joe Sable, here, and we're going to have some fun. You're going to watch me kill that greasy Jew, and then I'm going to fuck you like you've never been fucked before. It's been a while for me, and I'm looking forward to it. So that's the plan. What do you think?'

Helen twisted her leg in an effort to move Starling's hand. He laughed.

'We can't have you moving about too much. I

don't like unco-operative women.'

He reached under the bed and found a length of cord that he kept there. Helen, still confused from the savage blow to her head, put up no resistance as he bound her ankles.

'If you start using your hands, love, I won't tie them up, I'll just break both your arms. Got that?'

He leaned close to her face.

'Got that?' he shouted.

She nodded, and noted the smell of whisky on his breath.

He stood up and took a filleting knife from the top of a chest of drawers.

'And if you make a racket, I'll cut out your tongue with this.'

He rested the blade under Helen's nose. The odour of fish guts was strong.

'Where's Sable right now?'

He turned the blade from its flat side to its edge so that Helen could feel its razor sharpness on her lip.

'Star of the West,' she said weakly, and wondered if she'd spoken at all. Everything seemed so disembodied and remote.

'I'll telephone from the corridor. I can see you from there, so don't make a fucking move, and when I tell you to, I want you to call out his name so that he knows I've got you. Understand?'

Helen, who heard Starling's voice as if it were from somewhere distant, didn't understand. She said nothing.

'Understand?' he repeated, and slapped her. She nodded automatically.

Starling stood up, and when he turned to go into the corridor, he was momentarily startled to see a man standing in the doorway. He was holding a .22 rifle, which was pointed squarely at Starling's chest.

'I'd drop that knife if I were you, mate. The gun's loaded.' To underline the point, Eddie Rooney raised the barrel to the ceiling and pulled the trigger. The noise was deafening in the small room, and it took George Starling so completely by surprise that he dropped the knife. Gathering his thoughts quickly, he said, 'I'm a police officer, and this woman is a suspect in the murders in James Street.'

Whatever Eddie Rooney had been expecting him to say, it wasn't this, and in the confusion of the noise and of his noticing that the man's clothes were expensive, he pointed the gun at the floor. It was all the time that Starling needed to rush at the man and push him against the corridor wall. Eddie Rooney was tall and strong, though, and he didn't lose his grip on the rifle. Starling knew immediately that his only option was to escape into the street and into the darkness that would deny this man a clean shot. He took his chance, and Eddie Rooney followed him and saw him running away. He saw, too, in the light spilling from doors and windows, that the gunshot had drawn people out of their houses. Many of them had come to their gates; if he fired at the retreating figure, a bullet might find one of them. He returned to the bedroom, untied the cord from Helen Lord's legs, and telephoned Doctor Marriott.

14

Joe Sable sat with Inspector Lambert in his office at Russell Street police headquarters. It had been two days since he and Helen Lord had returned from Port Fairy. Helen, who'd suffered a severe concussion, and who hadn't yet given a full report of what had happened in the room in Port Fairy, was at home in Kew. Joe's report was on the desk in front of Lambert.

'Command is extremely unhappy that I placed a policewoman in physical danger. I've been told in no uncertain terms that this is a failed experiment.'

'Constable Lord wouldn't agree with you.'

'I know that, Sergeant, but Constable Lord is subject to the rulings of Police Command — as, in the end, am I. When she returns to work, it won't be to this department.'

'She hasn't said anything to me about this.'

'She hasn't been told yet. That's been left to me, and I want her to be fully recovered before I give her the bad news.'

'She'll know as soon as I walk through Peter Lillee's front door after work that something is up. She'll see it in my face.'

'That's true. I won't put you in that awkward position. I'll telephone her this afternoon. It won't be an easy phone call to make.'

'She'll take it badly. She already thinks we failed miserably in Port Fairy.'

'Inspector Halloran is confident they'll find Matthew Todd's killer eventually, but I don't share his confidence. Unless someone comes forward with information to break one of those alibis, or to confess, or to point the finger at a person no one even considered — and I can't imagine who such a person might be — I've got a feeling this will be an unsolved crime for some time to come. Port Fairy is a small community. If anyone knew the identity of Todd's killer, that person would surely have come forward. A secret like that can't be held for long.'

'It's deeply frustrating.'

'Your work and Constable Lord's work was excellent. There was nothing more you could have done.'

'Starling is still at large, sir. How did he know to find me in Port Fairy?'

Inspector Lambert reached into a drawer and pulled out a copy of *Truth*. He handed it to Joe.

'That's how. At least, that's what I'm assuming. You're clearly identifiable in that photograph.'

'You know what Constable Lord said about him, sir, about George Starling? She said that, when she looked at his face, all she saw was an ordinary man.'

'And we will find him, Sergeant.'

⋆ ⋆ ⋆

Sergeant Ron Dunnart and Sergeant Bob O'Dowd were drinking at the Sarah Sands Hotel in Sydney Road. Dunnart was known there. He'd done a few people a few favours over the years, and he rarely had to pay for his drinks. It didn't bother him particularly that the man who'd murdered Steven McNamara and Sturt Menadue hadn't been picked up. They knew who he was, and that was a result. Starling would turn up eventually. He took a piece of paper from his pocket and handed it to O'Dowd.

'What's this?'

'A way to put some money in your pocket. What do you see there, Bob?'

'A list of names and addresses.'

'I liberated that page from Sturt Menadue's notebook.'

O'Dowd smiled.

'Anyone interesting on this list?'

'I've done some discreet checking, and I've underlined what looks like a good prospect.'

O'Dowd ran his finger down the list.

'Peter Lillee,' he read. 'Who's he?'

'A very respectable man. He's rich. That's all you need to know. I think we should pay him a visit.'

* * *

John Abbot had buried his wife, and now he sat in the kitchen of their house. Johanna Scotney had continued to work on the farm. He was grateful for this; he couldn't have managed without her. A herd of dairy cows wouldn't pause to make way for a farmer's grief. But John Abbot felt more than grief. He felt trepidation. With every hour that passed, he thought there'd be a knock on his front door, and that the police

337

would finally come to arrest him for the murder of Matthew Todd. Rose had been angry with him over the things he'd said to Johanna, and he'd been ashamed. She'd told him, too, about Matthew's assault, and she'd said that she didn't know what to do about it. She'd talk to him, of course, and she'd told Johanna that it would be all right.

'But it won't be all right, will it?' she'd said. 'Aunt Aggie won't help. We need Johanna, John. We can't manage the farm without her. If I can't stop Matthew coming here, she'll leave. I know she doesn't want to, and her family needs the money, but she'll leave. And I wouldn't blame her.'

The news that Matthew Todd had physically assaulted Johanna Scotney had had a strange effect on John Abbot. What he felt wasn't outrage. It was, and he felt the disturbing force of this, closer to jealousy. Those feelings overtook him, and he'd made the decision, late on Sunday night, to drive into town and confront Todd. Rose had wanted to go with him, but he'd told her that all he wanted to do was make it clear to Matthew that the Abbot farm was off-limits to him. For all his uncouthness, Rose had never known her husband to be violent, and so she'd relented and told him that she'd wait up until he returned.

Sitting in his kitchen, John Abbot told himself that he hadn't gone into Matthew Todd's house intending to kill him. Matthew had been surprised to find Abbot on his doorstep at midnight. He'd been even more surprised when

Abbot had pushed past him into the house. In the end, it had been Matthew's smugness that had killed him. Abbot had told him that he knew what he'd done to Johanna Scotney, and Matthew had laughed and said, 'You're mad because I beat you to it.' He'd turned his back on Abbot, in a contemptuous gesture that sealed his fate. In no time at all, Matthew Todd was dead. Rather than panic, Abbot had picked up the body, put it in the back of his truck, and, in a moment of inspired retribution, had driven to Aggie Todd's house, where he'd propped the corpse in the front room. His only regret had been that he wouldn't see her face when she found stinking Matthew in the morning.

As no one had come forward to say that a truck had been heard near Matthew's or Aggie's house, the only person who could have told the police that he'd driven into town was dead. Was it really possible, he thought, that he could get away with murder? With every day that passed, it seemed that the answer to that question was yes. Yes, he *could* get away with murder.

We do hope that you have enjoyed reading this large print book.

Did you know that all of our titles are available for purchase?

We publish a wide range of high quality large print books including:
Romances, Mysteries, Classics
General Fiction
Non Fiction and Westerns

Special interest titles available in large print are:
The Little Oxford Dictionary
Music Book
Song Book
Hymn Book
Service Book

Also available from us courtesy of Oxford University Press:
Young Readers' Dictionary
(large print edition)
Young Readers' Thesaurus
(large print edition)

For further information or a free brochure, please contact us at:
Ulverscroft Large Print Books Ltd.,
The Green, Bradgate Road, Anstey,
Leicester, LE7 7FU, England.
Tel: (00 44) 0116 236 4325
Fax: (00 44) 0116 234 0205